Advance Praise for *Home Another Way*

"The people of Jonah are flawed and complicated, and Parrish allows readers to savor every moment of genuine, hard-earned human connection. With its vast array of richly imagined characters, its humor and its substance, this debut is sure to resonate with a wide and appreciative audience."

Publishers Weekly

* * *

"In a poignant tale that wraps around your heart, Christa Parrish brings faith home to the hearts of all of us—genuine, abiding faith that can only be found in the trenches of life. Her warts-and-all characters remind us of what the Christian life is really all about."

Michele Huey—columnist, author, radio host of *God, Me & a Cup of Tea*

* * *

"Realistic, and compelling, Christa Parrish's *Home Another Way* brings a magnetic new voice to the market that holds you fast and opens your world. I read it in one sitting. Christa Parrish is here to stay!"

Virelle Kidder—conference speaker and author of six books, including *Meet Me at the Well,* and *The Best Life Ain't Easy*

"Readers, get ready. This is the voice Christian fiction has been waiting for. In her debut novel, Christa Parrish breaks the ice with a story that is bold in character and rich in relationships. Like Sarah, I found myself melting, page after page, warmed by the glow of God's grace."

Allison Pittman—author of the CROSSROADS OF GRACE series, including *With Endless Sight*

* * *

"There's a bit of Sarah Graham in each of us: angry, defensive, and flat-out scared. In *Home Another Way,* Christa Parrish takes Sarah up a mountain and through a desert. Her fresh, direct voice draws us in, and gives us hope that we too can learn to listen and forgive. Leave room on your bookshelf. We'll be hearing a lot more from Christa—and loving every word."

Melanie Rigney—*Writer's Digest* magazine, former editor

* * *

"Christa Parrish has packed an epic's worth of realism and grace into powerful pages you won't stop turning. You are likely to be as changed at the end as Sarah Graham herself. Isn't that what great fiction is about?"

Nancy Rue—best-selling fiction author

CHRISTA PARRISH

HOME ANOTHER WAY

BETHANY HOUSE PUBLISHERS

Minneapolis, Minnesota

Home Another Way
Copyright © 2008
Christa Parrish

Cover design by Studio Gearbox
Cover photography by Chloe Dulude/Veer

Published by Bethany House Publishers
11400 Hampshire Avenue South
Bloomington, Minnesota 55438

Bethany House Publishers is a division of
Baker Publishing Group, Grand Rapids, Michigan.

Printed in the United States of America

Library of Congress Cataloging-in-Publication Data

Parrish, Christa.
    Home another way / Christa Parrish.
        p.   cm.
    ISBN 978-0-7642-0523-1 (pbk.)
    1. Young women—Fiction. 2. Fathers and daughters—Fiction. 3. For-
giveness—Fiction. 4. Villages—Fiction. 5. New York (State)—Fiction.
I. Title.
    PS3616.A76835H66   2008
    813'.6--dc22

                                                           2008028098

For Evelyn and Laura,

as He draws you to Him

A past winner of Associated Press awards for her journalism, CHRISTA PARRISH now teaches literature and writing to high school students, is a homeschool mom, and lives near Saratoga Springs, New York. This is her first novel.

www.christaparrish.com

chapter ONE

I had twenty-three borrowed dollars in my pocket, and the deed to a house in a town I couldn't find on any map. How long ago had I stopped at that gas station to ask for directions? It seemed like hours. The attendant had pointed to the top of the mountain and said, "Keep going up."

So I drove until the sun wilted into the horizon, dropping behind rows of shaggy, towering evergreens. Brown leaves skittered across the road; I swerved around them more than once, mistaking them for toads, or chickadees. Deer-crossing signs blazed yellow in my headlights around each turn. Snow appeared, as if growing from the ground. The windows began to fog.

I should have turned around before starting this absurd quest for—what? Revenge? Retribution? Whatever it was, a certain romanticism had crept into the ordeal—being on the road, alone, with just my thoughts and a cooler of Diet Coke. I always imagined myself the tragic heroine. That, and I had absolutely nowhere else to go.

Squinting, I saw a light ahead, attached to a worn, whale-shaped sign: THE JONAH INN

"Cute," I mumbled, turning into the driveway.

There was a story in the Bible about Jonah. My grandmother, a bit of a religious fanatic, had taken particular delight in giant fish and prophets and the complete stupidity of some guy living three days up to his knees in gastric juices. I must have heard it fifty times. "You see, you must always do what God tells you to do," she'd say. As a small child, I would nod and agree, and then ask for a cookie. Finally, when I was twelve, I demanded, "What about adultery? What about murder? What does God say about that?"

Grandmother's eyes had bulged. "Who told you?"

"Aunt Ruth," I said. "Don't you think God wanted me to know the truth about my parents?"

Grandmother didn't talk to me about the Bible anymore after that. She stopped talking to Ruth completely.

Lucky Aunt Ruth.

The inn's gray clapboard siding flaked like dead skin onto the front porch. I hoped the bed had clean sheets.

The door unlocked, I entered to a bell chime. A sleepy voice called, "One minute." I heard scuffling from the room to my left, and a woman limped out, hair the same sad color as the house. About fifty years old, she wore a too-big sweater with leather patches on the elbows, and thick fleece socks.

"This is mighty unexpected," she said, but smiled.

"I can go somewhere else, if you're not ready for guests."

Silent a moment too long, the woman realized she was staring. "Sorry, dear. I'm just a little fuzzed up with sleep is all. There's no place else to stay, except here." Pulling a ledger from the desk by the front door, she asked, "What's your name?"

"Sarah Graham."

"You a skier, here visiting?"

I cleared my throat. "Just passing through."

Under her flannel pajamas, the woman's bony frame stiffened at my lie. She finished writing my name in the book, and handed me a dusty key.

"I'm Mary-Margaret Watson. Folks here call me Maggie. You're welcome to do the same. That all you have, or do you need to go back out to your car?" She nodded toward my duffel bag.

"This is all I need tonight."

"Okay, then. Follow me."

The old stairs creaked in protest, unhappy to be bothered so late at night. Maggie opened the door to my room, pointed at another door just to the left. "That's the bathroom. Towels are in there. You'll need to let the hot water run a bit."

"Thank you."

"Yup. Pick up the phone in the room if you need something. You'll get me. Spare blankets are in the closet. Sleep tight," she said, and then disappeared back down the stairs.

I felt oily. I hadn't showered in three days but was too tired to clean up now. I didn't even change my clothes—just shook off my shoes, turned on the bedside lamp long enough to find the extra blankets, and climbed into bed.

I forgot to check the sheets.

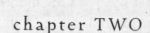

chapter TWO

Unable to sleep, Maggie listened to the floorboards crackle above her as Sarah tossed in the bed. Old houses, old bones, they're the same. Her hips ached—pain fueled by the raw autumn night.

She reached for a blue glass jar on the nightstand, a salve that Aggie Standing mixed for all the stiff joints in town. There were many. She rubbed on the cream, smelling camphor and eucalyptus, a hint of lemon, a dash of witch hazel. Then she took four painkillers. She was only supposed to take two, but two didn't do a darn thing.

Sinking back into the featherbed, she pulled her worn sweater tight around her spindly ribs and prayed silently for the pain to subside. Finally, the roar in her hips dimmed to a whimper.

Maggie had known it was Luke Petersen's daughter as soon as the sleep cleared her head. It wasn't so much how she looked, with hair the color of dried apricots and huge, dark eyes, but the way Sarah looked at her—still as a doe that smelled the hunter, but couldn't quite see him through the trees. Her father, however, had come into Jonah wind-beaten and searching for peace. Sarah seemed to want a fight.

It was Luke's sweater Maggie wore. He'd lent it to her one chilly night after church, and she never returned it. Day to day she told herself she just forgot, but on nights like tonight, when the pain made her honest, she admitted she kept it because it was his. For nine months, Luke had lived at the inn, until the ground thawed and he finished fixing up the house he bought. Maggie cooked for him, washed his socks and hemmed his pants, and talked with him late into the evenings. Folks had whispered in the beginning, but as they ate and shopped and worshipped with him, the rumors fell away, like woolen coats at spring's first thaw. Luke grew into the town, as if he'd always lived in that little cabin two turnoffs past McMahon's Sugar House, three-and-a-half miles down on the right.

She never expected to love him.

She never expected Sarah to show up in Jonah, at her inn.

Maggie reached over and set the alarm as her eyelids started to droop—not that, after all these years, she needed a clock to goad her out of bed. She would wake early to prepare a big breakfast, the kind she saved for Christmas mornings. She stirred love into those meals, and Sarah looked like she needed some of that something fierce.

chapter THREE

I didn't remember falling asleep, but I woke to sunlight carelessly passing through a frail paper window shade and jabbing at my eyes. I turned my head, stretched under the three layers of handmade quilts and glanced around the room. Pretty, but faded. Flowers dotted the wallpaper, pink and yellow. A few framed prints. No curtains. The clock read 2:14 p.m. I couldn't believe I slept so long.

The air was cold against my face. I didn't want to get out of bed, but I had to pee and my teeth felt slimy. Moving quickly, I grabbed my duffel and went into the bathroom.

I turned on the shower. It took five minutes for the water to warm up. While waiting, I brushed my teeth. The hot water soothed my car-weary muscles but didn't last long. I toweled off and blew dry my long red hair, my grandmother's tea-soaked voice echoing in my head. *Don't go out with wet hair or you'll catch pneumonia.*

Before going downstairs, I pulled the coverlet all the way down. The sheets were very white.

"Can I get you something to eat?" Maggie asked as I entered the front hall. She dusted the banister, the grandfather clock. "It's a bit late for breakfast, but there's French toast already made, and bacon and oatmeal. I can reheat it. Or I can make you a sandwich. You look like you need some stick-to-your-bones food."

"No, thank you, Maggie."

"Coffee?"

I pulled a well-creased envelope from my jeans, the one I'd ignored for the past eleven months. Fumbled to take the letter from it. "No, really, I'm fine. Could you just tell me how to get to 36 Main Street?"

"That's heading into town. You want to take a left out of here and make your first left. The road's steep and curvy, so you be careful. 'Bout three or so miles up, there'll be a fork. Go right onto the paved road. That's Main Street. You sure you don't want something hot? It's nippy out there. I can get you some coffee in one of those travel mugs."

"No, thanks."

As I stepped through the door, Maggie asked, "How long can I expect you here?"

"About a week."

I took a left out of the driveway as instructed, and then another. The pavement narrowed and turned to potholes. I drove slowly, looking at the houses that lined the road. No, not houses. Trailers. Soup cans with wheels and broken fences in front. An old man sat on a front deck made of barn wood and old tires, cheek fat with chaw. A coatless woman came quickly from her home and scooped a toddler into her arms, his mouth ringed with red Kool-Aid.

I drove past the fork and into town before my windows fully defrosted. Not that it was much of a town. A half-mile of hunched wood buildings, with a few brick storefronts between. I found 36 in the middle, next to a log diner. A hand-lettered sign hung near the door:

SMALL APPLIANCE REPAIR, TAXIDERMY,
NOTARY PUBLIC, LIVE BAIT.

Inside, a beefy man leaned over a table, screwdriver in his teeth. He wore canvas overalls, straps unhooked and crammed into his back pockets. All sorts of appliances and other mechanical doodads cluttered the shop—blenders and toasters, lawn mowers, televisions and pieces. Heads hung on the wall. I counted nine deer, two moose, and a bear. Some game birds and small rodents posed dramatically on a glass counter, wings spread or teeth bared.

"You must be Sarah Graham," the man said. "Only stranger to ever walk through my door." He didn't wait for a reply before straightening and pumping my hand in his, crunching my fingers. "Rich Portabella. Like the mushroom. Have a seat."

Rich pulled a chair out from behind the counter. "Coffee?" he asked.

"No," I said, handing him the letter he sent, and the deed. "I had an awful time finding this place. It's not on any map."

"Not on any recent map," he corrected me. "A handful of years ago, the county powers that be decided Jonah was too small to be its own municipality. Too much trouble keeping it separate on the tax rolls, or some nonsense like that. So, they merged us with the town below. Technically, we're Ogden. But no one around here thinks of us that way. We haven't changed the name on anything."

15

I sensed Rich the Mushroom could make small talk all day, so I asked, "What is there?"

"Of the estate? Well, the house, and everything in it. Quite a few books, I believe, furniture—"

"Money?" I interrupted.

"Some," he said, rolling the word over in his mouth.

"What?"

"Why don't we go see the house?"

"What does that mean?" I asked. My jaw tightened. After everything, I wouldn't even get the money?

"The house, the house. I'll drive. We'll talk there," Rich said, pulling on his coat, a fake-fur-lined parka. I wore a nylon windbreaker.

We climbed into an early-model Jeep with black vinyl seats. The cold seeped through the back of my jeans. Rich apologized for the broken heater, and then prattled on about birds and maple syrup, and his kids. I ignored him, seething, convinced I came all this way for nothing.

The house sat in the middle of a field, plain and lonely, with boarded windows.

"It's been empty more than a year," Rich said as he pulled up to the porch.

He unlocked the door and walked in, turning on the flashlight he brought with him. I peeked in from the bottom of the stairs. Sheets covered the furniture, ghosts of the past.

"You coming in?" Rich called.

"Yeah," I said, my voice disappearing into the wind. I closed the door behind me to keep out the cold. Or keep me from running back to the car.

I didn't know what I expected a murderer's home to look

like, but I certainly didn't think it would look so . . . normal. Floors, walls, ceilings. Yes, normal.

"So, what won't you tell me?" I asked.

"Want to look around first?"

"No," I said.

I couldn't move. Twenty-seven years of hatred and longing sank into my feet, weighing me to the plank flooring. I just wanted the money. No, I wanted the life I should have had. I'd take the money as a consolation prize.

"Well, Sarah." Rich spoke with care, the words tiptoeing off his lips. "When your father died, he had a bit over forty thousand dollars in the bank, and about the same in stocks and other holdings." He paused.

"And?"

"And, as part of the requirements set out in the trust your father established for you, you must live here, in Jonah, for at least six months. If you don't do this, you don't get the money."

I exploded. "What? Are you insane? Do you know what he did? Where does he get off, thinking he has the right to demand anything of me? He can rot in his grave. I won't do it."

Rich the Mushroom didn't flinch.

I flung open the door, and began walking back to town. I wanted to be alone, to stew in my own venom. Within fifty steps, though, the snow glued clumps of wet autumn leaves to my feet, my leather Mary Janes soaked through.

Rich pulled up behind me. He stopped. I got in. He said nothing. I said nothing. He dropped me off in town.

I'd lived on peanut M&M's and Diet Coke for the last three days, as the pounding in my head now reminded me. I went into the diner. A bell tinkled as I opened the door, and heads turned to see who was coming in. Within seconds, the chatter stopped. Patrons inspected me with darting glances.

The woman at the counter said, "Have a seat anywhere you want. Someone will be with you in a sec."

So I sat in a high-backed booth at the far corner. No one could see me, and that fueled the whispers. I put my head in my hands, rubbed at my temples.

"Hi. Can I get you some coffee?"

I looked up at the waitress, young and half pretty. The right half of her face was smooth and bright and scrubbed a sweet pink. The other side was scarred. Badly. It looked as if a plastic baby doll had been held too close to the campfire, skin melted tight and shiny. Her left nostril smushed flat into her cheek. She had no eyelashes or eyebrow on her left eye.

"Uh, no." My tongue caught in my throat. "Just water. Please."

"Sure thing," she said. "The menu is right there behind the napkins. Our specials are in there."

"Thanks."

"Not meaning to be nosy, but are you okay? You look really pale."

"I'm fine. It's just a bad headache."

"Can I bring you something? Tylenol? Aspirin? I have both in my purse."

"Tylenol, please."

The waitress disappeared for just a moment before coming back with a filmy glass and bottle. She dug her thumbnail under the cap and shook a couple of capsules into her hand, gave them to me. I tossed them in my mouth, swilling the ice water too fast. My headache swelled.

"I'm Beth. You must be Sarah," the girl said.

"Is this town that small?" I mumbled. Everyone was listening.

"Yes, but that's not how I know your name." Beth laughed. "You're staying with us. At the inn."

I looked at the girl again. She had Maggie's bird-thin frame.

"Can I take your order?"

"Cheeseburger, rare, with lettuce, onion, and tomato. And onion rings."

"Great," Beth said, and flitted away to the kitchen, humming. She moved like a bird, too, light and full of song.

I leaned my head back against the padded red seat and closed my eyes. Pieces of conversation floated through the French-fried air. By the time my food arrived, I'd learned that Mr. Winchell lost three goats yesterday, the diner's hash was too dry, and Ima-Louise Saltzman's youngest daughter had eyes for the town's pastor, but he wouldn't look twice at her.

"Here you go," Beth said, sliding a plate in front of me. "You can keep the Tylenol."

"Thanks."

I drenched the meat with ketchup and bit into the rarest burger I'd ever eaten, seared brown on each side, with an angry red center. The first few bites were coppery and slick, but I kept the food down despite the dripping grease, and the pickles, which I hadn't ordered.

Swallowing one mushy onion ring after another without tasting them, I mulled over my father's last request. He shouldn't have had anything, after what he took from me. He had phoned me once, after he was released from prison, asking to see me. At my request, Aunt Ruth told him I wasn't interested. That was partly true. I didn't want to meet and make small talk. I wanted to scream for a while, throw something at him and walk away forever.

I wouldn't give him the satisfaction of getting his own way now.

I needed that money, though. I had emptied my savings for the divorce. If David fought me, I'd owe my lawyer thousands more. And there were those nasty collection agents that kept calling, before the cellular phone company turned off my service for nonpayment.

Perhaps Rich the Mushroom was lonely and, with some strategically bared skin, I could persuade him to be a bit lenient with the terms of the will. I'd be happy with half, or even a third. I looked at my watch. Rich would have left the office. I'd go back tomorrow morning.

At the register I ordered a hot chocolate to go, and asked the cashier, "Where can a girl have some fun around here?"

The woman frowned. "Not sure what you're looking for."

"A mall? A movie theater? Anything?"

She gave me the change and the lidded Styrofoam cup, her knuckles cracked with eczema. "The closest mall is a couple hours down the mountain. But Westville is a little less than an hour from here, and they have a Super Wal-Mart."

"How about a bar?"

"You'll have to go to Gloverstown for that," she nipped. "The good folks of Jonah don't drink their money away."

Yeah, right. "And Gloverstown is where?" I asked.

"Half hour south on 22."

I spun to leave and bumped into someone behind me. The hot chocolate squashed between us, spilling onto my bare hand. "Ow," I said, dropping the cup. The rest of the liquid splashed on my jeans and shoes.

"Oh, no, I'm so sorry," the someone said, a tall man partly hidden in a wooly hat. The part I could see—chewed lips, dark eyebrows—did not impress me. In fact, I grew more annoyed because the guy's eyelashes were so long. What a waste.

"Your hand is red," he continued.

"Yeah, well, you just dumped twelve ounces of scalding liquid on it."

"Beth, get some ice," he said, and then reached for my hand. "Let me see."

"Thanks, you've done enough," I said, shoving past him and a few nosy onlookers.

"You need to get something cold on that burn."

"I'll stick it in the snow. There's plenty in this place."

I threw open the door, careful not to slip down the frozen diner steps. Getting into my car, I checked my hand. No blisters.

I drove back to the inn. Maggie had left the lights on for me and taped a note to my bedroom door. She was at Bible study, and if I was hungry I could help myself to anything in the guest kitchen, at the bottom of the stairs and down the hall on the right.

I dumped the contents of my duffel bag onto the now-made bed and picked through the clothes with the task of finding an outfit that both kept me warm and looked hot. Tossing my cocoa-stained windbreaker on the floor, I settled on gray trousers and a sheer blouse.

I left the clothes strewn over the bed. I had no plans of coming back tonight.

chapter FOUR

The pub was mostly empty, except for a few of the six o'clock people—those soggy, desperate types who have no place to go or no desire to go to the places they belong. I was one of them. But I wasn't there to get drunk, capable as I was of pounding back a few. Men were my diversion of choice.

Like mother, like daughter, I suppose.

I hoped I would have a better selection in an hour or so. Then again, I had no idea what would crawl in from the mountain. Not that I'd ever been picky. They did need to have showered in the last twenty-four hours, though, and have all their teeth.

I ordered a beer at the bar, a cheap domestic brew, and noticed an older man sitting there with a club soda, talking to a slouched waitress. He saw me, too, and I didn't like the odd way his mouth twitched as he pretended he wasn't looking.

"Hey," I said to the bartender, jerking my head toward the man. "He okay?"

"Who, Doc?" The woman wore three shades of purple eye shadow. "He's harmless."

I sat against the far wall, near two scraggly-haired men smoking and arguing across the billiards table. Another man hunched under a stuffed moose head, his table littered with empty shot glasses. The décor went past rustic; antlers jutted from the walls and the chandeliers.

I needed a second drink. Before I could signal the waitress, however, the man from the bar came toward my table.

"Can I join you?" he asked.

"No."

He hesitated for a moment, wiry eyebrows sinking slightly. I stressed my point, saying, "I'm not interested, old man."

"You're Luke Petersen's daughter," he said, sticking his hand out toward my face. "Crandall White."

I feigned disinterest. "The bartender called you Doc. Are you a real doctor?"

His hand fell. "If I answer yes, do I get to sit down?"

Kicking an empty chair toward him, I shrugged. "Whatever."

He sat, and motioned to the waitress. "Two more of whatever Sarah is drinking," he said.

It didn't surprise me he knew my name. He said nothing else until our drinks came, the waitress dropping them on the table. Beer sloshed onto my pants. Doc watched as I muttered a couple of obscenities and chugged half the glass.

"You look like him," he said.

"People always say I look like my mother."

"Do you?" Doc asked.

"No. But I guess they consider it bad form to say I look like a murderer." Like Rich the Mushroom, Doc didn't react to my words. "So, does the whole mountain know? About my father, I mean."

"Not the whole mountain," he said, taking a small sip of

his beer, "but all of Jonah. News travels fast in a place like that. From what I gather, Luke was quite open about what happened before he moved here. Told the whole church, which is just about everyone in town, except me. But I caught bits and pieces of the story from time to time."

I waited. Doc didn't offer any more, so I asked, "What exactly have you heard?"

"That Luke was in prison for a while. That he was convicted of killing his wife."

We fell silent. What more could be said about my father's sordid, not-so-secret past? Call me foolish, but I'd always thought uxoricide was something to be ashamed of, like beating your kid or drowning a sack of puppies. Luke appeared to treat it as if he had indigestion, a bit irritating but gone after a couple of Rolaids and a good night's sleep.

Shoving the mostly empty glass around the table with my thumbs, I asked, "You live there, then, in Jonah?"

Doc nodded.

"Why?"

"Doctors are scarce in this area of the mountain. I see patients in a dozen towns, and Jonah is fairly central."

So, he was really a doctor. I looked at him, in his threadbare sweater and outdated plastic-rimmed glasses, his middle-aged jowls drooping along a once-strong jaw. I could recognize a bleeding heart, having seen enough of them while living in New York City, in those save-the-world-hug-a-tree types. If it weren't snowing, Doc would probably be wearing leather-free sandals with organic cotton socks.

The noise in the small building distracted me, and I glanced up. The bar was filling, but not with the type of people I'd expected. These patrons wore expensive ski jackets and designer shoes. They laughed casually, drinking eight-dollar microbrews and mixed drinks with chic names like Pink Squirrel and Berry Mojito.

"Where are the mullets?" I asked, motioning to the growing crowd.

"Tourists," Doc said. "Skiers, actually. They're trying to experience the local flavor. Don't worry, they don't venture much past here."

"It doesn't matter. I'm not sticking around Jonah too much longer. I should be gone by the weekend. Monday at the latest."

Doc's mouth twitched again. He tossed a few dollars on the table. "Well, good-bye, since I won't see you again," he said, then handed me a business card with his address and phone number. "Just in case."

I watched Doc go, and then gulped the rest of his now-warm beer. Someone started the jukebox and '70s rock ripped through the room. Coats were tossed aside as women in tight jeans and tighter sweaters gyrated in bunches of three and four. I scanned the room, noticing some frat boys checking me out. I gave a long look at the group, flicked my hair, and pouted while holding my empty glass. One of the guys popped to his feet and came to my table carrying two full drinks.

His name was Brad. Or Brian. I couldn't understand most of what he shouted through the music, but he was good-looking with fresh-smelling breath, great muscles, and a tan.

We danced a bit and forced some half-heard small talk over a few more drinks. He just got back from Aruba, he told me. I said I was in town on business. He invited me back to his hotel room, college buddies giving him thumbs-up signs as we left.

I woke early, the sun low and orange. Brad-or-Brian snored, his back to me. I felt around the floor for my clothes, tugging them on without standing, and found my watch in my shoe: 6:57.

Outside, I remembered I left my car at the bar. I jogged there to keep warm, deciding I would head back to the inn for a bath and a nap before attempting to beguile Rich the Mushroom.

"What the—" I swore, coming to a halt in the parking lot. My car was gone. I didn't see any signs threatening towing but found scattered glass shards where it had been parked.

Raking my fingers through my hair, I headed down the road toward a lighted gas station. The clerk slept with his face in a textbook but bolted up when I opened the door. "I need to make a call," I said.

"Behind the building. Jiggle the cord if you don't get a dial tone," he said, wiping drool from his chin.

The clerk's advice worked, and my quarters disappeared with a hollow plunk. The telephone company had stuck a label with important emergency numbers to the receiver. I dialed the local police and told the answering Officer Davis my car had been stolen.

"Dark blue Toyota Corolla?" he asked.

"Yes. Have you found it?"

"Nope." I heard Davis munching something on the other end of the line—a donut, no doubt. "Someone reported seeing a bunch of hooligans break into it and speed off. Give me your name and number. We'll add it to the report and call you with any news."

"Sarah Graham. I'm from out of town, and I'm staying at the Jonah Inn. I don't know the number."

Davis assured me the inn was listed in the phone book and hung up.

I slammed the phone into the cradle, then picked it up and slammed it down again, and again. I pounded it until the clerk came out and told me to stop or he'd call the police.

Now what? I'd left my purse in the car. Not that it mattered. My credit cards were overdrawn, and I'd spent all my cash, except for—I fished through my pockets—three dollars and twenty-nine cents. And Doc's phone number.

I put in another quarter and called him. He answered after half a ring, and I calmly explained my situation.

"I'll be there in forty minutes," Doc said.

I went back into the gas station to defrost. The clerk eyed me cautiously as I bought a coffee and held my face over the open cup. Soon I could wriggle my nose again. I rubbed my cheeks briskly with my coffee-warmed hands. There was no place to sit inside the small convenience store—how convenient was that?—so I sank to the floor in a corner away from the front register, between loaves of Wonder Bread and diapers.

The clerk spotted me. "Miss, you can't just sit here. Is there some sort of problem?"

"Yes, there is a problem," I snapped. "I'm broke, I have hypothermia, my car was stolen, and I hate my father. Can't you have some compassion and leave me alone until my ride gets here?"

Apparently, the kid wasn't paid enough to deal with crazy out-of-towners. He went back to his book, looking up to check on me every few minutes. I didn't move. People came in for newspapers and bagels; they stepped over me.

Finally, I heard a horn honk outside. It was Doc, in a late-model Jeep. I got in the car and slammed the door.

"Shut up," I said, before he could speak.

He coughed, once, and drove me back to Jonah.

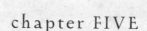

chapter FIVE

"Sarah? Sarah," Maggie called from behind the pocket doors as I entered the inn. I ignored her, taking the stairs two at a time, and shut myself in the bathroom.

I undressed, got in the shower, and wept from stress, from fatigue and loneliness. The tears slipped off my chin, dropping onto my feet before being carried down the drain. When the hot water ran out, I wrapped myself in towels and darted to the bedroom.

My clothes were folded neatly on the bed. After putting on running pants and a long-sleeve T-shirt, I shoved the pile to the floor and climbed under the covers. Maggie had changed the sheets; they were mint green with blue tulips.

Each time I closed my eyes, my father's face floated through my mind—what he looked like twenty-nine years ago in the only photo I'd ever seen of him. I found it after my grandmother died, when Aunt Ruth and I were cleaning out her house, rimpled and forgotten in a rarely used desk. It shocked me to see how much I looked like him—same red hair, same pale skin and dark eyes. Same splash of freckles

31

across the nose. In the photograph, my father had his arm tossed carelessly over my mother's shoulders. She was laughing, so happy. The date scribbled on the back read two years before I was born.

I rolled over, squashing the pillow around my ears.

I wouldn't be able to sleep until I saw Rich. I would walk there if necessary. Getting out of bed, I put on low-rise jeans and a V-neck sweater that barely covered my stomach. Gooseflesh prickled my arms and legs.

I hoped I didn't have to walk.

Downstairs, I knocked softly on the pocket doors. Maggie slid them open.

"Sarah, are you okay? I was worried when you didn't come home last night."

"My car was stolen," I told her. "There wouldn't be a bus that goes to Main Street, would there?"

"Oh, goodness me. Sweetie, I wouldn't have you take the bus, even if there was one. You can use my car. Let me get the keys."

She shuffled out of sight for a moment, returning with a jangling key ring. "It's this one here," she said.

"Thank you, Maggie. I really appreciate this."

"Not a problem, not a problem. I just feel so bad for you. Here you are, your first time coming here, and you got a bad taste in your mouth."

"Maggie, if it's not too much trouble, do you think I might be able to borrow a coat? Mine was in the car," I lied.

"Of course you can," she said, taking a heavy, calf-length parka from the closet in the foyer. "Oh, dear, was your wallet in the car? Do you need any money?"

"No, I'm fine." I wasn't desperate enough to steal from a little old lady. Yet.

"Well, the car is in the driveway. I'm not going anywhere today, so you can use it long as you need."

Maggie had a Jeep, too. I climbed into it, adjusted the seat, and turned up the heat. The air warmed slowly, but the coat helped. A thin sheen of ice covered the road, and the tires spun as I left the driveway. I popped the gearshift into four-wheel drive, keeping my left foot hovering above the brake as I drove to town.

I parked in front of Rich's office and left the coat in the car.

"You're going to catch your death if you don't dress warmer 'round here," Rich said when I walked in. He watched a small television on the counter, the picture flecked with static.

"Now, Rich," I said, smiling a bit, "you're a married man."

"Being married don't make me blind," he said.

"No, it doesn't." Elbows on the counter, I leaned over. "It certainly doesn't."

Rich moved across the room, fiddled with a set of antennas nailed to the wall. "Do you need something?"

"I do. But I'm broke. So, I thought if you needed something, we could work out some sort of deal." I straightened, tugging on the hem of my sweater so my navel showed. "Do you need something, Rich?"

"I got all I need," he said.

"Do you?" I asked. "Really?"

"I can't give you the money, Sarah."

"Well, you wouldn't have to give me all of it," I said simply, as if talking to a third grader. "Just a little. Half, maybe. You could give the rest to the church. And it would be our secret."

"I can't," he said.

"It's not like anyone would know."

"Nope."

"I—"

"No," Rich said firmly, eyes on my face.

"Why not? You're not working for free, are you? How much did he give you to make my life miserable?"

"Seems like you do a pretty good job of that on your own," he said.

I swore, kicking a metal bucket near my feet. It tumbled over, spilling rusty screws and other mismatched metal bits. I slumped into the chair, still in the middle of the room, elbows on my knees, palms pressed against my eyes. I heard Rich picking up the parts from the floor, humming, seemingly delighting in my agony.

There were few people I considered friends, and none who would drive to this frostbitten Siberia to come get me, and then let me crash on their sofa until I found a job making enough money to get a place of my own. I couldn't even afford a cab, and I refused to ask any of these inbred clodhoppers for help.

So, that meant what? Staying here? I would rather be that fox on Rich's counter—glass-eyed, full of stuffing, and most importantly, dead.

Yet, it would be the sweetest revenge to do what my father wanted and at the end of the six months walk away eighty thousand dollars richer and still hate him. Spiteful? Perhaps. Adolescent? Absolutely.

And really, what other choice did I have?

I stood. "I'll need that key, Rich. I'm staying."

He grinned. "Your dad would be real pleased to hear that."

"Good thing he can't."

Rich handed me an envelope from the cash register. "Here you go. The one key is for the house, the other for the truck. They're labeled."

I looked inside. "What's the little key for?"

Rich shrugged. "I don't know. He just left the envelope, and all three were in there. I suppose he meant you to have it."

I stuffed the keys in my jeans pocket, and saw something else in the envelope—a credit card with my name on it. "What's this?"

"Your father figured you might be strapped for cash when you got here."

I looked down at the counter, at my fingerprints smudged across the glass. So, Luke had kept tabs on me. A shiver of vindication crept down my arms, my legs. He'd seen what he'd done to me.

"As long as you're living in Jonah, I'll make the payments." Rich added. "The store across the street doesn't take charge cards. You can start an account there."

"Anything else I should know? About the house, I mean."

"Well, you saw it," Rich said. "Not much—galley kitchen, living room with woodstove, bedroom, and bathroom. No tub, just a shower stall. Luke kept it simple; he fixed up that place himself.

"The house is heated by the woodstove. There's some logs by the back door, but not enough to get you through the winter. Plenty of folks around here to sell you some. Also, there's a small water heater in the bathroom. Runs on fuel oil. You can get that at Brooks.

"You'll probably want to get that truck out of the shed. You'll need it for the winter. We get a couple more inches on the ground, and that little coupe of yours will be in a snowbank somewhere."

"My car is out of commission," I told him. "Will the truck start?"

"Probably not. It's been sitting about a year."

"Is there any way you can get someone to look at it, and drive it over to the inn when it's fixed?"

"I'll take care of it." Rich jotted a note on his pad.

"Fine. I'll see you May fourth. Early."

"I'll be waiting," he said. "Smile, Sarah. You may like it here."

chapter SIX

Brooks Variety Store had just that—everything from potato peelers to winter coats. Unfortunately for me, the coats only came in two styles of ugly—for the men, a swampy brown-green army surplus getup, and for women, ballooning nylon fuchsia. Two other shoppers watched me, whispering behind a tower of $1.49 disposable tin pie pans. One wore the bright pink parka.

I wasn't ready to tackle the house just yet, and I couldn't move in without certain necessities—winter clothes, shampoo, food. Not surprisingly, I would not find what I needed in Jonah.

The shopkeeper approached me, her crinkled bouffant stiff with hair spray. "Ms. Petersen, is there something I can help you find?"

"It's Graham," I said, "and no."

"I'm Nancy Brooks. Can I just say that I am so sorry about your father?" the woman continued, cannoli-shaped fingers on my arm. "He was such a wonderful man, and we all miss him so dearly. He was always willing to come over here and fix whatever was broken when my husband was sick with cancer. Carl's better now, praise the Lord, but when he was sick and the shutters were falling off, all I had to do was call Luke and he'd be right over with his toolbox and a—"

I turned away. "Lady, save it."

On my way out the door, I heard one of the pie-pan ladies say, "How rude!"

I remembered the diner woman telling me the nearest mall was a couple of hours away. Maggie did say I could use her car as long as I needed it.

I started down the mountain, stopping for directions in four towns. Finally, I pulled into a mall parking lot. Not the biggest I'd seen, but it had the basics. At the pharmacy, I stocked up on toiletries and cosmetics, Tylenol and flu remedies. It would be a long, cold winter.

Clothes next. I bought two pairs of boots, insulated work boots and rubber duck shoes. I also got running sneakers, fleece slippers and an armful of wool socks, long underwear, gloves, and mittens. I tried on flannel-lined corduroys, dismayed at the extra bulk they added to my hips and middle, but bought them anyway, as well as two pairs of tight, low-rise jeans and one impractically sexy dress. A green down parka, twelve turtlenecks, heavy sweaters, and blanket sleepers—with feet—brought my bill to over nine hundred dollars.

I'd never make it six months without an ample supply of peanut M&M's. After loading my things into the car, I asked directions to the nearest grocery store.

Fluorescent lights bounced off the frozen food coolers, shiny and modern. I found the candy in aisle eight. After layering the bottom of my cart with yellow bags, I threw in my favorite garlic potato chips, instant hot chocolate, ramen noodles, canned spaghetti. And Diet Coke, six-dozen cans.

During the ride back to Jonah, I listened to the radio; the stations, one by one, cracked and fizzled with the increased elevation. By the end of the trip, I was left with a choice between honky-tonk and NPR. I refilled Maggie's gas tank and returned to the inn, nearly crashing into the three vehicles parked on the driveway—a small SUV and two battered pickup trucks.

"You're just in time for dinner," Maggie said, coming from the innkeeper's quarters to greet me.

"No, I couldn't. I don't want to intrude," I said, my empty stomach kicking.

"No intrusion. I always make more than three people can eat in a week." She pulled me into her side of the house, through the sitting area and into the dining room.

Maggie's daughter—I couldn't think of her name—sat at the table, the mangled side of her face turned away from me. The cocoa-spiller from the diner was next to her.

"Sarah, you've met my daughter, Beth. And that's my son, Jack. This is Sarah Graham. She's staying here a few days."

"I hope you're feeling better," Beth said cheerfully.

"Ah, yes, thank you," I replied, sitting down across from Jack. Now hatless, his lips smeared with some sort of balm, he looked like the kind of guy I wouldn't mind meeting in a dark bedroom.

"I hope your hand is feeling better," he added.

I wiggled my fingers in front of him. "I'm fine. No lawsuit."

I piled my plate with ham and potatoes and, while listening to the gentle banter the Watsons tossed around the table, remembered why I hated family dinners.

I'd never had them.

"It's supposed to snow again tonight," Beth said.

Maggie sighed. "It seems like each year the snow comes sooner and deeper. Oh, Sarah, Luke's truck was brought over for you."

"Which one is it?" I asked.

"The black one," Maggie said.

"The cops didn't call here about my car, did they?"

Maggie shook her head and declared, "People today just don't have the fear of the Lord like they used to. Speaking of that, have you written your sermon yet, Jack?"

Jack sighed. "Not nearly."

"Well, last Sunday's was very good," Maggie said.

"Not just good. Beautiful," Beth insisted.

I looked at Jack. He shrugged. "It was okay."

"Jack's the town's pastor," Maggie said, voice alight with pride.

"Oh?" A preacher. It figured. "What was your sermon on?" I asked politely, to keep the conversation moving.

"The church at Philadelphia. Small but faithful."

Whatever that meant. Then I recalled the conversation I overheard at the diner. "Are you the only minister in town?"

"Well, I suppose. There's Reverend Joseph, but he's been retired about five years now," Jack said, picking up his glass.

"So you're the one that Ima-Louise Saltzman's daughter has a thing for."

Jack choked, milk dribbling from the corner of his mouth. He covered his lips with his napkin and, after managing to swallow, coughed several more times. Maggie and Beth laughed.

"I told you," Beth said. "Everyone in Jonah knows that Patty is still nuts about you."

"But how does *she* know?" Jack demanded.

"Small town, news travels fast," I said.

"I'd say," he grumbled, wiping beads of milk off his sweater. I wondered if he'd ever had a beer. Or a date.

"Well, since you seem to know so much about me, what about you?" Jack asked. "How long will you be part of this very wonderful, very small town?"

I hesitated, juggling several creative responses before I finally settled on the truth. "It looks like I'll be here a little longer than first expected. Through the winter, actually."

The three exchanged quick glances, and Maggie pushed away from the table. "How about dessert? I made pie."

"I'll help you," Beth said, picking up some of the dirty dishes and following her mother into the kitchen.

"Was it something I said?" I quipped.

Jack smiled, kind but tired. He'd never had braces. "They think that because I'm a pastor, I always know the right words."

"Do you?"

"No," he said, and took a deep breath. "Obviously, we all knew Luke."

"Obviously."

Jack bit his lip. I should have been nice to him, but I was in no mood for charity. He shifted in his chair, looking like a five-year-old boy who'd been caught stealing penny candy.

"Sarah, all I'm trying to say is, if you need to talk, any one of us is here to listen. You shouldn't go through this alone."

I clenched my teeth, getting angry. Not only because some man I'd known for ten minutes thought he knew what

I needed, but because of the way he said my name. *Sarah*. Like he cared about me, about what happened to me. No one had ever said my name like that. Not my grandmother, not Aunt Ruth or David, not Brad-or-Brian from the night before or any other sweaty fling. It was the way my mother would have said my name, if she had lived.

If my father hadn't killed her.

"And what am I going through?"

"Sarah—"

"Stop saying my name," I said, "and leave me alone. You have no idea. And you don't want to."

I went upstairs to my room. The bed was made, as if I were never there.

I wanted to leave. I wanted to cry. Mostly, I wanted to spit in Jack's face. I saw in his eyes how he pitied me, and how he loved my father.

No one should have loved my father.

My head pounded again, pulsing at the temples to my heartbeat. I dug through my bag to find the Tylenol Beth had given me the day before. There were five left. I took them all. Then I put on my pajamas and got into bed. The sheets were cold against my bare feet. I should have kept my socks on.

chapter SEVEN

Jack reran his conversation with Sarah over in his mind again and again, until his words blurred and all he clearly remembered were her eyes—brown and haunted with the ghosts of too many lost dreams.

Could he have said something different? Probably not. It had been a long time since she trusted anyone, and her walls wouldn't fall over a plate of mashed potatoes and an "I'm here for you," no matter how well his mother cooked, or how sincere his words.

Yes, he had sworn to Luke that, if Sarah found her way to Jonah, he would look after her. But she was more to Jack than a promise to a dying friend; she offered him a chance to prove his days could be counted in more than sermons and breakfast specials.

A sermon. He still needed to finish his for Sunday. With a groan, he took a legal pad and pen from his desk and sat in the squeaky antique chair. He flipped open his Bible, scrawling a few uninspired sentences, then tore off the defaced sheet of yellow paper and threw it across the room at the blotchy watercolor one of the church members painted for him. He would not be writing anything tonight, and so closed his book with a defeated thud.

Jack pushed back from the desk, rolling to the center of the cramped room because the old floor bowed so badly. The chair wheels caught on the corner of the braided rug and stopped. Not much larger than the church's fifteen-passenger van, the room pulled triple duty as his office and living and eating areas. The sofa, supple brown leather with matching ottoman, had been an impractical splurge, but he'd salvaged the dinette set from Goodwill. It didn't matter that the chipped top was an ugly '70s avocado green, and the uneven legs caused the table to rock like the apostles' rowboat in the storm. He rarely ate at home, and when he did, he stood at the counter in the equally modest kitchen.

The tight surroundings irritating his cluttered brain, Jack bundled up and walked out into the night. Undisturbed, the snow in the field to his left undulated softly toward the woods. He stepped into it, sank to his ankles. Then he continued walking, marring the snow, which, despite the almost full moon, did not look white but gray scale. After fifty paces he turned his head to glance back at his footprints, small black pits intruding on the otherwise smooth landscape. Leave it to man—to him—to screw up God's perfection with his muddy feet.

Yes, he was wallowing in good ol' self-pity, as much as he hated to admit it. His confrontation with Sarah played just a small part in a melancholy that had persisted for, well, too long. Not that he had any doubts about serving as pastor in Jonah. He didn't. He belonged here. Still, it remained, the feeling he should be doing something bigger than shuttling senior citizens to the market or judging pie-eating contests.

Jack wanted to have a Christmas pageant again. Four years had passed since the fire, and the town still mourned. He hadn't yet pressed the issue with the congregation, but after considerable prayer, he believed it was time to try.

The wind rasped bitterly, sweeping the clouds over the moon and cutting through his pants. Turning, he walked back to the apartment, careful to step only in the boot prints he'd already made.

chapter EIGHT

For too long, my days had been about sleeping and waking, about beds and blankets and who, if anyone, would be next to me. The hours between were stuffed with life, a tedious blend of walking, talking, and sometimes food.

It started again that morning. I woke, dressed in the dark, and snuck out of the inn. My bags were still in Maggie's car. I put on my new coat and tossed the rest into the cab of the truck, and then drove into the center of town, past the variety store. It opened in an hour, at eight, so I went to the diner. I wasn't hungry, but I needed a warm place to wait.

The same woman at the counter again told me to sit where I wanted. A few men in red-checked wool coats filled their thermoses with hot coffee. I walked to the back of the diner to *my* booth.

Jack was there.

In my haste not to be noticed, I turned and bumped against the table with my hip. Jack's milk tipped, flooding the paper place mat and his breakfast. He jumped from the booth to avoid getting his pants wet, pulling his briefcase with him.

"Sorry," I said.

He grinned. "For now or yesterday?"

"Both."

"Don't worry, my boss is big into forgiveness. Have breakfast with me."

"Oh, I can't—"

"Please," Jack said. "My treat. And I promise, no questions. I'll limit my conversation to the history of the town, and to the snow."

A waitress pushed past me to sop up the milky mess. I flopped into the booth, with Jack sitting across from me.

"So, there's snow out there," he said.

I couldn't help but smile. The waitress finished cleaning and came to take our order. About sixty and sour-faced, she looked at me disapprovingly. "Reverend, can I get you another plate?"

"Yes, thank you, Ima-Louise. I'll have the same. With orange juice this time."

"And you?" she asked me.

"Coffee, and whatever Jack is having."

Ima-Louise's scowl deepened. "The reverend is having the breakfast special. Two eggs, toast, sausage, bacon, and oatmeal."

"That's fine," I said.

"And your eggs?"

"Scrambled."

"Uh-huh," she said.

"Um, what was that all about?" I whispered as Ima-Louise headed into the kitchen with our order.

"No one around here calls me Jack, except my sister and my mother," he explained. "I'm sure Mrs. Saltzman found the familiarity inappropriately disrespectful."

"I'll remember that, Reverend."

Jack chuckled quietly.

Ima-Louise returned with our drinks. I put cream in my coffee, and sugar, eight packets. I hated coffee, but it was too early for soda and I needed caffeine. I stirred the sludge and looked at Jack as he held a pencil in his teeth and rummaged through his briefcase. Unshaven, with restless hair, he looked more like a beach bum than a minister. He pulled out his datebook and paged through it.

"Is your social calendar so full that you need to write things down?" I asked.

"You joke, but you don't realize that even in a little place like this, a pastor stays busy, especially when nearly half my congregation is over sixty. There's always someone who's sick, or who has a leaky roof or needs a ride to a specialist down the mountain. Believe you me, some days I start to think I'm just a glorified errand boy."

The food came, hot and shiny with grease. "Tell Rose this looks wonderful," Jack said to Ima-Louise. She continued to frown.

I tasted the eggs—salty, a bit runny, but good. Between mouthfuls, Jack told me about Jonah. Founded as a loggers' camp in the early 1800s, the menfolk, lonesome on those cold mountain nights, began bringing their wives and building houses. Now, most of the locals worked at the paper mill or state prison, both about an hour's drive.

"Few people leave the mountain once they're here, though they may move from town to town," he added.

"Really?" I asked, very surprised.

"I know we don't have all the amenities, but who needs cable TV with views like this?" Jack said, gesturing to the snowy evergreens. "There've been some brave souls who have fled to the lowlands after high school, for college or adventure, but most folks are settled and happy. Kids grow up, marry their grade school sweethearts, have babies, and the whole thing starts again."

"You didn't leave."

"No," he said.

The door burst open, and Beth fluttered in. "Goodness, it's chilly this morning," she announced cheerfully to no one in particular. "Jack, where are you?"

Her brother called, "Back here," and Beth came over.

"Oh, Sarah, hi."

I gave a little half wave, too early for me to share her exuberance. Half her face glowed white from the wind, her scars a molted purple.

"Scoot over," she told Jack, and he did. She took the toast from his plate and ate it.

"Help yourself," he said.

"You never eat your toast."

"Maybe that's because you never give me a chance," Jack shot back, tugging on her stubby ponytail. The simple motion made my nose tighten in that oh-no-I'm-going-to-cry way. I sniffed and shoveled cold oats into my mouth.

"When do you start work?" Jack asked.

Beth sighed. "Now. I'm running late. The garage door froze close. I was out there with a hair dryer." She took a few bites of egg.

"Do you want my bacon, too?"

"If you don't," she said, and grabbed the fatty strips. "You only like it crunchy, anyway."

"You know me better than I know myself."

"I'll see you later," Beth giggled, and was gone, into the kitchen.

"I wish I had her energy in the morning," I groused, throwing back the rest of my coffee in two sharp gulps.

"She's always been like that. Sunshine, my father called her," Jack said. "She and Mom. If I had my way, I'd still be in bed. Mornings are not my thing."

"Your father, he's . . ."

"Dead. It's been nearly ten years. Beth was just a kid, and I was in college. Mom was devastated. She and Dad were a couple of those grade school sweethearts."

I pushed the rest of my eggs around my plate. Jack looked at his watch. I hadn't put mine on.

"So," he said.

"So."

"So," he said again.

"You just said that."

"Well, I've covered the weather and the town's history, so there's nothing left for me to say."

I looked him straight in the face. "I doubt that."

He met my gaze for a moment but lowered his eyes as Ima-Louise came to pick up the dirty dishes. She stacked them loudly, one on another.

"Ted Armstrong just rang," the waitress said. "His eyeglasses broke, and he can't see to find his old ones. He wanted to know if you could stop by and help, when you were done."

Jack wiped his mouth and tossed some money on the table. "If he calls again, tell him I'm on my way."

"There needs to be a sign when you come into town, warning that Big Brother is watching," I said.

"I eat here every morning of the week, same time. Except Sunday." Jack pulled on his coat, hat, and matching gloves

51

I was sure his mother knitted for him, or some other blue hair. "People know where to find me."

He extended a wooly hand. "Bye for now. I'll see you again. There are only so many places to hide in Jonah."

Through the frost-streaked window, I watched him get into his truck and drive away. He was nice, in a milk-drinking, boy-scouting sort of way. I wondered how long it would take me to get him in a compromising situation. I had no doubt I could, and really, Jack would probably thank me. If Patty Saltzman was anything like her mother, he desperately needed another option.

chapter NINE

It took me the entire morning to remove the boards from the cabin's three windows.

I'd only used a hammer once before, and that was when I chased David around the house, swinging it at him. We had been married about five months, arguing about whose turn it was to wash the dishes. I found, now, that I was much less adept at using the tool for its intended purposes. The nails bent when I hit them, broke as I tried to pull them out of the plywood. I repeatedly gouged the cedar siding and my fingers.

Finally finished, I unloaded the cleaning supplies from the truck. Mrs. Brooks at the variety hadn't given her condolences this time, or blathered on about her husband's cancer. She bagged my bleach and sponges with a hushed "Thank you," and "Please come again." When I asked to use her phone to call the utility company, she mutely pushed it across the counter. The service representative assured me the power at the house would be turned on tomorrow.

Inside the cabin, my breath visibly curled from my nose. I opened the woodstove, stuffed in some logs and crumpled newspaper, and tossed a lit match onto the heap. The paper smoldered, glowing red around the edges, then fell away in sooty flakes. I rubbed my hands in front of the flames, but my eyes burned. I blinked once, twice, trying to clear my blurred vision.

The air in the cabin thickened and turned gray. Smoke tumbled from the open stove. I slammed the door, cast iron clanging, but the smoke continued to escape. Opening one of the windows, I hung my head outside, coughing, and gulping the frostbitten air.

"Fool city girl," I heard behind me. "Got the flue closed."

Through teary eyes, I watched a very short, very fat woman clomp over to the woodstove and turn a small knob at the base of the chimney. She then opened another window before plopping down on the sheeted couch. Dust puffed around her. She swatted perspiration bubbles from her upper lip.

"Uh, who are you?" I asked, somewhat perturbed, despite the rapidly dissipating smoke.

"Memory Jones, I am. Memory Jones, and you ain't never gonna forget me. No one does—that's for sure. Boy, you sure are rude. Just like folks say. Not even a thank you or nothing. Nope, not nothing. You ain't like your pa, no, no, no."

She hauled herself to her feet with a grunt and "Amen," then banged her heels against the wood floor, knocking the ice from her grubby boots. She shook her dark blond hair, the kind that always looked unwashed, and thin, so her ears poked through.

"You need to get yourself a grateful spirit, yep. Ain't never gonna be happy without one."

"Look, I'm not trying to be rude or ungrateful," I said,

though I was clearly being both, and was quite unbothered by it. "I just wasn't expecting . . . visitors."

Memory's fleshy cheeks rolled up over her eyes as she laughed from her gut, mouth wide open and full of white teeth. "Miss Mary-Margaret didn't tell you we was coming?"

"Who?"

As if on command, a gaggle of women poured through the front door, tugging on mops and pails and empty cardboard boxes. Maggie led the fuchsia-coated parade; I counted seven out of twelve grandmas wearing that fashion atrocity.

"Sarah, cleaning is no fun alone," Maggie said. "So I got some of the ladies from the church to come help you."

"How did you know I was here?" I asked.

"Maggie's got spies all around," Memory hooted.

I stood there and shook hands as Maggie orchestrated introductions. Beatrice Rawlings had the smooth, soft hands, Editha DeMay's hands were gnarly tree roots; I gave up trying to remember after that. Instead, I watched as strangers dusted furniture, washed windows, and cleaned out closets and cupboards. Memory scrubbed the wood floor on her hands and knees, ample belly sopping up soap.

"What would you like done with Luke's clothes?" someone asked me, the woman with the nicotine-stained fingernails. Abby? Alice?

I shrugged, looking at Maggie.

"We can give them to Doc White, if you don't mind, Sarah," she said. "He can pass them out during his rounds."

"Fine," I told her.

"Box them up for Doc, Adele," Maggie called.

Adele. Right. Adele, with the yellow fingers.

"What about this fiddle?" Adele asked, holding up a peeling leather case.

"Leave it," I said without hesitation, without thought.

The pine-scented cleaner clogged my sinuses, and I stepped onto the front porch, surveying the land. Naked trees clawed the overcast sky. Gray branches stuck up from the snow, dead leaves clinging to the tips. I was those leaves, shivery and desperate, waiting helplessly to be swept away by the slightest breeze.

"We're about done in there," Memory said, coming out onto the porch wearing a scarf and mittens, no coat. The boards croaked under her weight.

I didn't answer.

"I said, we're about done in there," she shouted close to my ear, her wide face webbed with capillaries.

"I'm not deaf," I huffed.

"Then don't act it," she said. "Oh, it's chilly out here. I best be getting back to my boy. You coming for supper?"

"What?"

"Not deaf, eh? I said, are you coming for supper?"

"Is that supposed to be an invitation?"

"I seen what you got in those cupboards. You need some hospitality. Ain't you never had anybody be nice to you?"

Not recently. "Thank you, Ms. Jones, but I still have things to do here."

"I ain't Miss anything. I'm just Memory—don't you forget." She snorted at her repeated pun. I didn't.

"Well, thank you anyway, Memory."

"I expect you'll be by when you're not so busy. Have fun eating those noodle things in a can. Don't know how you do. Look like worms to me." She slapped me on the shoulder and shuffled to her car.

The other women spilled outside, each hugging me or patting my cheek. Maggie invited me to dinner, too, but I pleaded fatigue and locked myself in the cabin.

I screwed new batteries into the flashlights and unrolled my sleeping bag onto the couch. The sun had dipped into the mountains, soaking the living room in deep purple shadows. I added two more logs to the fire and settled down for the night with a six-pack of Diet Coke and a bag of chips.

One hundred and seventy-nine days of hibernation left to go.

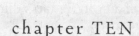

chapter TEN

Memory hobbled and huffed up the nine stairs to her house. Some days she wished for less—like five, or better yet, two—but most days she was thankful she could manage the nine without her lungs bursting like paper firecrackers.

The storm door on the three-season porch had no handle; Memory kicked the bottom until it bounced open, and she stuck her elbow inside. The frayed screens and hole in the roof rendered the porch useless in any season, from spring-time thunderstorms to pesky summer mosquitoes, to the heap of icy pine needles Memory now stepped over to get to the front door.

It hit her as soon as she walked into the living room, the smell of disinfectant, tinged with urine. It didn't matter that Memory scrubbed the house until the bleach water pickled her hands. The smell remained. She blamed the pressboard floors—the porous wood sucked in odors, held them, grew them—and had started making rag rugs. The Bethel Baptist Church, two towns west of Jonah, had a bag day at its thrift store on the third Wednesday of the month, two dollars for as much clothing as she could stuff into a plastic grocery sack. Memory took only the stained T-shirts. Still, the feeling lingered that, maybe, it was a sin to cover her floors with shirts somebody might still be able to wear.

The rugs didn't help, anyway. They prettied the house and made it warmer to walk barefoot but did nothing to reduce the offending odor of a grown man's diapers.

She found Beth in front of the fireplace, reading to Robert from a Beatrix Potter storybook. Robert's bloated tongue hung out of his mouth.

"I'm home, sweet boy," Memory said, kissing his forehead.

Beth closed the book. "I think he's getting hungry."

"To be sure. It's nearly three."

"Do you want me to stay?" Beth asked.

"Nah. You worked all morning. You must be beat like a potato."

"You, too."

Memory smoothed Beth's hair tenderly. "You go home."

Beth nodded, zipped her coat and tied her boots. "How'd it go today?"

"That cabin is shiniest in Jonah."

"I bet, with all you ladies going at it. What about Sarah?"

"Bristly as my legs when I can't afford a razor."

"I'm praying for her."

Memory nodded. "That's 'bout the only thing that'll help that girl."

After Beth left, Memory went to the kitchen to prepare Robert's lunch. Hers, too. She pulled two cans of Ensure formula from the cupboard, and then took leftover split pea soup from the refrigerator. After heating the soup in a pot on the stove, she poured it into a plastic bowl, which she put on a tray with the formula, a spoon, and a catheter tip syringe.

"Are you hungry, Robert?" Memory asked, putting the tray on a small table next to his bed. "I sure am."

She unbuttoned the bottom of her son's shirt, exposing his gastrostomy tube, filled the syringe with one can of formula, and inserted it into the tube. Slowly, she depressed the syringe, just a little. Then she said grace and spooned some soup into her mouth. For an hour, she told Robert about her day, until both cans of formula were gone. The green pea puree went mostly uneaten.

Everyday she did this, every four hours, around the clock. The state insurance wouldn't pay for a continuous feeding pump. Memory cleaned Robert's face and swabbed around the g-tube with warm water. The incision looked red and sore, so she dabbed on some Maalox antacid and covered it with gauze.

Memory heard Robert's snore, a wet wheeze familiar to the point of maddening. Then she changed his diaper. She always did so, if possible, while he slept. The doctors kept telling her, in their faithless, starched-coated way, that he had nothing going on in his head. Still, cognitive or not, no thirty-one-year-old would want his mother wiping his rear.

chapter ELEVEN

I spent five days on the couch, eating myself out of my jeans and into sweatpants. The cushions had molded around my body, and I got up only to go to the bathroom, add logs to the fire, and grab more junk food. With just a few packages of instant soup left, my insides rancid from lack of substantive nutrition, I would have to venture out of the house soon.

I know I slept more than I was awake, a combination of exhaustion, boredom and sheer escapism. During those rare times my eyes stayed opened, I stuffed my face and watched Luke's 15-inch television. The old, gray box had rabbit ears and picked up one scratchy channel. The daytime lineup— hours of pet psychics, voyeuristically televised blind dates, and *Who's My Baby's Daddy?* talk-show episodes—was more effective than any therapist I'd seen. Clearly, I was not the most dysfunctional person on the planet.

The knocking had begun my first morning at the cabin, and continued well into the evening of day two. Some people pounded steadily on the door for minutes at a time, others rapped softly, once, twice, and then were gone. A few called my name. I figured someone would soon break a window and climb inside, worried I had hung myself or been eaten by wild dogs, so I nailed a note to the door: *I'm fine, go away.* After that, there were just footsteps as those concerned townsfolk tromped up the snowy steps, then tromped back down after they had read my admonition.

I checked the fire, shoving in the last two logs I had stacked next to the woodstove. I unlocked the front door and nudged my head outside, seeing only three logs on the porch, and added firewood to the list of necessities.

Smelling of stale laundry and the mothballs I found tucked in the couch crevices, I wandered into the bathroom and started the water in the tiny shower. The stall's door was glass, transparent and icy. I soaped and shaved under the steaming water for almost an hour. My clothes, however, were still crumpled in shopping bags. I put on a bathrobe and, wrapping my hair in a towel, scooted to the living room closet where I had piled the bags.

Crouching on the cold pine floor, I scoured through the sacks, selecting wool socks and a velour jogging suit. Kicking the clothes back inside, I knocked over the fiddle case, which I ignored as I yanked the socks over my frozen toes. I couldn't shut the door, though; the case blocked it. I bent over to nudge the instrument into the closet, but found myself popping open the latch. Inside, cradled in musty gold velvet, was a violin. I picked it up, hands trembling slightly, and turned it over. The one-piece maple back was deeply flamed, the varnish muted with age. I peered into the f-holes to find the label. There was none.

Lifting the violin to my chin, I ran the bow over the strings. Flat, but just a little. I tweaked the boxwood tuners and tried again. Brilliant, sinewy tones resonated through the house. This instrument rivaled my own vintage Leon Mougenot. Of course, I had hocked that violin last year.

Taking a deep, shaky breath, I began Bach's Concerto in A Minor, a piece I'd memorized in junior high school. I played the first movement, hands and arms tense, strings cutting into my skin, calluses having peeled away months ago. However, as the *allegro moderato* rolled into the *andante*, I melted into the music, and my fingers remembered.

I completed the *allegro assai*, and immediately shifted to something more befitting my mood, the brooding Shostakovich concerto from opus 99. I skipped the first two movements and began with the *passacaglia*. Pounding away at the accents, jerking my head until the towel unraveled and my hair flopped around my face, I played until I had the eerie feeling of someone watching me.

I spun around.

Jack leaned against the front door. "The door was open, and I heard you playing, and . . . wow," he blurted.

Gathering my robe tight at the neck with one hand, I fumbled to get the violin in the case with the other, saying, "I found it in the closet."

He moved a few steps closer. "You don't have to stop."

I closed the instrument in the closet. "Did my—Luke play?"

"Not like that."

"I'm out of practice. It was awful," I said, my face hot and prickly.

Jack shook his head faintly, "No, it was, wow. Wow."

"You said that."

"I know. I mean, Sarah, you're wonderful."

I brushed away the compliment with a brisk "Thanks"

and picked up my jogging suit. "Excuse me. I was about to get dressed."

Jack, realizing suddenly that I wore only a bathrobe and socks, blushed and turned his head. "Oh, I'm sorry. I didn't notice."

I locked myself in the bathroom. There was only one mirror in the house, the medicine cabinet above the sink. I climbed up on the vanity and, kneeling precariously on the Formica top, obsessed over my puffy stomach, which I pinched and pulled for several minutes. I would have to add lettuce and prunes to my current I-hate-my-life diet, or six months from now I'd leave here looking like Memory Jones. Well, half of her, anyway.

Fortunately, my running pants had a drawstring waist.

Jack continued to wait for me in the living room. I heard him sneeze a couple of times. Sitting on the edge of the toilet, I leaned forward and squished my head between my knees, hoping to soothe the uneasiness in my gut. I never played like that in front of people. My public violin performances were terse and controlled, with impeccable technique and counterfeit emotion. Privately, music provided my only means to love, to grieve, to rage, and to be utterly vulnerable.

Now I felt like a fool. I had poured myself into that music, and Jack had heard. I couldn't have been more exposed if I had opened my robe and flashed the good reverend.

"I read your note," Jack said as I came out of the bathroom. He still stood by the closet. "I don't mean to be a bother, but I wanted to invite you to Jonah's annual fall fun night. It's tomorrow. There's food and games for the kids. Some dancing. Basically, it's an excuse to get out of the house before everyone gets snowed in."

"Before? There's already a foot of snow out there," I said.

"More like four inches. That's just a dusting."

"How much do you get here in a winter?"

"You don't want to know. The festival is at the Grange hall, and starts at five. So, I'll see you there?"

"I'll think about it," I said, a polite no.

He took the hint. "Well, I better get back to work. Do you need anything? I think your woodpile is low."

"Yeah, I know. I'm heading into town this afternoon," I said with a groan. "Do you think Maggie would mind if I used her phone? I need to make a few calls."

"Mom's not home. She and Beth took a trip into civilization and won't be back until late. But the inn's open. Just go in. Until tomorrow night, then."

Wordlessly, I closed the door behind Jack, but not before feeling a gust of frigid air. I put on another pair of socks and thermal long johns under my clothes, my boots, coat, hat, scarf, and gloves. I stumbled out to the truck, started it, and waited back inside the cabin for another fifteen minutes until it warmed up.

At the variety store, I took a plastic shopping basket and inspected the meager produce section: iceberg lettuce, already limp and turning brown, onions, potatoes, knobby carrots, and seven varieties of apples. My intestines screamed for roughage, so I grabbed three heads of lettuce and the carrots, finding the prunes next. I added a loaf of bread, peanut butter, some pasta, cans of sauce, and Jell-O to the basket, and brought my booty to the man at the counter.

"Excuse me," I said with a huge, friendly smile. "I'm staying at Luke Petersen's cabin. Would you know what kind of fuel I need for the water heater there? Luke probably bought it here, and maybe you remember?"

"I remember," he said, packing my groceries.

"Oh, great. That really makes my life a whole lot easier," I said, words coated with saccharine. "Um, you wouldn't happen to remember how much I would need?"

"Yep," he said.

I let out a deep breath. "Wonderful. I'll take however much I need. I have an account here, under Graham."

He scribbled on an invoice. "I know who you are."

"Of course. One more thing. Could you explain how I put the fuel in?"

"I'll do you one better. I'll come over and show you."

"You don't have to do that. I don't want to be any trouble," I told him, not meaning a single word.

"Luke would have done the same for me. Did do the same for me," he said.

Please, don't let this guy break into some Saint Luke monologue. "Well, thank you, really. Are you Mr. Brooks?"

"Yep. Carl Brooks. You need anything else?" he asked.

"Actually, you wouldn't sell firewood here, would you?"

"No, but I can get you some, have it delivered."

"Perfect. Just put it on my account. Or, have the bill sent to Rich Portabella. He'll take care of it," I said, reaching out my hand for the receipt.

Carl tore the top sheet off his pad. "You know, you weren't so nice to my wife when you came in here that other time."

I bit the inside of my cheek. I didn't want to take cold showers for the next six months, so I smiled tightly and said, "I am sorry. I was just having a bad day."

"Well, if that were true, my wife would sure like to hear it." Carl gave me the slip. "I'll be there Saturday to help you with that water heater."

Stuffing the paper in my coat pocket, I picked up my food with a pert nod and went out to the truck. I needed to call my lawyer to check on the status of the divorce, since I now had the means to settle any unpaid bill. At the inn, I dialed information, wrote down the number, then called Vincent Voykowski, Esq. I had picked him out of the yellow pages several months earlier because his ad boasted cheap, fast service.

"Vinny Voykowski. Speak to me," he answered.

"This is Sarah Graham. I'm calling about my divorce."

"Where you been, Sarah. I've been trying to reach you for days."

"I'm at a new number. Let me give it to you."

"Not gonna need it," he said. "You're finished with me. The divorce is done. The husband, ex-husband, I mean, signed the papers last week."

Vinny's words wriggled their way into my ear and lodged against the back of my skull. Mouth dry, I managed to ask, "What do I owe you?"

"Two thousand."

I gave him Rich's address. "Send the bill there."

"Sure thing. Hope I don't hear from you again soon."

"Yeah, thanks," I murmured, hanging up. Standing at the desk, thoughts churning like sweaty socks in an off-balance washer, I picked up the phone again, and dialed quickly.

Maybe he wouldn't be home.

Two rings, then, "Hello."

"David," I forced out.

"What do you want?"

"Just to see how you're doing."

"Give it up, Sarah. I signed the papers, so leave me alone."

Click. Buzz.

Good-bye.

chapter TWELVE

I found the Grange by driving around and around in the dark until I turned down a road lined with SUVs and pickups. A building at the end, windows long and orange, glowed like a four-eyed jack-o-lantern.

Pulling over, I sat in my truck, headlights off, engine idling. I couldn't stay another moment in the cabin. David's words continued to fester, no matter how loud I turned up the television to mask his voice that continued to roll around my head.

I had expected a flood of relief after the divorce, the bubbly tingle of freedom and a yearning to celebrate. Instead, cement filled the spaces between my ribs and I found it difficult to breathe. So, this was brokenheartedness, a phantom dial tone in my ear and not a single party hat in sight.

I didn't know why I felt so miserable. I had never loved David, despite our to-have-and-to-hold promises in front of judge and family after three missed periods. And he didn't—couldn't—love me. The miscarriage, six years of failed monogamy, and a three-thousand-dollar retainer should have squelched any residual doubt. But here I was, fifty yards from a hoedown, wondering if I did the right thing.

Marriage, if nothing else, gave the illusion of love. And some deranged part of me wanted that fairy tale. I remembered reading the cards from my parents' wedding. They were tucked in my grandmother's attic, in a trunk with my mother's baby clothes and training bra. The inscriptions, some written with large, looping letters, others in precise block print, varied on the same theme: *I've never seen two people more in love.* What a joke. That love left my mother bleeding on the new carpet, shot twice in a jealous rage.

It was well past seven when I finally ventured inside the hall. Children's artwork and felt banners proclaiming *Jesus is Lord* and other religious niceties covered the water-stained plaster walls.

Tables of food wrapped around the room, cakes and brownies, ziti and other casseroles. The home cooking tempted me, but I'd had to lie on the floor to zip my jeans earlier, waistband cutting into my gut. Anyway, I didn't know who prepared what, and looking at the unwashed clothes and grimy knuckles, I couldn't be sure what might be baked into those pies.

I skirted the crowd. Music reverberated from a pair of battered speakers, some whiny country tune. People stepped this way and turned that way, touching their shoulders and shaking their hips. Looking for Jack or Maggie, or even Memory, I drifted into a corner at the front of the building.

"Sarah, I'm surprised to see you here," a voice boomed behind me.

I turned and found Rich the Mushroom, balancing a heaping plateful of food on one hand, and holding onto a toddler with the other. The little girl hid her face against Rich's thigh, and he wore a necktie, the thin back tail several inches longer than the front and stained with tomato sauce.

"Yeah, well, I do love the nightlife," I said.

"Ha, ha. Honey," he called, "come here and meet Sarah."

A pudgy, gnomish woman ambled over, lugging an infant in a side sling. "Hi there, I'm Shelly Portabella."

I shook her hand.

"This little princess is Penny," Rich said. "She's almost four. And that's my son, Lane. He's five months old."

"He would have named them Yoko and John if I'd let him," Shelly said, giggling and rubbing noses with her husband before kissing him moistly on the lips. "When I was pregnant with both these two, he put headphones on my belly and blared *Magical Mystery Tour*."

Rich speared a meatball with his fork and took a bite. "Oh, you have to try these," he said, waving the saucy blob in front of Shelly. She nibbled a little before her husband stuffed the rest in his mouth. "You want a bite, Sarah? I have a bunch here."

"Uh, no. Have you seen Jack Watson?"

"Check the office. It's over there." Rich pointed.

I crossed to the opposite corner and shimmied between the piano and pulpit blocking a door marked PASTOR. Without knocking, I stepped into the dark room and swept my hand up the wall until I found the light switch.

The small study area smelled of old paper and aftershave. Unmatched bookcases flanked an antique desk and a computer. Words scrolled across the monitor:

> His lord said unto him, "Well done, thou good and faithful servant: thou hast been faithful over a few things, I will make thee ruler over many things: enter thou into the joy of thy lord."

I touched the Space bar and the screen saver disappeared, revealing an unfinished game of solitaire.

Two framed diplomas hung on the wall above the desk, both awarded to John Paul Watson: a Bachelor of Philosophy in Religious Ethics from Columbia University, summa cum laude, and a Master of Divinity from Manhattan Theological Seminary, magna cum laude.

So, not only was Jack a minister, he was disgustingly smart. That would explain all the books with titles longer than my arm. And how many Bibles did he need? KJV, NIV, NASB, HCSB, NLT—the acronyms continued across two shelves. Only alphabet soup strung more letters together.

Nestled in one corner of the desk were three photographs. The largest captured Maggie, tawny hair draped over one shoulder. She sat posed in front of a painted backdrop in a short, paisley dress, legs crossed self-consciously. A man stood behind her, his crooked smile nearly identical to Jack's, his sideburns dark and stubborn.

In the second picture, a young boy waded knee-deep in a muddy river, hair twirling in the wind. He clutched a fishing rod in one hand and a squirming steelhead in the other. The photo paper was wrinkled behind the glass.

I picked up the third frame. Beth, probably fifteen or so, laughed candidly in front of a white country church, steeple pointing into the clear, perfect sky, her face clear and perfect. I wondered how she could now look in the mirror each day without screaming. I wondered if she looked in the mirror at all.

"Sarah? What are you doing in here?" Jack asked, coming through the door.

"I was looking for you," I said. "And snooping."

"Honesty. That's refreshing," he said, taking the frame

from me. "Isn't she beautiful?" His voice was wistful, broken.

"Is that your church?" I asked, trying to segue to a more pleasant topic.

"It was," he said, setting the photo gingerly on the desk, "before it burned down."

I winced. *Smooth, Sarah.* Still, curious, I asked, "Is that what happened to—"

"Yes." Jack bit his lip. "Almost four years ago, Christmas Eve. Beth and her friend Danielle were in the basement with a few kindergarteners, getting on costumes for the annual pageant. We're still not sure what happened, but the old church lit up like kindling. They were trapped downstairs.

"By some miracle, Beth survived. But no one else." He swiped at his eyes, sniffled, now his turn to redirect the conversation. "So, what do you think? You like my place?"

"You don't live here, do you?"

"Is it that awful? Admittedly, it's a bachelor's pad, but I'm not using empty pizza boxes for a coffee table, or anything like that. The pastor's residence was attached to the church building. After the fire, Mom wanted me to move back into the inn, but people come looking for me at all sorts of crazy hours. I didn't want her to deal with that. Anyway, we hold services here at the Grange now, so it's convenient. Roll out of bed and onto the pulpit."

"Do you even have a bed?"

"The couch pulls out," Jack said. "Zip your coat. You can't come to Jonah's fall fun night without trying a traditional lumberjack delicacy. After that, you're free to go."

He led me from the room, hand pressed lightly against the small of my back. Heads turned toward us in unison, people elbowed each other and whispered behind their plastic punch cups. Jack seemed unfazed by the rubbernecking, stopping every few steps to chat and introduce me. I kept my eyes on the slush-streaked floor.

Outside, the rimy wind wove its fingers through my hair, stretching it into the night, a fiery tempest. I flicked up my hood and slumped deep into my parka. Children—gloveless, hatless, and rosy-cheeked—shouted playfully and threw snow at one another.

I followed Jack to a man standing at a gas grill, ice cream scoop in his hand. "How'd ya do, Reverend?" he asked.

"I'm wonderful tonight, Tom. And you're doing well?"

"Can't complain. Except Karen is in there dancing with that Reynolds boy. What ya think of that?"

"Charlie Reynolds is a good kid. So is Karen. I wouldn't worry," Jack said.

"That's what the wife said. 'Course, I reminded her that her mama told her daddy the same thing, right before me and her ran off and got ourselves married."

Jack laughed. "Tom, this is Sarah Graham."

Tom touched the brim of his baseball cap. "Tom Hardy. Sure do miss your dad."

My head twitched in acknowledgment. "Yeah."

"Two, please," Jack said.

"No problem," Tom replied, scooping packed snow into paper cups. He put on an oven mitt and grabbed one of the metal tins from the grill, dumping some brown liquid onto the snow.

Jack handed me one of the cups, and a spoon. "This is jack's wax."

"Your what?"

"No, jack as in lumberjack. Hot maple syrup over snow,

the perfect dessert for poor loggers deep in the mountains. Let it cool for a minute."

I took a bite of the now-chewy syrup, mouth puckering at the sweetness. "It needs a shot of something stronger."

"I'm sure it's been done," Jack said. "Are you cold?"

"Very."

"Let's go in."

The warm Grange air promptly thawed my nose, and it started dripping, tickling my upper lip. I sniffled.

"There you are," Maggie said, rushing over to us. When Jack turned to speak with her, I wiped my nose with my glove and stuck it in my pocket. I'd wash it later.

"Iris Finn is going crazy. You haven't returned your votes for the bake-off." She paused. "Where have you been all night?"

There was something in her voice—the question chafed with motherly vigilance. Jack seemed to notice, too. He removed a handful of paper strips from his pocket. "I was mingling," he said, his tone deliberate, his eyes steady on his mother. "Then I showed Sarah around the place and introduced her to jack's wax. Here. Would you make sure Iris gets them?"

Maggie took the ballots. "I'll find her now." She started to walk away, but stopped, turned back. "And don't worry about the kitchen. Us ladies will take care of it."

The crowd had dwindled. A few dozen people bopped around the speakers or milled near the food. "I can see if there's any coffee left," Jack offered.

I dropped my coat on an empty chair.

"Dance with me," I said. "Or aren't you allowed?"

Jack wavered, eyes sweeping the room, and then said, "Sure, why not?"

"How progressive. Do you let your pregnant women wear shoes, too?"

"Funny," he said, piling his coat on mine. "Actually, our denomination permits shoes. And dancing, even by pastors."

"You don't kiss snakes and roll around on the floor, do you?"

"No, that's not us. Most would say we're somewhere between a bit conservative and downright boring."

We moved into the group of couples. Jack's hand gently, chastely, settled on my waist, just above my hip. I tightened my stomach. His other hand was warm in mine.

I noticed a woman glowering at us, arms akimbo, hair so black it shimmered blue, like raven feathers. But before I could question Jack about her, he asked, "I have to know, how long have you been playing the violin?"

"Since I was six. I was at a rummage sale, and wanted to buy something with my own money. I had a nickel, and the only thing I could afford was an old Jascha Heifetz record. After that, I begged my grandmother for lessons. She made me earn them by polishing her silverware, scrubbing the floors. Dusting. Whatever." I shrugged. "I really don't play anymore."

"But you love it."

Instead of answering, I slid my hand from his shoulder to the back of his neck, closing the space between us. Jack tensed as I leaned into him and tucked my head under his chin. Each time he swallowed, I felt his throat bob against my brow bone, his stubble coarse on my skin.

As soon as the music stopped, he took two large steps away from me and nodded toward the kitchen. "I should go help the ladies clean up back there."

"Sure, yeah," I said.

He paused. "Now that you know how to get here, maybe I'll see you Sunday?"

"Not a chance."

"Well, I have to try. It's that pesky pastor in me," he said with that uneven, chapped-lip grin I was beginning to find infectious. "Have a good night, then."

I stood there, in the center of the floor, watching Jack leave. The fluttery, warm feeling I had while my cheek was pressed against his chest—the stuff first dates are made of—withered away, replaced by a roomful of intrusive, skittering eyes. I yanked on my coat and drove back to the cabin.

I was alone. Again. But this time, for some reason, it stung.

chapter THIRTEEN

Jack wedged a rumpled paperback under one table leg, a folded washcloth under another. "How's that?" he asked, on his knees beneath the tablecloth.

"Much better," Ephraim Joseph said.

After brushing off his pants, Jack sat across from the retired minister, who proceeded to fold his hands and pray over their lunch. Then Ephraim passed a tray of deviled eggs. Jack spooned four onto his plate and ate them quickly, gulping iced tea after each bite. Still, the gritty yolks coated his tongue.

"Tell Clara thank you for these, but she really doesn't need to go through all the trouble," he said.

"It's no trouble at all," Ephraim said. "Quite the contrary, she tells me she enjoys making them for you. She knows you love them."

Jack hated deviled eggs.

Not long after he returned from seminary, the Josephs had invited him to dinner. Clara made the bluish-white blobs, amply garnished with paprika and snipped parsley. Jack managed to swallow a couple without retching, and told her they were delicious. Since then, the thoughtful woman unfailingly sent several dozen with her husband each time he and Jack met for lunch, every other week.

Oh, the folly of lying, even with the best intentions. His stomach would gripe all evening.

"And how are things with Sarah Graham?" Ephraim asked. "She appears to be quite fond of you."

"We just danced."

"Yes, I have heard several detailed reports."

"No doubt," Jack said. "Maybe Sunday's sermon should be on gossip."

Ephraim's mouth lifted slightly at the corners. "I know your eyes are heavenward, Jack. I've never doubted that, not for a moment, not even when you were a child. But that girl's eyes are elsewhere."

Jack sighed. He pressed his two middle fingers on the bridge of his nose, where it met the forehead. "No, you're right. You're right."

Sarah was looking for something, and it certainly wasn't Jesus. He had seen her flaunt herself consciously, unconsciously—one too many open buttons on her blouse, a loitering glance, a smile—using her body as a sword, to draw first blood. As Kevlar, to protect that soft underbelly, for fear that someone should reach through and find himself too close to her heart.

Jack walked a tenuous line, struggling with how to best reach out to her, wanting to be accessible but not overly involved. But if he waited until she asked for help, it wouldn't be until she needed some strong arms to pack her truck in May.

Her music stayed with him, coursing through him as he stared at the black ceiling during the night, sleep buzzing in his ear like a hungry mosquito that wouldn't be caught.

Something resonated in each of Sarah's notes, each pass of the bow on those steel strings, something so close to hope, and it hid under the tattered memory of a little girl with a five-cent record album.

Could someone connect with her through those notes? Brenda Hardy played the fiddle, but it was bluegrass twang, pig Latin to Sarah's poetry. Jack knew of only one other person in Jonah who had any sort of classical music knowledge—Patty Saltzman. She and Sarah in the same room was a bad idea, like a fox in a hen house.

Who would be the fox and who the hen, it was difficult to say.

"I'm open to suggestions," he told Ephraim.

The elderly man considered this for a moment, brow deeply creased. "I think your sister would be good for her."

"She'd eat Beth alive."

"No." Ephraim shook his head. "Beth isn't a child anymore, as much as you like to pretend otherwise. I think she would be very good for Sarah."

"I'll talk to her."

"Good. Is that all?"

Jack pushed back his plate. "The Christmas pageant. I want to have it again this year."

"I agree it's time."

"Will anyone else?"

"Perhaps not. But it is your decision."

"I'll make the announcement tomorrow after the service."

After Ephraim left, Jack tugged on his boots and wrapped the leftovers in aluminum foil. He'd bring them to the Baldwins—one mother, two jobs, five small children and no ends met; they loved deviled eggs.

chapter FOURTEEN

I'd forgotten to buy an ice scraper.

A thin frozen crust encased the truck, caused by an unseasonable afternoon drizzle and plunging overnight temperatures. I used a steak knife to chip the ice from around the driver's door, and found only a snowbrush in the cab. I would have simply started the truck and cranked up the heat until the ice melted, but I was worried the gas would run out in the process—the fuel gauge hovered at E.

Inside my gloves, my fingers prickled from the cold as I scraped the windshield with a plastic spatula. The handle snapped and I tossed the pieces into the snow. A metal tablespoon worked better, though it took twenty minutes to clean all the windows.

After all this trouble, I'd better be able to find a job.

With my eyeballs rotting in my head from too much television, and my paunch undeterred by a three-day lettuce diet, I knew that only some type of daily, scheduled activity would keep me out of a straitjacket. Self-motivated, I was not. I doubted, however, there was a hiring frenzy in town.

I didn't mind working. I'd put in my share of menial

labor, the kind usually reserved for high school graduates and single mothers. I even busked in college. Many of the Juilliard music majors did, including the trust-fund bunch— something about suffering for one's art. Basically, it was an easy way to earn a few dollars for beer while putting in the practice hours. I clearly wouldn't be standing on any street corners here. Anyway, I doubted a single person in Jonah could tell the difference between a Dvořák symphony and the dueling *Deliverance* banjos.

Well, maybe Jack could.

Jack. I thought that he might come by Sunday morning, attempting to goad me into a pew. He didn't, and that was the problem with nice guys—they actually did what people asked. I would have much preferred his showing up on my porch, and my dismissing him with a "Didn't you listen to a word I said? I don't want to be bothered." At least then I would know he was thinking of me.

Like I was thinking of him.

Since the dance, Jack had impinged on my thoughts, mostly blurred recollections I swiftly quashed. Occasionally, though, my mind wandered down unhealthy paths that included two cats, joint checking accounts, and a picket fence.

"Enough, enough, enough," I growled, stabbing the key into the truck ignition and twisting.

The engine sputtered, gasped, and then turned over. Gas first.

The station was a few miles south of the inn and offered a full-service pump. It cost nineteen cents more per gallon, but who cared? My father was paying the tab.

A stocky young man with piceous eyes plodded to the truck. He reminded me of a garden slug, thick and slow. I rolled down my window and handed him the credit card. "Fill it up."

He did. The name patch on his jacket read *Dominic*.

Now, where was I going to find a job?

Sunlight flared through the windshield, blinding me. I flipped down the visor and a small white card fluttered to my lap. I turned it over. Doc's card. Well, it was as good a place to start as any.

I found the office on Main Street. A receptionist—the tart, midnight-haired woman from the dance—paged through a celebrity news magazine at the front desk.

"Can I help you?" she asked.

"Is Doc White in?"

Her eyes narrowed slightly. Maybe a few years older than me, her lips gleamed with deep claret lipstick. "You don't have an appointment."

"No, but could you please tell him I'm here?"

"You can wait. He's busy now," she said, turning back to her reading.

I sat, shuffling through the dated magazines and tabloids, finding one with headlines announcing proof positive aliens had landed on earth. Probably here. That would explain things.

Doc came out of a back room. "Patty, I thought I heard— Oh, why didn't you tell me Sarah was here?"

"She doesn't have an appointment," the receptionist said.

"Sarah, come on back," Doc said, handing Patty some envelopes. "Please go mail these."

"Okay, I will."

"Now."

Patty pulled on a yellow parka and trudged out the door.

"Loud," I said.

"You're telling me." Doc led me into an examination room.

"I meant her coat."

"I didn't," he said. "That girl has the biggest mouth in town, and the biggest ears. Worse than her mother, and that's difficult to believe, if you know Ima-Louise Saltzman."

"I had the pleasure of meeting her last week, at the diner," I said. "I don't think she liked me."

"You were sitting with Jack Watson. That would do it. Can't help but overhear; my ears are big, too. They already have Patty's wedding dress picked out, you know. She's been trying to get her Jezebel red fingernails into the reverend for years."

I laughed. "That's not very nice."

"I'm not very nice. Anyway, I'm not making it up. Her nail polish is called Jezebel Red. I watch her touch up several times a day." He cleared his throat, a gloppy, guttural haw. "I thought you were leaving."

"Change of plans," I said, wringing my fingers in my lap.

I looked around the room. Cheap paneling, shabby brown carpet, and none of the generic pastel landscapes expected in doctors' offices. The exam table was brown, too, and the synthetic cover had cracked and been taped several times.

"I need a job. You don't even have to pay me."

"An altruist. I'm shocked."

"I'll go insane if I don't have something to kill time through the winter."

"The diner might be hiring."

"Heck, no," I gagged.

"I'm joking. I do have something for you. The winter weather is hard on many of my patients, and I have some who need to be looked in on more frequently than I have the time for. I'll give you a hundred dollars a week to do it."

"Do what, exactly? I don't want to be emptying bedpans."

"Visit folks. Talk to them for an hour or so. Make sure they're eating, and that their heat works. That sort of thing."

"You're talking companion. Not nurse."

"Yep. Be here tomorrow at nine, and dress warm."

I was gone before Patty and her big ears returned.

chapter FIFTEEN

I pulled in front of Doc's office at twenty-eight minutes after nine. He was waiting for me in the Jeep, engine on.

"You're late," he said.

I yawned. "Sorry."

"I bet," Doc said, skidding onto the road. "We'll go north today. Start with Ben Harrison and his wife, Rabbit."

"As in bunny?"

"Ben has a diabetic ulcer on his foot and can't hunt. It's killing them to depend on someone else. Normally, he hunts year round. She has a vegetable garden in the summer, and jars the surplus for the winter."

Pine trees packed the woods on each side, crowding the road, which now rose headlong into the sky. Pressure swelled in my ears. I pinched my nose and blew.

"There's gum in the glove box," Doc said.

Cramming two sticks of Juicy Fruit in my mouth, I balled the foil wrappers in my palm and flicked them onto the floor with several others. Doc took a left, and another, and then turned right at a junkyard. Weeds, sinewy and taut, lashed hunks of rusted metal to the snow. A school bus tilted drunkenly on two flat tires amidst the scrap heaps.

"I won't remember how to get here," I told him.

"I'll draw you a map."

The Jeep lurched through the woods. I rested my forehead against the window. Condensation bloomed around my nose and mouth, and I closed my eyes, dozing until Doc nudged my shoulder. We were parked in front of a ramshackle shed; it listed to the right, one wall bowed like a hunchback. The lone window was broken, with several layers of green garbage bags taped over it. The shingles rippled under a moldy nylon tarp. Doc wrapped his scarf over his ears and climbed out of the car.

"Where's the house?" I asked, briskly rubbing my face to wake up.

"This is it. Grab that bag on the back seat."

He knocked once and opened the door. I followed, carrying the grocery sack, bracing for some horrible stench or towers of empty cat food cans. Instead, the one-room home was tiny but neat, except for the tangle of blankets on top of a mattress. Two bentwood chairs and a potbellied stove filled the remaining space. The floor was dirt and recently swept, broom bristle lines still visible.

A sun-dried woman sat in one chair, sewing a patch on a corduroy jacket. Her hair hung to her waist in two stringy, uneven horsetails.

"Doc, his foot ain't no better," she said.

Barely glancing at me, she crossed the room in four strides, peeling back the pile of blankets to reveal a bearded man. He moaned. "Get off me, woman."

She slapped the top of his head. "Hush. The doc be here."

The man propped himself on his elbows. "Oh, Doc, I ain't going nowhere with you. You can take my leg off right here, but if you tries to get me to a hospital, I'll shoot you like a stew squirrel."

"Keep your gun on the wall, Ben," Doc said. "I'm just here to take a look."

I peeked over Doc's shoulder as he unwrapped a bandage, exposing a fist-sized ulcer on the ball of Ben's foot. Callused skin, putrid and yellow, ringed a meaty crater. "Rabbit, I need that pan," Doc said.

The woman lugged a cast-iron pan from the shelf above the stove. Doc lined it with a large sterile pad and put Ben's foot in it. He took a bottle of clear liquid—*saline*, the label read—from his bag and flushed the wound, and then applied a cream. "If you get queasy, Sarah, you shouldn't watch," he said, wiping his instruments with alcohol. Using forceps to lift the edge of the dead skin, he sliced off a chunk with a scalpel, continuing until the rotted skin was removed. Then Doc took a blunt metal rod and probed the raw flesh.

"You still smoking?" he asked Ben.

"I tries to quit, but, Doc, you be making me lay here all day. Ain't nothing else to do."

Doc dabbed on another ointment and dressed the wound. He gave the tube to Rabbit. "Apply this twice a day when you change the bandage. And here. This is an antibiotic. Have him take one pill at breakfast and one before bed. Ben, listen to me. No smoking. And no alcohol."

"Come on, Doc."

"I mean it. Now, this is Sarah Graham. She'll be checking in on you once a week and bringing your groceries."

"Oh, no." Rabbit shook her head, oily hair slapping against

the cabin walls. "I don't be wanting that girl here, spitting on how we live. You come."

"You know I can only get here once a month."

"But—"

"Do you want your husband to lose his foot?"

Rabbit's mouth snapped shut. She crouched, twisting her gangly arms around the paper bag. "I have to be putting this meat in the snow," she said, the flimsy door slamming behind her.

"Don't pay Rabbit no mind," Ben said. "She's a jealous one. Don't want no other woman looking at me." Grinning through thorny whiskers, he added, "It don't bother me none."

Rabbit was nowhere to be seen as we got back into the Jeep.

"That man should be in a hospital," I told Doc.

"And you care?"

My nostrils flared, and I ground my teeth together, staring straight ahead. He was right. If Ben had his foot lopped off tomorrow, I would continue to eat, drink, and be merry. Well, as merry as I got.

Doc shook his head. "Most of the people around here, they don't have insurance. Some of them don't even have indoor plumbing. They're like Ben and Rabbit. All they know is this mountain.

"Yes, Ben should be in a hospital. Can I force him there? Should I? I do what I can, Sarah. I treat my patients with samples given to me by drug reps, with old pharmacy stock and things I pick up from garage sales. Heck, I even pull from my own medicine cabinet.

"It took me months, years in some cases, to get these people to trust me. They're proud. And they don't take handouts. Mostly, I'm paid in venison and jars of apple butter, a handful of loose change now and then. Someone offered me a chicken once. A live one." Doc laughed a little. "And Hiram Dennison gives me old *National Geographics*. I have no idea where he got them, but so far I've collected April 1957 to December 1961."

"You're the altruist."

"No, not me."

"Yeah, right. Why else would you be here, schlepping around in the snow, eating dead deer?"

Doc seemed to age twenty years with my question, shoulders crumpling as he turned down another rutted path. "We all have skeletons. Do you want to share yours first?"

I adjusted the heat vent, listening as the birch twigs whipped against the side panels of the Jeep, scratching the paint. Hot air blew into my face. I unzipped my jacket a little, an embarrassed sweat dampening my neck.

"Where to now?" I asked finally, my voice raspy, unsure.

"Back to that school bus."

"Someone lives there?"

"Welcome to the mountain, Sarah."

Someone did, indeed, live in the school bus, though it had been converted to a house. Sort of. Hiram Dennison had a refrigerator, heater, and electric lights that ran off a generator he had built from junk parts. A coarse-furred mutt slept on a mound of magazines.

After that, Doc took me to four other homes, giving a brief history before each visit. Like Hiram, these patients were poor and brittle, their faces etched with mountain living. I went back to the cabin that night feeling like a wet cardboard box stored too long in a cellar, drooping and smelly. Before falling onto the couch, I set my alarm. I had another appointment with Doc, to meet the rest of his geriatrics ward.

Arriving five minutes early the next morning, I hauled my aching body into Doc's Jeep, sore from yesterday's backroad adventure. He handed me a covered mug of coffee.

"This is disgusting." I coughed the liquid back into the cup. "What'd you do, scrape it from the bottom of the pot?"

"You're welcome," he said, taking a sip of his own drink.

We kept to the towns, visiting two winter-eaten trailers in Jonah, a cinderblock building in Deer Lake, a garage apartment in Greeley, and a huge, crumbling farmhouse on the outskirts of Bethel with Volkswagen-sized holes in the floor and rats that scampered in the ceiling.

Finally, Doc announced the last stop.

"Zuriel Washington. She's almost a hundred and near blind, but her mind is sharp."

The home, a cluster of ill-matched additions, squatted in a copse of blue juniper. Threads of smoke dribbled from the stone chimney.

"Careful. The second step is rotted through. Zuriel," Doc called as we stepped into a sparsely furnished sitting area. One vintage brocade chair faced the room's single window, and beside it, a lacquered dark-wood table with carved lion's feet. Billie Holiday's moody croon drifted from the back of the house.

I heard squeaks and clunks, and a woman appeared in the doorway. She clutched a metal walker. "Doc, you've brought someone," she said.

She looked older than her one hundred years, if that

was possible. Her skin, the color of cinnamon sticks, hung loosely over her skull, as if she borrowed it from someone much larger, or bought it off a clearance rack. Age spots clung to her cheeks like leeches. Filmy, sightless eyes peered out from between rheum-caked eyelids, and her earlobes hung nearly to her chin.

But her voice was a lullaby of fireflies and snickerdoodles. My tense muscles relaxed under her words.

"This is Sarah. She'll be stopping by once a week."

"It is a pleasure, my dear," Zuriel said. "But you know I don't need to be checked in on, Doc. Someone from my church brings over a hot meal every night."

"Yes, but do they read to you?" Doc asked.

The old woman's right hand flittered to her throat and rubbed at a gold cross pendant dangling there. "Thank you," she whispered.

"Are there any particular books you'd like Sarah to bring next week?"

"Oh, anything is just fine." Zuriel said. "What day can I expect you, my dear?"

"Tuesday," I said.

Oddly enough, I was looking forward to it.

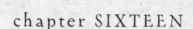

chapter SIXTEEN

A dusky figure stood against the cabin door when I returned from Zuriel's. I thought it was Jack at first, hoped it was. I jammed my forearm against my stomach to stop the cartwheels.

I wasn't even wearing mascara.

But the twilight fooled me, as it's prone to do. My headlights deflated the shadow. It was Beth. She waved at me as I parked.

"Sarah, hi. I don't want to bother you or anything, but I know you don't have a phone. Do you have a minute?"

I groaned inwardly, wanting only to change to warm pajamas, burrow into my sleeping bag, and snooze until Tuesday. But even I had a problem saying no to a cripple. "Come on in," I told her.

I hung my coat on the hook by the door. Beth kept hers on. "I have something to ask you," she said, gingerly removing her hat. "A favor."

"Uh-huh?"

"The church is having this Christmas Eve service, and

I'm going to sing. Jack told me you play the violin." She hesitated. "Would you accompany me?"

"I don't know . . ."

"You don't have to if you don't want. But to be honest, I'm really nervous about it. I haven't sung in front of people in a few years, and I thought that, if you played, everyone would be paying attention to you and, maybe, they wouldn't notice me so much. Jack said you're wonderful."

"He exaggerates."

"My brother doesn't know how to exaggerate."

My eyes drifted over her face. The upper rim of her left ear was missing. Pity rose in my mouth—a salty flood of saliva—and for a moment I was thankful my own wounds were well concealed, on the inside and away from scrutiny. I, at least, could pretend I was whole.

Darn that cripple thing.

"Okay," I said.

Beth sprung forward and hugged me. "Really? Oh, thanks so much, Sarah."

I twisted away from her and went to the woodstove, chucking in another log, flames nipping my fingers. The air quivered feverishly against my cheeks. I was six inches and a dizzy spell from looking like a napalmed marshmallow. From looking like Beth. "Do you have your song picked out?"

She pulled a hardcover from her pocket, gave it to me. "Hymn 171."

Most of the pages were no longer sewn into the binding. I shuffled through, the aged paper shedding corners and edges, and a few printed words here and there. I found it—"It Is Well With My Soul." I hauled Luke's violin from the closet, opened the latches in three curt pops. "Are you ready?"

"You want me to sing now?"

I raised an eyebrow. Just one. I had practiced this for hours as a child, sitting in front of a mirror, holding my left brow still while twitching my right up and down. "That's what you came for." I snuggled into the chinrest, my body responding to the cool wood, the scent of rosin.

Beth fumbled briefly with her zipper, slipped off her ski jacket, and, drawing a wobbly breath, began to sing. Her voice wasn't striking, but there was a poignancy to it, and a delicate vibrato tinkled like a sterling jewel box—the kind with the spinning ballerina in the lid.

I'd always wanted one of those, but my grandmother thought dancing was one of Satan's most clever seductions.

I played the melody along with Beth until she began the second verse, and then dropped to the harmony line, folding my notes around hers. The tune reeked of pews and padded kneelers, so I improvised the remaining verses—some double stops here, a few trills there, a handful of gaudy flourishes. By the end, however, Beth tired, sucking quick, coarse breaths between syllables, her words full of holes. She shrugged. "I ran out of steam, I guess. Can I have a drink?"

"I'll put a cadenza in the middle, between the third and fourth verses. It'll give you a chance to rest."

"What's that?"

"Basically, a chance for me to show off. Diet Coke okay?"

"Thanks," she said. "Please don't tell my mother what I'm singing. It's sort of a gift for her, one of her favorite hymns."

"Yeah, no problem."

She popped the metal tab, soda can opening with a hiss. Foam oozed between her fingers, onto the counter. "And don't tell Jack. He's horrible at keeping secrets. Not that he doesn't try, but he can't tell even a tiny fib. If Mom questions him and he knows, his face will give it all away."

"I don't think that will be an issue. I haven't seen your brother in days." Since Friday night, but who kept track of such things? "How is he?"

"Busy. Always busy. I couldn't do it. Last year, for his birthday, I tried to get him a day to sleep in, asking everyone not to bother him until at least noon. I think his first phone call came at seven-thirty, which is about two hours later than usual." She laughed, but added, "I'm sure if you needed to talk or something, he'd be here."

"I'm fine." I sponged up the wayward soda.

Beth picked up her coat. "Do you think we could practice again sometime? I know you'll be busy now with work, but—"

"Work?"

"For Doc. Was I not supposed to know? It seemed common knowledge around town."

"Right. This very wonderful, very small town," I said, tossing the dishrag at the sink. It somersaulted off the edge, to the floor.

"You'll get used to it."

"I certainly hope not." I set the violin in the case, but did not close the lid. "Monday, Wednesday, and Friday nights. Be here at seven, unless you have a hot date." Immediately, I wished I could reach out to snatch my words and stuff them back into my mouth.

Beth, however, seemed unfazed. "Not hardly," she said, struggling a bit to get her coat on. Her left arm moved stiffly, heavy almost, as if an invisible weight hung from her fingertips and she was too weak to lift it. "See you Friday, then."

I picked up the dishrag and went to dump the half-empty can of soda down the sink. But my Diet Coke supply was dwindling, only eight left, so I poured the warm liquid into a glass and drank it. The gas ballooned in my throat. I belched.

The violin stared at me from its perch on the back of the couch, f-hole eyes dark, squinty. I went to it, ran my fingers across the strings. They moaned softly, beckoning me to pick up the instrument, to cradle it, play it. But I couldn't. Not tonight. I'd had too much life this week.

chapter SEVENTEEN

Beth dropped her wet boots on the doormat and found her mother in the overstuffed tapestry chair, pillows stuffed around her hips and spine, knitting a sweater sleeve.

"How did it go?" Maggie asked.

"Good. Very good, actually."

"Are you going to tell me yet?"

"No, it's a surprise. You'll find out Christmas Eve." Beth kissed her mother's forehead. "Good night."

In stocking feet, she skated down the hallway on the freshly polished oak floor. A prick of static ignited between the metal doorknob and her fingers as she went into her bedroom, still decorated with her girlhood eyelet canopy and pink walls.

Beth had thought about getting a place of her own, some postage-stamp apartment in one of the surrounding hamlets. But Jonah was her insulation, her swaddling cloth. And she could never leave her mother alone in this hulking Victorian. She would grow old here, caring for Maggie when the arthritis drove her to bed, and occasionally renting a room to wandering leaf-peekers. Perhaps one day she'd be known as the Spinster of the Inn, the one who left her Christmas lights up all year, and a dead balsam wreath on the door well into August.

Beth changed to her nightgown. When the bandages were first removed, she had put on her clothes in the dark, fumbling at her buttons and sometimes finding her underwear on backwards. With the tags sewn into the side seam, she could never remember if they went on the right or left. She had showered with the lights out, too, wearing bath gloves to wash, not wanting to feel how her skin puckered and folded like a pile of dirty towels kicked in a corner.

Hiding, she soon found, was exhausting. She grew tired of wearing turtlenecks on summer days, and darting behind trees to avoid being seen by passing cars during her evening walks. She had woke on the morning of her eighteenth birthday to an overcast sky, and realized, with both shame and repentance, that God didn't spare her life so she could live as if she were dead. She dressed with the shades up, ate a stack of warm peach pancakes, and drove to the diner to apply for a job.

Now, more than a year since that epiphany, she could no longer close her eyes and picture herself before the fire. There were things, however, she couldn't forget. The peppery stench of charred nose hair. The sight of her skin curling in ribbons from her arm. The daily burn baths, when the nurses scoured her body, their hands steel wool on silk, washing away dead flesh and infection. She would wail and moan, sometimes vomiting from the pain, her morphine drip as effective as orange juice. Later, lying in her hospital bed swathed in fresh gossamer dressings, she'd listen to the shrieks of the other patients, and be grateful it wasn't her.

Beth remembered, too, the stretches of sleepless nights as she healed, when the itchiness grew so unbearable she would bite her tongue until it bled. Maggie would stay awake with her, slathering antihistamine lotion over her skin and singing old-time hymns, one after another, always ending with "It Is Well With My Soul." She grew to hate the song, imagining its author, Horatio Spafford, and his ironclad faith, scribbling those words while sailing over the watery grave of his drowned children merely days after their deaths.

She had hated herself, too, for her inability to muster even a crumb of his conviction. But now she could say with sincerity that things were well. Not perfect. Well. How she wanted to prove that at the pageant, to have people listen not just to her words—Spafford's words—but to the peace infused into them. She wasn't that scared little burned girl anymore.

Burrowing into the freshly changed sheets, Beth inhaled deeply. She loved clean linens, all crispy against her, smelling white and sunny, even though it was too cold to hang them on the line. Her mother added lavender oil to the wash, and herbal fabric softener. Beth never remembered to throw in a dryer sheet. She hoped she wouldn't be taking over duties at the inn anytime soon. Maggie was a much better housekeeper.

chapter EIGHTEEN

I had no reason to be awake at eight-thirty on a Sunday morning, but I was, tossing and sighing, too hot with the sleeping bag zipped to my neck, too cold with my limbs sticking outside of it. The couch, short and unforgiving, forced my body into odd contortions, and I often woke with my head hanging off the cushions, or my arms folded under me, crushed and numb.

I could not bring myself to sleep in Luke's bed.

The knock came just as I kicked off the blankets again, three short raps at the front door. It had to be Jack. He couldn't see me like this, hair snarled around my shoulders, drool crusted in the corners of my mouth. "One minute," I shouted at the door, snatching yesterday's jeans from the floor and running into the bathroom.

I splashed a couple handfuls of icy water on my face to shrink my sleep-swollen nose. Dragged a brush through my hair, and swirled Listerine over my tongue while dabbing on a bit of eye shadow. And lip gloss. I dropped the blush in the toilet while fumbling to open the little case, so I pinched my cheeks for color. Jeans, sweater. Done.

"I'm coming," I called again, and fluffed my hair before opening the door.

"Morning," Doc said. "Did I wake you?"

I deflated. "Yeah. You did."

"Well, you're dressed now. Get your boots on," he told me. "I have another job for you."

"It's Sunday morning."

"You have someplace to be?"

I tied my boots on over two pairs of socks, pulled on a second sweater, and cocooned into the rest of my outdoor survival gear. Doc sped off in his toasty warm Jeep, and I followed him, truck still an icebox.

We stopped in front of a house set into a hill, with nine terraced steps up to a dilapidated screened porch. Memory Jones answered the door.

"Doc? It's Sunday, ain't it? We don't got nothing going on today."

"We're here because it is Sunday. You know Sarah. She's going to sit with Robert so you can get to church."

Memory's grin stretched across her flabby face, thin-lipped and shimmering with teeth. "Well, paint me pink and call me a ballerina. Come in, come in. I got oatmeal in the pot, still warm, if ya want some."

The hallway stunk of Clorox and pine cleaner, and something else, something bitter. Ammonia, perhaps, or vinegar. I tried to breathe through my mouth.

"Go get dressed," Doc said. "I'll make the introductions."

Memory swished around a corner, nightgown flapping at her ankles. I followed Doc into another room, with a couch, coffee table, and hospital bed. "Sarah, this is Robert, Memory's son."

The man in the bed didn't move. Slack-jawed, with his

neck crooked backward and his arms pulled into his chest, he looked like a fossilized dinosaur, one just excavated from a prehistoric tar pit, all papery skin over bone.

"What's wrong with him?" I asked.

"He's in a minimally conscious state due to traumatic brain injury."

Memory lumbered in then, dressed in what I assumed was her Sunday best—a long-sleeved gray tent with a black turtleneck beneath it. Red thermal underwear stuck to her legs, fire hydrants in galoshes.

"Sweet boy, I'm off to church. Sarah here's real nice, and she'll stay with you 'til I'm back." She kissed Robert on the cheek, seemingly oblivious to his gutter breath, which I could smell across the room. "He likes to be read to. There's some of his favorites. And I always turn on the Gospel Grace show at ten. Radio's already tuned in."

She left, battered Bible under her arm, covers held together with rubber bands. Doc started out, too, but I grabbed the end of his scarf. "You can't leave me here with him," I said.

"Relax. All you have to do is sit for an hour or so," he said, and was gone.

So I sat, listening to Robert gurgle and smack, wondering if I should at least wipe the growing puddle of saliva from the front of his shirt. At ten, I turned the radio on, and listened to the scratchy hollering of some preacher about his good friend, JEE-zuss. Robert opened his eyes and stared at the ceiling, his tongue flopping about like an epileptic eel.

I went to use the bathroom. It was shockingly clean, white, except for permanent mineral stains in the sink and bowl. A showerhead protruded from one wall, but there was no tub, just a drain in the tile floor. Memory bought the cheap toilet tissue, wafer-thin and gritty. I pressed the flusher handle. Nothing happened.

Returning to the living room, I plowed into Memory.

"Your toilet won't flush," I said.

"That little chain busted a couple months back. You gotta stick your hand in the tank and pull up the flapper thing." She laughed, I think at me, as my face puckered with disgust. "I'll do it. You're a guest. Can't have my guest getting their elbows wet. That ain't hospitable. No, it ain't."

"Well, okay. Thanks. I'm going now."

"Wait one minute. I sure ain't gonna let you off without feeding you. I got mac and cheese loaf, sliced thin, and a jar of mayo. Bread, too."

"I really need to go."

"Well, then, I'll make sure to double stuff you on Thursday."

"Thursday?"

"Thanksgiving, girl. You don't got nowhere else to be, right?"

I opened my mouth, but no excuse came out.

"Good," Memory said. "See you here at two."

chapter NINETEEN

I made the local rounds Tuesday, checking in on Doc's patients and spending five, maybe six minutes with them, saving Zuriel for last. On my way through her house to find her, I peered into doorways; the rooms were empty, mostly, with an occasional chair or dresser pushed against a wall and filmy with dust.

"Zuriel." I found her in a back room, the largest room, settled in a bentwood rocker, cockled hands nimbly tatting a doily.

"Oh, Sarah, I'm so glad you came. How are you?"

Her voice glided around me, and she waited for my reply, sightless eyes on my face. "I'm fine," I said.

Zuriel let out a long, light breath. "I have faith you'll mean those words one day," she said. "Please, sit."

I did, in the rocker next to her.

"My grandson made these chairs. Comfortable, aren't they?"

"Yes." And they were. The back slats contoured to me, as if the seat was designed for the curves of my spine only.

Furniture cramped this large room, unlike the others.

Zuriel spent most of her time here, I could tell. A handmade bed with a log headboard filled one corner, and a matching wardrobe stood in another. Next to my chair was a curiously shaped piano, flat-topped and nearly square. It had been there a long time, as the floor buckled under the carved legs. But it did not belong in this place, with its exotic, tiger-grained wood and filigree music desk. I picked at the keys, producing several delicate notes reminiscent of a Mozart pianoforte.

"Do you play?" Zuriel asked.

"Not really, no. Unless you consider "Chopsticks" playing."

She smiled ruefully. "I suppose the old girl will keep mute a while longer."

I pulled a couple of books from a plastic grocery bag, a mystery and a legal thriller I had taken from my father's extensive library, and asked Zuriel which she preferred. "Growing up, I had only two books to read. The Bible and Webster's dictionary," she said. "So you choose. I can listen to anything, any number of times."

Flipping to the beginning page of the John Grisham, I began to read. For an hour, it was just my voice and the squeak of the old woman's rocker moving back and forth, back and forth. I could have stayed all afternoon in Zuriel's halcyon presence, but she said, "I think I'll have a nap now."

I helped her into the bed and folded the coverlet under her hoary chin. "I'll see you next week," I said.

On Wednesday, I forced myself out of the cabin before noon, and drove first to Ben and Rabbit's home with groceries. I banged on the door without answer, so I left the food and finished the visits, collecting my first magazine payment from Hiram Dennison.

I tossed the rumpled *Field & Stream* behind the seat of the truck.

Thursday. Thanksgiving. I dreaded the dinner with Memory, sitting there with her turnip-headed son gurgling while she stuffed herself with hills of gravy-soaked turkey. I considered, briefly, bringing some sort of dessert or side dish, but found only instant rice and spaghetti in the cabinets, and a half loaf of fuzzy green bread.

Memory greeted me in a yellow sweat suit and an apron, once white, but now a Rorschach test of lard splatters and colored purees. "Just in time," she said. "Meat's just about set."

Pots and bowls cluttered the small kitchen counter, buffet-style. "Hope you don't mind eating in the den," Memory said, handing me a plate. "I always eat with my boy. Go 'head and help yourself."

There were sweet potatoes just the way I liked them, heavy with butter and molasses, and mixed vegetables suspended in some dome-shaped gelatinous blob. I took a sliver of that, and a heaping spoonful of homemade cranberry sauce. The bird wasn't a real turkey but a boneless pressed breast of white and dark meat. I grabbed two hot yeast rolls and went into the den, where TV trays stood beside Robert's bed.

Memory's plate had no more food on it than my own. She covered it loosely with a napkin and pulled up Robert's shirt, where a little tube stuck out of his stomach. She filled a huge syringe with canned formula, and said, "Well, we better give back thanks before we eat. Lord, oh Lord, we thank you for this, the meal you saw fit to bless us with today. Thank you that Sarah came to be here with us, and that me and Robert is spending another year together here on earth. Keep us all warm as the winter comes in. In the name of our precious Savior, our Lord Jesus, amen."

I sat. Memory said, "You start eating. I just gonna get Robert's dinner started here." She put the syringe in the tube, pressing some of the creamy liquid right into his belly. And she spoke to him, telling him that she burned the bottom of the rolls, that she finished another rag rug, this one a swirl of purples and greens, a gift for Willa McClure. She talked to me, too—small talk about snow and Thanksgivings past and how to make a gelled veggie casserole.

"You don't say much," she said.

I finished the last of my meal, craving more, but not ready to admit I enjoyed it. "I really don't have much to say."

She made a sound, "Hmpf," like a bicycle tire spitting out a quick burst of air. "I bet you find it boring 'round here, after that big city and all. Bet you think all us 'round here is dim and dumb. Maybe that's so, but I ain't gonna swap it for any of your fancy living. 'Specially if it turned me into the likes of you—all crabby and waspish and whatnot."

"Oh, yeah? That means a lot, coming from you."

"Rude, rude. If my mama were alive, she'd wallop you one upside the head, being fresh and all."

"Well, that's my problem right there. I didn't have a mother to instill proper manners in me."

"Go 'head, blame your sourpuss attitude on that rotten childhood of yours."

"What do you know of it?"

"Nothing. Nothing at all. 'Cept you ain't the only one ever had a bad run of it." Panting, she hefted herself around the bed, cleaned Robert's feeding tube and tucked his striped shirt into his pants. "Maybe you'd like to swap places with me, or Robert, or maybe Beth Watson—see how that tastes."

I crossed my arms over my chest and slid down a bit in the chair. Memory tucked a crocheted afghan around her son, lumbered into the kitchen, and returned with a wedge of chocolate cake dusted with confectioner's sugar. She slid the plate onto my tray. "Now, we don't have any moping here on a day of thanks."

I poked the dessert with my fork. "Aren't you having any?"

She shook her head. "Nope, all full up here." As my nose twitched with disbelief, she added, "Don't look at me like that. I'm fat for sure, but that don't make me a pig."

It was the moistest cake I'd ever had, rich and sticky. I pressed the last crumbs into the back of my fork and stuck them in my mouth before dumping my dirty dishes into the sink. Memory handed me several foil-wrapped plates and an index card with a recipe scrawled on it   *Hot Water Cake*.

I offered my halfhearted appreciation for the meal and went home. Memory probably finished the rest of the cake as soon as I left.

chapter TWENTY

The building was packed; young children wove between their mothers' legs, ran up the center aisle, and spilled around the rows of metal folding chairs. Men with camouflage baseball caps and toothpicks stuck in the corner of their mouths whacked each other on the backs as they bragged about the twelve-pointers they bagged that season, and the wives lamented their hunting-widow status.

I searched the crowd for Beth. A few people stopped me to wish me well—Shelley Portabella, Tom Hardy, some women in fuchsia coats whose names I couldn't remember. I locked myself in the restroom, quickly tuned my violin and played a few scales to loosen my fingers. Then I left my instrument with the others in the corner next to the piano.

I'd spent the last month as a creature of habit. Woke around eleven in the morning. Took a shower until the hot water ran out. Dried my hair and visited two or three of Doc's patients. I went to Ben and Rabbit's shack on Mondays; she still hadn't unlocked the door to me, but the bag of food was gone each week, so I figured they were alive and eating. On Tuesdays I sat with Zuriel for at least an hour, usually longer. Sometimes I read, and sometimes I just listened to her tales of mountain life.

I still sat with Robert on Sundays. When she returned from church, I ate lunch with Memory, too, sandwiches or "leftover pie"—all the week's uneaten food baked into a crust, which Memory would decorate with little lopsided hearts molded from the dough scraps. We'd always end up arguing about something, but the next week she'd greet me at the door with a muffle-jawed grin, and never mentioned the insults I'd hurled at her Sunday prior, or that I'd stormed out without clearing my plate.

And three days a week I practiced for the pageant with Beth.

Beth. I liked her. It shocked me to realize that one night when, after rehearsal, she popped a movie in the VCR she had smuggled over from the inn, and we watched some dumb horror flick, throwing popcorn at the television in disgust and laughing until our cheeks hurt. In fact, Beth laughed often, and about everything.

I'd never really had any close girl friends. Not that Beth and I were close—we didn't paint each other's toenails or share secrets, or anything. But I'd found myself looking forward to the evenings I knew she'd be coming.

I stepped on the hem of my skirt, lurching forward, arms flailing, then I peeked around to see if anyone noticed my gaffe. I wore borrowed clothes, having nothing of my own appropriate for a recital. Beth had come one evening with a selection of long, black skirts—I didn't ask her where she got them, afraid to know. But one of the skirts fit well and had some style to it, with tiny buttons running down the back, and an airy crinoline underneath for a bit of poof. My blouse, however, was a horror. I had planned to wear a black cashmere sweater, but Maggie insisted she had the perfect shirt to lend me—a gold polyester thing printed with ferocious crimson poinsettias. And I wore it, if only because I felt I owed her for letting me use her washing machine as often as I needed.

I spotted Jack across the room. He talked easily with several people. Patty Saltzman stood too close to him, her sleek hair draped over his shoulder. She touched his arm, said something. Everyone laughed. I wanted to kick her in the mouth.

Jack saw me and waved but didn't approach. I gave a little wave back. We'd rarely seen each other since that night we danced. I wasn't avoiding him, really. I just didn't go where I knew he was—no diner breakfasts, no town events, no afternoon Sunday suppers at the inn. I'd run into him twice at the variety store while grabbing groceries, and once at Doc's office. I'd been there giving Doc a weekly report on his patients, and Jack was playing taxi for one of his congregants.

I jostled through the crowd, finding Maggie at the front, pinning angel wings on a chubby preschooler. She told me Beth was changing in the office. I went in without knocking.

Beth stood in the center of the room, wearing nothing but her underwear. She froze—we both did—then spun and dropped her dress over her head, but not before I saw her fire-gnawed body.

The scars dripped down her face and neck, over her left shoulder and to her wrist. They swept across her chest—no breasts, just pearlized skin pulled taut over her rib cage, stomach, and right hip, trailing down her leg to the knee. A thick rope of tissue bulged in her armpit, and I understood why she couldn't lift her arm above her head. On her back and thighs, I saw tidy, symmetrical patches where skin had been removed for grafts.

"I'm sorry," I said.

"It's okay, really." She turned to me with a smile. "Toss me those pantyhose, will you? Thanks," she said, straightening her blackwatch-plaid dress, a simple A-line with a scoop neck. She took a deep, wavering breath. "I'm nervous."

So was I. I hadn't performed in years.

A light knock came on the door, and Jack poked in his head. "Five minutes, you two."

"You can come in. We're done making ourselves beautiful," Beth said.

"Nice tie," I said to him. It was tree-shaped and flashed with tiny Christmas lights.

"A gift from my dear mother. She bought it at the same place she found that lovely blouse you're wearing." He laughed. "Otherwise, you look very nice."

"I feel like I have an orange poodle nailed to the back of my head," I said, touching the ringlets I'd spent two hours creating with Maggie's twenty-year-old curling iron.

"No, I like it," Jack said.

"Hey. What about me?" Beth asked, twirling for effect.

"Hmm. I think something's missing. Here, try this." He pulled a strand of champagne-colored pearls from his jacket pocket, fastened them around her neck. "They were your Christmas gift, but I think you need them now."

"Jack, they're perfect," Beth said. She threw her arms around him. "I love you."

"You too, kiddo. Now don't start crying. You'll mess your makeup." He ran his thumbs gently under her eyes. "And don't expect anything else tomorrow. I can't stretch my meager salary that far."

Jack ushered us into the public area. Kids sat on their parents' laps, people shared chairs and leaned against the walls. Beth and I made our way to the back of the room, where seats were reserved for the performers. Suddenly, she stopped. Her shoulders stiffened, and I heard her whisper, "Please, Lord, help me."

I came alongside her, touched her elbow. "What's wrong?" I asked, following her gaze to the man who approached us.

It was the sloe-eyed gas station attendant.

"G-good luck t-t-tonight, Beth," he said.

"Thanks."

They stood there, him shuffling his feet, her twisting her new pearls in her fingers. Finally, I stuck out my hand. "Sarah Graham. And you are?"

"I'm sorry, Sarah," Beth said, shoving her hair behind her ears with trembling hands. "This is . . . this is Dominic Draven."

"Pleasure," he mumbled, and then brushed by us, a fog of motor oil trailing behind.

Beth hurried to her seat. I squeezed next to her. "What's wrong?"

"That was Danielle's brother. Danielle, my best friend, who . . ." Her voice contorted with the memory. "He hates me."

"Beth, no."

"Yes, yes. He hates me because I'm still alive, and his sister is dead."

"Calm down. You won't be able to sing with your nose all stuffed up."

She shook her head, quick, little tremors. "I can't do this."

"Yes, you can."

"No. I'm going to throw up."

The lights dimmed. From the corner of my eye, I watched Jack on the platform, adjusting the microphone. He tapped it once, twice.

I grabbed Beth by the shoulders. "Look at me. I didn't practice for a month so you could let some dumb grease monkey scare you off the stage."

"That's not very nice."

"I'm not very nice," I said, stealing Doc's line. "You should know that about me by now."

A smile lifted the right corner of Beth's mouth. "I do. I just thought you might behave better in public."

"Never." Then I said seriously, "I know you can do this."

She nodded and closed her eyes. Head lowered, she put her fist against her lips, catching the skin of her knuckle between her teeth.

The pageant began. Jack introduced each act. There was the obligatory nativity scene, with a bunch of screechy kids singing "Silent Night," some sort of fairy ballet, tap dancers, jugglers, and a guy who played a saw blade. And, much to my displeasure, Patty Saltzman proved to be a competent pianist. Not Juilliard caliber, but much better than your average ten-year piano lesson veteran.

Jack seemed to clap loudest for her.

Beth and I were last. We made our way to the stage, stepping over stray feet in the aisle and puddles of melted snow. I wiped my hands on my skirt, checked to make sure

the violin was still tuned, and played the introduction. Beth
began to sing:

> When peace, like a river, attendeth my way,
> When sorrows like sea billows roll;
> Whatever my lot, Thou has taught me to say,
> It is well, it is well, with my soul.
>
> It is well, with my soul,
> It is well, it is well, with my soul.
>
> Though Satan should buffet, though trials should
>   come,
> Let this blest assurance control,
> That Christ has regarded my helpless estate,
> And hath shed His own blood for my soul.
>
> My sin, oh, the bliss of this glorious thought!
> My sin, not in part but the whole,
> Is nailed to the cross, and I bear it no more,
> Praise the Lord, praise the Lord, O my soul!
>
> For me, be it Christ, be it Christ hence to live:
> If Jordan above me shall roll,
> No pang shall be mine, for in death as in life
> Thou wilt whisper Thy peace to my soul.
>
> But, Lord, 'tis for Thee, for Thy coming we wait,
> The sky, not the grave, is our goal;
> Oh, trump of the angel! Oh, voice of the Lord!
> Blessed hope, blessed rest of my soul!

And Lord, haste the day when my faith shall be
    sight,
The clouds be rolled back as a scroll;
The trump shall resound, and the Lord shall
    descend,
Even so, it is well with my soul.

It is well, with my soul,
It is well, it is well, with my soul.

I watched Beth as she sang, muscles rigid, hands fisted at her sides, eyes fixed on the back corner of the room where the wall met the ceiling. Her voice, however, had changed. It was no longer timid, but luminous, infectious. I found myself, for the first time, truly hearing the words of the hymn. I didn't understand half of them—all those *thees* and *thous* and holy talk. But I knew it was about hope, and for a moment I could almost feel it. Almost. If someone had asked me, right then, if I believed in God, I might have said yes.

She finished, and for one static second the room fell silent as vapor. Then, all at once, the ovation began, tumbling around us. "Bow," I told Beth, and she did. So did I.

We stood there together, in the rain of applause, the porcelain skin of the unmarred half of Beth's face glowing as if lit from within. For an instant, she was the girl from the photo on Jack's desk, untouched by flame and sorrow. And I was performing at Carnegie Hall.

The clapping stopped—not all at once, as it began, but in trickles. The lights snapped on, and squinting at the sudden brightness, I caught a glimpse of Doc sneaking out the door. Beth hugged me and thanked me, still beaming as the audience crowded onto the stage, offering words of congratulations and handshakes, and wilted carnation bouquets. Beth and Maggie wept together.

There were too many people around me. The heat and the smells—body odor and perfume, skin and peppermint candy—turned my stomach. I wriggled out of the throng and packed my violin in its case.

"You're not sneaking out, are you?" a voice asked from behind. Jack.

"I don't really do crowds," I said.

"Please stay. There's punch and cookies coming out."

"Tempting, but not tempting enough."

"I know it would mean a lot to Beth."

I looked back to the stage where Beth still stood, talking and smiling, surrounded by people who loved her. She had more joy than anyone I'd ever known; not that I'd known too many happy people. But I'd met plenty who had reason to be happy—talented, rich, beautiful people with big houses and blond children, and yearly vacations on tropical islands. Beth had none of those reasons, and less.

I was envious.

"I just have to go," I told Jack.

"I'll see you at breakfast tomorrow, then?"

"Well . . ." I fumbled around for some excuse, not sure why I'd ever agreed when Beth invited me last week. I had no warm Christmas memories to relive, and certainly didn't want to sit there listening to the joyous Yuletide tales of relative strangers.

"You're not getting out of this one. If you're not at the inn by nine, I'm going to come drag you over," Jack said.

I sighed. "Can you make it ten?"

"Okay, ten." Jack laughed. "It'll be brunch instead. And Sarah?"

"Yeah?"

"Thank you. For everything."

I thought for a moment he was going to hug me. He jerked forward, but stopped, finally deciding to pat my shoulder with a "See you tomorrow," and went off to find his sister.

While buttoning my coat, I saw Dominic standing at the back of the hall, one leg out the door. His eyes clung to Beth, drinking in her every movement, a desert cactus sucking up the rain after months of parching heat.

He loved her. I could tell.

"Dominic," I called, pushing through rows of folding chairs. He looked at me, then bolted from the building. By the time I stepped outside, he was gone, his taillights blushing in the darkness as he drove away.

chapter TWENTY-ONE

Maggie covered a cardboard box with bright Christmas paper, and filled it with home-baked muffins and cookies, yeast breads, Starlight Mints and hand-knitted slippers. Then she sighed, pinching the bridge of her nose, and poured boiling water over a teabag and spoonful of honey. She watched the chamomile-scented steam curl over the rim of the cup before sitting and taking a sip.

Her arthritis raged tonight, bones throbbing, as if someone jammed a bottlebrush into the hollowed-out centers, thrusting up and down, scraping out the marrow. She'd worn the wrong shoes to the pageant, shiny black ones with an unforgiving sole. Pure vanity. Her clunky orthopedic sneakers looked horrid with her dress.

She heard a noise in the hallway, and Beth floated by, humming softly, in a pink nightgown, pearls still on.

"Can't sleep?" Maggie asked.

She nodded. "I thought I'd have some warm milk," Beth said, taking the carton from the refrigerator and fishing through the cabinet for her favorite mug, the black one with the New York City skyline stamped on it in gold, though the tops of the tallest buildings had long since been washed away by Maggie's scouring sponge. "Done with those boxes yet?"

"This is my last one. Here, I'll make the milk for you," Maggie said, gripping the edge of the table as she creaked to her feet, loose joints of the old wood chair scritching in concert with her knees. A soft groan escaped from between her clenched teeth.

"It's okay. I can do it," Beth said.

"Humor an old lady, will you? I hate watching you heat it in the microwave. It's not right."

"Mom—"

"I said I'll do it," Maggie snapped. She untangled a copper pot from the rack above the stove and dumped some milk into it. The burner *clicked, clicked, clicked* in the late-night silence before bursting into a blue, gassy light. The color reminded her of Beth's eyes. Always did.

"I'm sorry," Maggie told her daughter. She leaned against the counter, Formica cutting into her back.

"I can get your medication," Beth said softly.

"No, no. It's fine. I'm heading to bed in a minute or two anyhow." She'd already taken her pills, and they were wearing off, after only three hours. She gave Beth her mug. "You were beautiful tonight."

"I can't stop thinking about it. I just wish Sarah hadn't run out so quickly."

"She didn't mean anything by it, I'm sure. Bet she's not used to having so many people fuss over her."

"I know." Beth yawned. "I think I'll take that milk to my room."

Maggie kissed her on the cheek, the scarred one—still, after four years, she noticed how that skin felt different against her lips—and watched her pad down the hall. She wanted to finish her tea but didn't dare sit down again. She knew she wouldn't be able to stand back up. It had happened before. She had gotten stuck in the living room chair all night, unable to lift her stiff, achy body out of the deep cushions, and too stubborn to call out to Beth for help.

After dumping her half-full cup into the sink—and leaving it there, unwashed—Maggie limped to her bedroom. Luke had given her a cane once; he'd carved it from a twisted hickory branch, and the thick handle fit her hand perfectly. She had tossed it into the fireplace while he stood watching. Only old, useless women used canes, she'd told him.

Stubborn pride, plain and simple.

She fumbled with the six buttons on her blouse, her cramped fingers kneading the smooth plastic disks through the holes. She shrugged the shirt off her shoulders and left it where it fell, on the floor in front of the dresser. Tomorrow, after a good night's sleep, she'd be able to bend over and pick it up.

chapter TWENTY-TWO

An ice storm besieged Jonah early Christmas morning. Outside my window, saplings genuflected beneath the frozen weight, heads on the ground, and mighty evergreens drooped with cracked branches. I refused, however, to wear my frumpy, flannel-lined jeans, opting instead for low-rise flares and black cashmere sweater—the one I had planned to wear last night. I kicked my waterproof boots under the couch and zipped on my black leather ankle ones with the three-inch heels. Then I brushed the tight curls from my hair; it now fell around my face in soft waves.

I hurried from the cabin to the truck, which I'd given ample time to warm, and skidded out of the driveway. The road stretched before me, a smooth, glassy sea of asphalt and ice. I hugged the shoulder as I drove, keeping my passenger-side tires in the crunchy snow, for traction, I hoped.

A stop sign loomed red at the next corner. Gently, I pressed the brake, but the truck slid, picking up speed into the intersection. I jammed my foot down, spun to the right, jerked the steering wheel to the left. The truck pirouetted once, twice, and crashed into the drainage ditch on the side of the road. My seat belt prevented me from flying through the windshield, but I was still jostled, and had bit my lip. Blood dripped off my chin. I found a napkin shoved between the seats and applied pressure to the cut. When the bleeding stopped, I checked the wound in the rearview mirror. Teeth marks perforated my lower lip.

Opening the driver's door, I squeezed a handful of snow into a ball and held it to my lip to reduce the swelling. Then I closed myself back in the truck, idling the engine to keep the heat running, cracking the window so I wouldn't die of carbon monoxide poisoning. I waited twenty minutes. No one drove by.

It was a couple of miles to the inn. I twisted my scarf around my head, leaving slits for my eyes and nose, and started hiking. Slipping twice on the icy road in the first three yards, I climbed onto the frozen snowbank and walked easily upon the dingy crust for several minutes, until my foot hit a soft spot and I fell through. Shards of icy soot jammed up my pant leg, all the way past my knee.

"I hate this place!" I screamed. My voice echoed through the vacant streets. I jerked my leg out of the snow and continued walking, jaw set, nostrils frozen together.

I saw the inn's sign, a truck pulling from its driveway. Moments later, Jack stopped in the middle of the road. "Sarah?"

"I crashed. In the ditch down there," I said, pointing.

"Are you okay?" He helped me into his truck. I unwrapped my face. "You're bleeding," he said, taking my head gently in his hands, moving it this way and that.

"I'm fine. I just bit my lip."

He ignored me, cupping his hands around my eyes. "Does your head hurt? You could have a concussion."

"The only thing that hurts is my tailbone. I fell on it about a dozen times." His hands felt warm and dry against my skin, a little rough, masculine. I moved them away. "I'm okay. Really."

"I told you I'd come looking for you if you didn't show up."

The clock on the dashboard read 10:47. "You said ten. If you'd come looking sooner, I wouldn't have a sore butt."

"Let me look at your truck. I have a chain in the bed. Maybe I can pull you out."

The truck, however, was wedged into the ditch. It needed to be towed, Jack said. "I'll take you to Draven's garage now."

"Can't we just call from the inn?"

"Phone lines are down, because of the ice. The garage is just around the corner."

We drove to the full-service gas station—the only gas station in Jonah. "Wait here," Jack said, and he went up the stairs on the side of the building, which I assumed led to an apartment above the garage. He returned in a few minutes. "Dominic's getting the tow truck."

Dominic followed us to the accident site. Wordlessly, he pulled my truck from the ditch, started it. "Sounds fine."

"What about the dent?" I asked.

He shrugged. "Don't stop it from working."

"But can you fix it?"

He shrugged again. "Bring it by next week."

Jack waited for me across the street, in his truck. "I'll follow you," he called, and I held up one finger. I knocked on Dominic's window; he rolled it down. "You can send the bill to Rich Portabella. He'll pay it."

Dominic nodded.

If I was going to say something, I had to do it now. "I saw the way you looked at Beth last night." He stared straight ahead.

"You know," I added, "she thinks you hate her."

Dominic still said nothing. But he swallowed. Hard. And rolled up the window.

Maggie had prepared a huge breakfast—pancakes and home fries, bacon, venison sausage, cheesy egg strata and fruit salad—and it waited on the table when Jack and I arrived, reheated and beckoning. We sat down and Jack prayed. I peeked around the table at the Watsons, noting that Beth and Maggie both scrunched their eyes tight and Jack kept his face turned upward.

I glutted myself on the delicious food while Jack recounted my morning, with Beth and Maggie providing worried gasps and the occasional "Oh, no" at the appropriate times. Maggie looked drawn and yellow. She chatted as usual, but pushed her pancakes around in the syrup without eating them, and more than once glanced at the clock—the one made from a cast-iron griddle—on the counter. Beth, however, still sparkled from the night before. She wore jeans, a blue Nordic-pattern sweater, and a white turtleneck tucked under her new pearls. Plush penguin slippers covered her feet—a gift from her mother, she said.

"Speaking of gifts," Maggie said, stirring her coffee gently, "maybe we should give Sarah hers now."

"Yes, we should," Beth said, grabbing my arm and pulling me onto the living room couch. "Here, open mine first."

From under the tree she pulled a cellophane bag filled with red shredded paper and plastic candy-cane confetti.

"I don't have anything for you," I said, feeling foolish. It wasn't that I didn't think of it, but what could I possibly get at the variety store? Oven mitts? Dish soap?

"Just open it," Beth said.

Digging through the fill, I found a cassette tape.

"It's our greatest hits," she said. "Well, hit, anyway."

I looked at the tape. Beth had tucked a small watercolor of a ship inside the front cover; it sailed on a calm, early-morning ocean, pink sunshine coloring the waves. "Did you paint this?"

"Yeah," she said.

"It's good," I said, and I meant it.

"I tell her that all the time," Maggie said, "But she doesn't listen to me 'cause I'm just her mother. Mine next. It's that one, Beth, with the gold bow."

Usually, I tore off wrapping paper in wild, ragged chunks. But I couldn't do that to Maggie's gift, with its perfect corners and ribbon tendrils, and the little glass ornaments tied to the top. I slipped my finger along the seam, pulling the tape up without damaging the paper, and took a lovely sage-colored sweater from the box. Hand-knitted in the softest yarn I'd ever felt, it had wide, romantic wrists and a slanted hemline, and fastened at the neck with a carved mother-of-pearl button.

"This is beautiful, Maggie."

"Do you like it? I thought the color would go perfectly with your hair."

My throat prickled with impending tears. I coughed and held the sweater close against my face, as if gauging the softness against my cheek or, odder yet, smelling it. The threat passed, and I folded the sweater more neatly than anything I'd ever folded in my life.

"One more," Jack said, placing a thin, book-shaped package wound in wrinkled green paper on my lap. "Wrapping is not one of my talents."

I pressed the gift to my ear. "It's a Bible."

"Come on," Jack said. "I'm not that predictable."

"Yes, you are," said Beth, giggling and ducking her head to avoid the needlepoint pillow her brother tossed at her.

I dug my fingers through the layers of blue painter's tape. It was, in fact, a Bible, with a pebbly brown leather cover and my name embossed in the lower right corner. *Sarah Isabel Graham.*

He knew my middle name.

"Don't feel like you have to read it or anything," Jack said, stuffing stray wrapping paper into a trash bag. "It makes a really good coaster. Or a doorstop. Or a—"

"Projectile?" offered Beth. She and her mother laughed.

"Oh, come on. I was eight years old," said Jack, but he, too, chuckled.

"Sarah, you have to hear this story," Maggie said. "One November when the boys were eight, my husband, John, and I took them camping in the mountains. Well, John had gone out early to hunt, very early, like four in the morning. And not too long after that, me and the boys heard this sound outside the tent, this growling and rustling. There were a couple of coyotes out there, scrounging around in the trash that someone forgot to tie up in a tree."

"That was Timothy. Not me," Jack said.

"Before I could find a pot and spoon to bang and try to scare the coyotes off, Jack was out of the tent, Bible in hand, shouting things like, 'Get thee behind me, ye hounds of hell,' " Maggie said. "Those coyotes stood there, looking at Jack like he was crazy as a loon, I'm not kidding. So he threw his Bible at them. When they didn't leave, he threw Timothy's Bible at them. Finally, I think they just got tired of some kid screaming and tossing books at them, and they walked off into the woods."

"It could be worse. I could still be thumping coyotes with Bibles. Or people, for that matter," Jack said.

"Well, there was that one time you threw your Bible at me when I was a baby," Beth said.

"I accidentally dropped it on you. And there wasn't any permanent damage. I don't think, anyway," he teased, hitting her with another pillow.

"See. Still throwing," Beth said. "You should've played for the Yankees."

"All right, I've had enough of this torment. Let's change the subject." He turned to me. "Sarah, do you have anything nice to say about me?"

"Nope," I said, adding to the laughter. "But I was wondering who Timothy is."

My question sucked the merriment from the room. Maggie's eyes flickered toward Jack, and he leaned toward her, saying quietly, "The subject never came up."

Maggie picked up a photo from the end table and handed it to me, the same one from Jack's office of the young boy with the fish, hair battling the wind. "Timothy was Jack's twin brother. He died when he was twelve."

I stared at the Christmas tree, a plump, long-needled kind, with tinsel and metallic garlands twirled around it, and several strands of colored lights flashing at uneven intervals. A motley assortment of ornaments, handmade mostly, but with an occasional glass ball nestled here and there, brightened the velvety-green branches. "I'm sorry. I mean—"

"You didn't know," Jack said.

The front doorbell jingled, and someone called, "Maggie?"

"In here, Adele."

The yellow-fingered woman rushed in, hair and clothes stale with cigarette smoke. I sneezed.

"The roads are thawed, Maggie. We can get those boxes delivered now," Adele said.

"Wonderful," Maggie said. She struggled up from her seat. Jack reached his arm out to her, but she brushed him away. "Sarah, don't mean to be rude and all, but each year some of the ladies at church put together boxes of baked goods and little gifts for some of the families 'round here who can't afford much of anything. Usually we get them all delivered before breakfast, but with the storm and all—well, they're still sitting in my bedroom."

"I should probably go anyway," I said.

"No, stay," Jack said. "Who wants to be alone on Christmas? And I'm not allowed to help with the baskets. It's a girl thing."

Beth gave me a warm hug as she left the room. Maggie's embrace seemed quicker, cooler somehow. She said, "We won't be long," her eyes on Jack, her words pointed there, too.

Jack and I sat for several minutes, listening to Bing Crosby and to the women tramping in and out as they loaded their vehicles. He nursed a glass of eggnog, homemade by Maggie, of course.

"Your mom's upset with me," I said after the ladies drove away.

"No. You're fine. That last look was for me."

"About?"

"Don't worry. Nothing important."

My toes cold, I tucked my feet between the couch cushions, resting my chin on my knees. The fire smoldered; Jack added a couple more logs, and sat beside me.

"So, what happened? To your brother, I mean."

"He drowned. The river was high from all the spring rain and thaw, and moving fast. We shouldn't have been playing near it, we both knew better, but . . . Anyway, Timothy fell in and was swept away. I ran along the bank, following him, and slipped in, too. I was pulled out by a couple of loggers. Timothy was found stuck in some branches about a mile past where I was rescued.

"We were so different. Mom called Tim spirited, but that was probably being nice." He smiled wryly. "It didn't matter. He was my best friend. We were inseparable. I was always trying to talk him out of something."

"It must have been hard."

"The hardest part was the whispers, the side comments. No one actually came out and said it, but there was a general attitude of 'Thank God it wasn't Jack.' I've been carrying that with me for the last twenty years. The expectation that I was spared for something . . . I don't know . . . something bigger. Some divine purpose. I just can't—"

He stopped, took a breath. "I don't know why I just told you that. Anyway, my folks never thought that way. Mom was crushed. I can't imagine what it would be like to lose a child. You just don't get over that. If she hadn't gotten pregnant with Beth, I honestly don't think she would have made it."

I raised an eyebrow.

"Believe you me, I did the math. She got pregnant about three weeks before Tim died. It was just too early to know. It really was an act of God's grace—she'd had seven miscarriages between us and Beth."

"Grace?"

"Yeah. A gift. A miracle, really."

I shook my head. "I don't follow your logic. Your brother dies, and you see having another baby to replace him as a gift?"

"I wouldn't put it quite like that."

"My grandmother would've seen some sort of punishment in all this."

"I would have to respectfully disagree with your grandmother. And I'd tell her to read John, chapter nine, verses one through three."

"My grandmother's dead."

"I'm sorry."

"I'm not."

Jack didn't respond, so I said, "She wasn't like you. She was . . ."

I stretched my legs, knees popping. Thinking about my grandmother, even now, five years after her death, made me feel as if I were six years old again, sobbing because she refused to hug me. Crossing the room to the window, I watched the melting ice drip off the inn's rusted gutters, and pushed my hand against the glass. A ghostly haze formed around my fingers. I pressed a little harder, wondering how much weight was needed to break through. The pain of glass shards in my palm would be a relief from any memory of my childhood.

"She called me her burden," I said to the street outside. "She said I was her constant reminder that she raised her daughter to be a whore."

Jack came up behind me; he stood close, not touching but

close enough that I felt the air warm between us. I thought briefly about sinking back into him, like two spoons in a drawer, but knew if my body touched his, I would shatter.

"Sarah." He took my shoulders and spun me to face him. I looked at his feet, in gray socks with green stitching over the toes. Putting his thumb under my chin, he nudged, saying, "Look at me."

"I can't," I said, stiffening the muscles in my neck. And I couldn't. I wouldn't.

The phone rang. And rang, its persistent cry shrill and pleading. Jack sighed and answered it. "Jonah Inn . . . Calm down, Editha . . . Did you call Bill Hendrickson? . . . I know . . . it's Christmas for me, too . . . No, no, don't do that. I'll be there in ten minutes." He covered his face with his hands, pulling his cheeks down until I could see the reds of his lower eyelids, looking like one of those baggy-skinned dogs. "I have to go rescue someone from her overflowing toilet."

"You're a plumber now?"

"You would be surprised at the extent of my knowledge and skill," he said, tugging a knit hat over his curls. "Sit. Enjoy the fire. Mom and Beth should be back soon."

"I'm going to get out of here."

Jack glanced at me, at the tree, out the window. He chewed a flap of loose skin from his bottom lip and shook his head quickly, as if trying to shake a stubborn thought from it, the kind that pursued, and the faster a person ran from it, the more determined it became.

I had them all the time.

"I'll stop by the cabin in a couple of hours," he said.

"No."

"Sarah—"

"Don't."

"Okay," he said with a deflated nod. "Okay."

We left together. He opened my truck door, closing it softly, silently, behind me. I turned left out of the driveway; he turned right. I watched him in my mirror until he shrunk to nothing.

Already the daylight was creeping away, the last strands of sunlight tangled high in the treetops. I loved and hated the short winter days for the same reason—longer nights. More time to sleep, to escape. Or play. But also more time to relive the past, if sleep refused to come, and there was no one to play with.

I only wanted to sack out now, and changed to my pajamas as soon as I got back to the cabin. I crawled into the sleeping bag, saw the Bible on the coffee table where I dropped it, with my other gifts. What did Jack say to look up? I flipped though the pages. Matthew. Mark. Luke. John. My grandmother had made me memorize all the books of both testaments. There it was, John 9:1–3: *"As he went along, he saw a man blind from birth. His disciples asked him, 'Rabbi, who sinned, this man or his parents, that he was born blind?'*

" 'Neither this man nor his parents sinned,' said Jesus, 'but this happened so that the work of God might be displayed in his life.' "

I tossed the book back on the table. Jack was right. It would make a good coaster.

chapter TWENTY-THREE

Jack sat in his truck outside Luke's cabin, engine off. Icy gusts pierced the cab, and inside his gloves he curled his fingers into his palms to keep his hands warm. He'd been there twenty minutes, staring at a dull light flickering in the front windows. From the television, he thought, but he didn't know if Sarah was watching it. She had told Beth once she slept with it on, for company. He didn't want to wake her.

She'd told him not to come, anyway.

Every time he saw Sarah, her wall sprung another crack. She worked to patch them as soon as they came, with the mortar of a sharp word, or a turn-and-retreat. Still, he knew she wouldn't be able to hide behind that weakening barricade forever. He prayed it would crumble here, in Jonah, where someone stood waiting to catch her. Only God knew how many bones would break if no one padded her fall.

Jack swallowed a trickle of disappointment. He had wanted Sarah to invite him over. He more than enjoyed talking with her. She didn't know he had wet his pants on the first day of kindergarten, or that he forgot his only line— "It's a long way to Canaan. Can't we stop and rest?"—in his

145

third-grade Sunday school play. She didn't know that, when he turned eleven, he went out into the wilderness of his backyard for a forty-day fast, only to have his father drag him back into the house after a week, when an autumn downpour threatened to wash Jack's pup tent down the mountain, and he was so weak from hunger he couldn't walk more than a couple of yards on his wobbly knees. With Sarah, he didn't have to act the part of Jack Watson, best thing to come out of Jonah since, well, since never. He could be the someone no one knew him to be.

And he was attracted to her.

Jack closed his eyes, sighing, and banged the back of his head into the unpadded headrest, once, twice. *Idiot, idiot*, the thuds echoed. When the feelings began, he didn't know. But in the past week, since he watched her on the stage next to Beth, her violin transforming his sister from pauper to princess, he found himself thinking of her too often. Not just her music. Her. How her hair blazed in the light. How her fingernails always looked short and frayed, from her chewing them, no doubt, though he'd never seen her do it. The way she hid her smile beneath the back of her hand when she laughed. The thoughts were fleeting—he refused to let them dawdle, instead going to his knees or running out on some errand. But he was a minister, not a eunuch. And he was lonely.

Lord forgive him, he was lonely.

Allison's face darted behind his closed eyelids, surprising him. Jack hadn't thought of her in months, more than a year, maybe. His stomach bucked as if he swallowed pounds of deviled eggs. The weight of guilt. He pushed it away. He'd been forgiven of that. And it wasn't something he'd repeat. Not with Sarah. Not ever.

The old pickup started loudly, rattling from the leaky exhaust he'd yet to have repaired, unable to justify spending three hundred dollars on a twenty-five-year-old junker. He kept his lights off so they wouldn't shine into the cabin windows. He'd rather not have Sarah know he'd been there, peering, waiting. What would she think of him then?

chapter TWENTY-FOUR

I stopped by Doc's office to meet him New Year's Eve day. Two people sat in the waiting room—a woman with her ankle wrapped in a beige compression bandage, and a man with glasses at least an inch thick, paper clips dangling from where the screws should be, holding on the arms.

I hadn't seen Patty since the pageant. I decided if she said something about my performance, I'd give a thin, courteous compliment on hers. If not, she'd get nothing.

"You're late," she said, cutting photos of floral arrangements from a bridal magazine.

"I'm always late," I said. "Doc back there?"

"Where else would he be?"

I found Doc in the only exam room, folding dingy cotton hospital gowns and stacking them in a metal cabinet. I hopped up on the table, white paper wrinkling beneath me, legs dangling off the side.

He sighed. "I wish you wouldn't do that," he said. "I'll have to rip that paper off after you leave. It's wasteful."

"You don't pay me enough to care," I said.

"This coming from someone who said she'd work for

nothing." Doc shook his head a little, a smirk lighting one corner of his mouth. Every week I sat in the same place, and every week he told me not to.

We had a peculiar understanding, Doc and I. We tiptoed around the old wounds both of us so obviously had, but neither wanted to share—nor did we want them to close. We pecked at each other's half-healed scabs with sarcasm and contrivances, until they started to bleed again, and we hurt just enough to remember why we didn't belong in polite society.

I so wanted to know what Doc hid from up in these mountains. Whatever it was, it had to be delicious.

"All your old folks are fine," I said. "At least, I think they are. Rabbit still won't let me in."

"I saw them a couple days ago. Ben's foot is healing. But slowly. I expect it will be two, three months before he can be up on it again, unrestricted. Anything else to report?"

"No. But I was wondering, how much is Robert really aware of? I mean, does he recognize people by sight, or voices? Or sounds?"

"I honestly don't know. It's nearly impossible to diagnose how much of his response is simply reflexive and how much is deliberate. Why do you ask?"

"No reason. But I think Memory believes he understands every word she says."

"Memory's not a fool. She's just doing what she needs to do to get through each day. You should understand that." Doc handed me a spray bottle, and then threw a rag at me. "Make yourself useful."

Another weekly ritual. I slid off the table, tore off the paper I'd been sitting on, and coated the vinyl with the disinfecting mist. "I thought I saw you at the pageant the other night," I said, "trying to sneak out before the lights came up."

"That was me."

"What'd you think?"

He looked at me then, not like a man who'd known me for only a couple of months but as if he were someone who'd watched me grow through the years—someone who'd been there for that first missing tooth, or who waved me off to the prom. I almost expected him to pull out his wallet and show me photos of myself at all those milestones. Instead, he turned away and began filling a glass apothecary jar with more cotton balls. "You play well."

"That's it?"

He moved to the next jar, dumping in a box of tongue depressors. "You're better than your father. Is that what you were looking for?"

It wasn't.

I crunched up the discarded paper, tossed it toward the trash can. He hadn't mentioned Luke to me, not since that first time we met. "How do you know?"

"I heard him once."

"When? Why? I thought— I mean, I was under the impression you had nothing to do with Luke."

"We weren't friends. We hardly said half a dozen words to each other over the years. I—" Doc stopped, took his glasses off and rubbed one eye with the fat, fleshy part of his hand, just beneath his thumb. "I didn't know him."

I wanted to ask more, to be nosy, but he said, "Go home, Sarah. I have patients."

I'd never made popcorn without a microwave. I'd watched Beth do it several times, fluffy kernels bursting out from under the aluminum lid like an Orville Redenbacher commercial.

Grab a pot, pour in some oil, add the popping corn, wiggle the handle around over the heat so nothing would burn. Done. How difficult could it be?

Twenty minutes later, I held the pot over the trash pail, scraping greasy, blackened kernels off the bottom with a knife. Beth could make more when she arrived. She and I planned to watch movies until midnight, then go outside, banging pots and hooting like banshees in the new year. A tradition, she insisted, and fun, too.

I'd humor her.

I did have brownie mix in the cabinet. I dumped the mix in a bowl, sneezing as the chocolate dust puffed into the air and up my nose. I added three eggs for more cakelike brownies—the way I liked them—and spooned the batter into my only pan.

The front door swung open, and Beth bounded in, shaking snow from her hair. "Sarah."

"You're early," I called, leaving the pan on the stovetop. "Don't laugh. I'm baking."

She flung her arms around my rib cage and squeezed the breath from me. "Thank you, thank you, thank you."

"You're welcome, I think." I pried her off. "Did you leave your car running?"

"It's Dominic," she said, with a smile that was coy and shy and radiant all at once. "He told me. Oh, Sarah, do you mind if I— That is, could we reschedule?"

"I don't think the new year will wait. But I've said before, hot dates take precedence. He's not taking you to the diner, is he?"

"No." She giggled. "He said it's special, but he won't tell me what."

"A surprise. Sounds romantic."

Beth pulled her head down into her shoulders, tortoise-like, and covered her face with her hands, fingers splayed, giggling some more. "I know. Sarah, I can't believe what you did."

"It's no big deal. I just talked to him. I didn't even exhaust my entire vocabulary."

"No, it's not that." She shoved her hair behind her ears.

"Then, what?"

"Never mind. It's nothing."

"Beth, what?"

She looked at me then, her blue eyes on mine, her face divided nearly down the middle. And I realized how long it had been since I'd noticed her scars. I'd seen them, but they were no longer something freakish and grotesque; they were Beth.

"What you did for me," Beth said. "It was . . . I mean, I knew you had a heart, Sarah. I just never thought I'd see it."

I felt my forehead scrunch at that thumbprint-sized place between my eyebrows, folding and unfolding quickly, almost instantaneously. Then a ripple of understanding, another. I don't know what look passed over my face, but Beth stammered, "I'm sorry. I didn't mean . . ."

"It's okay." My lips kinked into what I hoped looked like a smile. It wasn't okay. It wasn't. "You go on your date. But I want to hear all about it tomorrow."

"I'll come by early."

"Not too early. Go on. Dominic will run out of gas if you stay here gabbing too much longer."

And she went. And I stood in the middle of the room, ordering myself to take deep, slow breaths.

I'd been called heartless before. Sometimes with blatant disgust, by those I had—in their own estimation—handled too carelessly. And other times with admiration for my deft ability to remain unmoved, untouched. Either way, I'd always taken the observation as a compliment.

But Beth . . . she said it in such a plain, compassionate way, like a mother explaining to her crying toddler that the butterfly had died because his chubby, clumsy hands closed too tightly around it. As if I didn't know better but still should learn to be more cautious.

I knew better. I just didn't care.

I wouldn't think of Beth anymore. I crammed a movie into the VCR, and when it ended I remembered I never baked the brownies. After shutting them in the oven, I squirted detergent into the popcorn pot and scrubbed the last burnt remnants from the bottom. Moving with determination, I dried the pot, added more oil, heated it, and emptied the bag of kernels into it. The oil sizzled, and as the corn started popping, I held the pot just above the burner, swirling it around and around until the *ping, ding* and *pop* ended. I drenched the popcorn with two sticks of melted butter and a handful of salt, carried the pot and several sodas into the living room, and started another video.

Sometime during the movie, a bitter, fudgey smell plugged my nostrils. I jumped up, ran into the kitchen, and yanked down the oven door and reached in for the pan, wearing a mitt on only one hand. My naked fingers touched the metal and I swore, twisted on the faucet. Cold water washed over my hand as the hot oven air—I'd left the door open, brownies tottering on the edge of the wire shelf—toasted my legs.

I couldn't do anything right.

No, I could do one thing right.

I stumbled to the closet, tore open the door, and jammed the violin against my chin. My jumbled mind didn't know what to play. But my hands did, and in a few moments, despite the blisters growing on my left fingertips, the familiar strains of Giuseppe Tartini's Sonata in G Minor—*La Sonata del Diavolo*—infected the silence.

I had planned to perform this piece at my Juilliard graduation jury. But not the popular Romantic-era Fritz Kreisler arrangement, with a piano accompaniment that oozed Viennese charm and warmth. After hearing Andrew Manze's blazing solo rendition, I, too, wanted to play it alone on an authentic Baroque instrument. Just eighteen minutes of me, the violin, and Tartini's devilish trill.

According to musical folklore, the devil came to Tartini in a dream, and in the dream the devil played a sonata on the composer's own violin. Tartini, awed by such ambrosial strains, forced himself to wake and tried to replicate the music he'd heard while sleeping. The result was *The Devil's Sonata*, though Tartini insisted it was far inferior to the music in his dream. If he could have found another way to support himself, he would have smashed his violin and given up music forever after hearing the virtuoso from Hades, a mastery he could not touch.

I played with my eyes closed, leaning against the back of the sofa so I wouldn't lose my balance, and tried to conjure up an image of Tartini in his bed, in a nightgown and sleeping cap, as Satan stood at the footboard, bow flying over the gut strings, heel tapping. Instead, I saw myself under the blankets, and my own devil—my father—playing before me.

"What do you want from me?" I dropped the instrument onto the couch. Why did he want me here? Was it so I'd come to some appreciation of his reformed life through the gushing praise of the people in this place? Did he hope I'd regret shutting him out of my life, perhaps even forgive him? I thought about my arrival in Jonah, how the credit card waited for me, and recognized my father had watched me, had known I was broke and miserable and shiftless. I'd felt vindicated then—but now I was ashamed, almost. Because I'd shown him I was nothing more than a murderer's daughter.

I'd let him get the better of me.

The cabin seemed to shrink around me, walls and ceiling pressing in. I saw Luke's ghost in every corner, mocking me. My heart thumped against my rib cage, and a heavy, tingling sensation rushed down my arms. I flung open the door. The puffy flakes attacked my face in tiny, cold pricks. I flicked the switch to turn on the outside porch light. The bulb lit, surged, and went out with a snap.

The darkness swallowed me. I sprinted, coatless, shoeless, to the truck and pulled the headlight handle. Two thin streams of gold light reached into the night. I climbed onto the hood of the truck, socks caked with snow. My thighs stung, jeans no protection against the frigid metal beneath me.

"I hate you. I hate you," I whispered. To me. About me. I maimed everyone I touched. And I did it purposely, to soothe the furor within. Each nail I drove into someone else deadened another nerve in my own heart.

Was I numb enough yet to stay out all night? I could just lie down against the windshield and sleep.

But Beth would come tomorrow, bubbling over with news of her date, and find me, curled up like a cocktail shrimp, all blue and hard, and dead. I couldn't do that to her. She'd been through enough.

Snow whirled in the headlights, luminous flecks of glitter. I watched, captivated, seeing sparkles of pink and green and blue mixed with silver. Then I wriggled off the truck, punched out the headlights, and went back into the cabin.

In the distance I heard the clatter of pots and pans.

chapter TWENTY-FIVE

The beautiful, dainty snowflakes from the night before accumulated to thirty inches. I groaned and, snow shovel in hand, went to dig myself out. I cleared the steps, shoveled a path around the truck. By then, I was panting. The driveway to the cabin was at least twenty-five yards long. But I finished, clothes plastered to my sweaty skin, my whole body smarting, and most of the daylight hours gone.

Back inside the house, I made a box of instant mashed potatoes. I didn't have any milk, or butter—I'd used it all on the popcorn last night—so the spuds tasted like flour paste. My muscles, unaccustomed to manual labor, stiffened as I ate. Gimping into the bathroom carrying a kitchen chair, I twisted the showerhead to massage. I put the wood chair in the stall so I could sit and relax while the steamy water pelted my skin.

I dressed and, too lazy to blow-dry my hair, pulled my wool hat over my head. Then I turned on the television before sinking into the couch. College bowl players pounded each other between the fuzzy lines of poor reception. I hated football but wasn't getting up to turn it off.

Someone knocked on the door.

"Come in," I said. I wasn't getting up to answer it, either.

"You shoveled the whole driveway?" Beth asked, plopping next to me. She kept her coat on.

"Don't remind me. I officially hate snow."

"Jack told me once that Eskimos have something like four hundred words for snow."

"I have a few, too." I kneaded my cramping hamstring.

She laughed. "I'll ask Dom to put you on his plow list."

"Dom, huh? I guess that meant your date went pretty good."

"I have something to tell you. Mom is the only other person who knows." Beth's face reddened, her left cheek brighter than Dorothy's ruby slipper. "Dom and I are getting married."

"What are you talking about?" I rubbed my ears, convinced I heard wrong.

"He asked, and I said yes."

"Two days ago you couldn't even look at each other."

"I know. But"—she shrugged, giggled—"it was a very good first date."

"No, no buts. What are you thinking? You don't even know him."

"Sarah, I grew up with him."

"You can do better."

Beth frowned, voice quavering as she said, "Better than what? A dumb hick grease monkey?"

"I didn't mean it like that," I said. But I did.

"I'm not ever leaving Jonah, Sarah. Until yesterday, I thought I'd be alone for the rest of my life."

"I just don't want you to settle because . . . well, because . . ."

"I've been in love with Dominic since I was twelve. I used to go over to Draven's garage and pretend I was waiting for

Danielle to come home, even though I knew she had piano lessons every Thursday after school. I'd sit on the steps, with my homework open on my knees, and watch Dom under the cars. Sometimes he'd ask me to get him a wrench. I'd make sure our fingers touched when I handed it to him," she said. "I'm not settling."

I crossed my left hand to the opposite shoulder, crooked my right toward my head and twisted it in a circle. Oh, did I ache. "Then I'm happy for you," I said.

"Really?"

No.

A sour concoction of jealousy and regret ballooned in my stomach, pushing against my diaphragm. I tasted it, snaking up my throat and around my tongue, metallic and sticky, like blood. I wanted to be the one in love, the one giggling and glowing, and picking out monogrammed bathrobes.

"Yeah, really," I said, looking at the television, at the bronzed, lithe cheerleaders, all big-toothed and bouncy on the sidelines.

"Okay, then, I have a favor. Be my maid of honor?"

"Me? Shouldn't it be someone you've known longer than two months?"

"You're the one who got us together. Please, Sarah?"

I held a small spark of Beth's happiness in my hands, and having so little control over my own life, I coveted this bit of power. And I felt mean at that moment. I wanted to say no, to close my fist over that spark and squelch it. To watch Beth's face crumble, so she might know—for a day, a minute, a few seconds, perhaps—how I felt all the time.

Something stopped me, though—a nearly unrecognizable sense of self-reproach. My latent conscience jolted to life, like Frankenstein's monster, bound to the table, twitching and straining to break free. I stomped on people all the time, but this was Beth. In all my callousness, I cared about her.

"Fine," I said. "But you better not make me wear some nightmare of a gown. No bows. No pink and purple polka dots. I've heard the horror stories."

"That's so great," she squealed, hugging me.

"I'm guessing you've already set a date. When is it? Tomorrow?"

Beth laughed again. It came so easy for her. "February twenty-second. That gives us almost eight weeks to get ready."

"Are you sure this is what you want?"

"Sarah," she said, rolling her eyes.

"Okay, okay. I won't ask again," I said, holding up my hands in mock surrender. "What do you think your brother will say?"

She grinned sheepishly. "I asked Mom to tell him."

Beth left to meet Dominic and his parents for dinner. I willed my sore body off the couch and into my still-damp parka. I'd go see Jack and try to convince him to talk some sense into his sister.

The paths to the Grange hadn't been shoveled. I wondered, briefly, if I should turn around and go home. My desire to see Jack, however, propelled me from the truck, and I plodded, knee-deep in snow, to his door.

"She told you," he said, letting me in.

I stomped my feet on the welcome mat, black and growing a rainbow assortment of plastic flowers. "How did you know?"

"Small town."

"Right. And news travels fast."

I hadn't seen Jack since Christmas Day, having intention-
ally stayed away, ashamed at the vulnerability I allowed to leak
out on him and all over Maggie's living room floor. I braced
for a moment of awkwardness between us. But he smiled at
me, and my guts kinked with delight, as if I were the only
person who could make Jack flash that tasty, tilted grin.

"Do you want some hot tea? You look cold."

"Okay. And maybe a towel, so I can dry my jeans."

"You're soaked through. I can give you something to
wear, and hang yours over the radiator."

He opened the dresser in the corner, his clothes folded
and piled in neat stacks in the drawer, and tossed me a pair
of sweatpants. "Bathroom's in there," he said, pointing.

Both my jeans and long underwear were wet. I peeled
them off and changed into Jack's pants. Then I flushed the
toilet so he wouldn't hear me rummaging through his medicine cabinet. Half empty and not nearly as neat as his dresser,
I found nothing scandalous—deodorant, a tube of toothpaste,
squeezed from the middle, a scraggly-bristled toothbrush,
and a bottle of Brut aftershave. And a square, green tin of
something called Bag Balm. I read the label. *Use for bunches,
caked bags, cuts, sore teats, chapping, and inflammation. Also excel-
lent for horses, dogs, and other pets.*

A steaming mug waited for me on the dinette table, a
quart of milk and bag of sugar next to it. "I didn't know how
you liked your tea," Jack said, draping my clothes over the
old cast-iron heater.

I stirred in milk until the brown liquid turned creamy
beige, and added two spoonfuls of sugar. "Thanks, this helps,"
I said. "Are you having some?"

"I'm not the one who's frozen." He sat in the other chair,

across from me. "So, tell me. What did you think of my darling sister's big news?"

"It's crazy. Can't you do anything about it?"

"What should I do?"

"Talk her out of it. She'll listen to you."

"You're the one who set them up."

"I never expected this. I figured they'd go out, maybe have a few drinks, have . . . I don't know . . . whatever fun people like them have. Then, maybe in a year or two, the marriage subject might come up. It's crazy."

"You already said that."

"Jack, seriously."

He exhaled thickly, lips vibrating, making a buzzing sound. Then he closed his eyes, sighed and raked his fingers through his hair, grabbing the curls at the back of his neck and tugging. "I've been fighting the urge to wield my brotherly power the entire day. To tell Beth to wait. But that's my own bruised ego speaking. I've been the most important man in her life for so long. It's hard to be replaced. Especially after just one date. But I guess I'm going to have to learn to share."

"I don't think he's good enough for her," I said.

"That's one thing I'm not worried about," Jack said. "I couldn't have chosen a better husband for my sister. Dominic's a hard worker; he's kind and good-hearted. Most importantly, he loves the Lord. Of course, if he got out of line, I'd have to go over there and kick his you-know-what."

I had tea in my mouth when he said this, and the words shocked me so much that I coughed up my drink; it spewed from my mouth and nose, back into the mug. Jack jumped up, grabbing a handful of napkins. I wiped my chin and shirt.

"Sorry," he said.

"Pastors say things like that?"

"You act like we're a different breed of people. I'm not perfect, Sarah."

"Could've fooled me."

"I don't think you want this anymore," Jack said, reaching for my cup. He took my wrist instead, turning my hand over. "What happened here?"

I rubbed the pad of my thumb lightly over the blisters. I'd sliced them open last night, pressing on the strings while playing, and they'd crusted over. "I burned myself cooking. It's nothing."

"You'd better watch those hands of yours. They're valuable," he said, carrying the mug into the kitchen. "Juilliard hands, right?"

"I never told you that."

"Luke did."

I looked at my fingers again. I always imagined a true virtuoso's hands to be carved by Michelangelo, long and strong with embroidered veins. Mine were stubby, all crooked fingers and broad knuckles. "I never graduated," I said.

Jack shrugged. "Just getting in there has to be worth something."

Yeah, a two-week stint in the pit orchestra of some lowbrow, off-off-off-Broadway musical. "Maybe. I don't know."

I couldn't remember the name of the musical now, or what the plot had been. But a year after I dropped out of school, I'd run into a Juilliard acquaintance who told me about the pit orchestra job. Actually, I served him a poppy seed bagel and iced coffee. He came into the Dunkin' Donuts where I worked. He served as set designer for the show, and said they were desperate for musicians.

After the way I left Juilliard, I didn't think I'd ever want to touch a violin again. But I loved it, and the mention of music started my fingers curling around a phantom bow, my chin tingling with the pressure of a phantom chinrest. I thought, perhaps, a pit orchestra job would be an easy, mindless way to find my way back to my first love.

I was wrong.

After two weeks, I quit. I couldn't take it anymore. I hadn't practiced away my entire adolescence, skipping school dances and movies and make-out parties, to be entertaining a theater full of half-wits who couldn't get tickets to *Cats*, and who hadn't a single ounce of appreciation for my art. I refused to go on, day in and day out, and play the same trash over and over again. This was not my love's music. It was the cadence of a quick fling in some drunk's rusted-out Pontiac parked behind the bar—and I'd had plenty of those already.

"Earth to Sarah," Jack said. "You look lost."

"Sorry. Just thinking."

"About what?"

"It's hard to explain."

"Try me."

I hesitated. Every time Jack and I spoke, I tore off a piece of myself and gave it to him. Crumbs at first, and now chunks, a bit bigger. Eventually, if I let him, he'd have all of me. And no one had ever known me like that. A good boy like Jack Watson couldn't handle seeing all the filth that churned around my soul.

"Not today," I said, and I left, jeans still hanging over the radiator.

chapter TWENTY-SIX

"Come on in," Memory shouted from somewhere inside her house, after I knocked. I was greeted by the scent of cinnamon-oatmeal spoon bread—a kind of scoopable cake sweetened with raisins and brown sugar. She knew I liked it, and had a pan waiting for me every Sunday morning.

"Don't know why you keep pounding on that door. It's always open," Memory said, galumphing into the kitchen as I dished the oatmeal into a bowl.

"Because it's polite to knock before entering, just in case you're not dressed or something. Aren't you constantly reminding me of my lack of manners?"

"I ain't walked around the house naked since I was three," she said. "And there's a dog's egg chance I'll ever do it again. Anyhoo, family don't knock. And you're family now."

"I'm not sure that's a good thing," I said, mouth full of food. Memory whacked me on the back, and I coughed some oats onto the table.

" 'Course it's good," she said with a chuckle. "Just as long as you don't be calling me Mama."

"There's about a dog's egg chance of me doing that," I said, echoing one of her favorite expressions.

She squawked, "Girl, there's hope for you yet," and left with her Bible, porcine hips scraping the doorjamb.

I washed my bowl and, opening the cabinet to put it away, found an index card hunched tentlike on top of the stack of bowls. I unfolded it. *Don't you be putting that bowl away wet*, it read in Memory's hen scrawl. Snickering, I swiped the bowl with a dish towel.

It took me by complete surprise, how Memory and I had knotted ourselves together, one Sunday at a time, one argument at a time—knit one, purl two—until we'd tangled ourselves into some ugly granny-square afghan, with misshapen edges and dropped stitches throughout. In many ways, despite Memory's earlier joke, we were like mother and daughter—albeit in a dysfunctional family sitcom, where the mother harassed the daughter about her grades and hairstyles and boyfriends, and the daughter stole money from her mother's purse and filled her vodka bottles with water after sneaking some, but everyone hugged by half hour's end.

When it was almost ten, I went to turn on the radio for Robert. He stared at the ceiling, blinking occasionally. When the introductory music began—an amateurish orchestral rendition of Beethoven's famous Ninth Symphony—he opened and closed his mouth several times, like a carp, grunting, twitching. Once the preaching started, however, his eyes crossed slightly, and his head sunk into his shoulder.

I'd noticed this pattern a couple of weeks ago, and since Doc couldn't tell me how pulpy Robert's mind was, I decided to try an experiment of my own. I'd brought my violin.

"Robert. Robert," I said, clapping my hands next to his ear. He didn't respond, so I raised the violin and ran the bow over the strings. His head lolled in my direction. I began playing *Ode to Joy* while walking slowly around the room, and his eyes followed me. When I stopped, his eyes stopped and he sucked his tongue. I played the song again, faster this time, and he squealed, piglike, legs jerking sporadically.

I paced until Memory came home, hoping Robert's response hadn't been a well-timed fluke, or that he hadn't used up the little brain juice he had left. I wanted this for her—a single minute of joy in the dreary, wasted hours that had become her life.

Memory stumped into the house, humming, carrying an aluminum-foil packet. "Who's hungry?" she said, heading to the kitchen. "Got some deviled eggs from Reverend Watson. You think it's fitting to eat deviled eggs on the Lord's day?"

I met her in there. "I need to show you something," I said, "in the den."

"Is my boy all right?"

"Watch this."

This time I played Bach—*Jesu, bleibet meine Freude* from Cantata 147—and Memory looked on, mouth agape, tears caught in the rolling folds of her face, as Robert followed me with his eyes.

She dropped to her knees with a thud; the lamp on the end table rattled unsteadily. "Oh, my precious Lord Jesus, what a gift. Thank you and praise you, heavenly Father. Oh, my boy. My boy," she said, rocking slightly, one hand on the floor, the other raised, open-palmed, toward the ceiling.

She stayed there for some time, lips moving silently. I packed my violin and went to leave, but she said, "Wait, Sarah." Jiggling to her feet, she took both Robert's hands, covering them with kisses. He had fallen asleep.

"Sarah," she said, but couldn't finish. I watched her, crying, leaning over her son's bed, back heaving, and thought I should give her a hug, or at least touch her shoulder. But my feet took me to the kitchen, and I sat in the gold vinyl-cushioned chair, listening to the sniffs and hiccups from the other room. Memory came in a few minutes later.

"Guess you need some lunch," she said, wiping her eyes on the cuff of her flannel shirt. She fixed two bologna and mustard sandwiches on stale homemade bread and slid a plate in front of me. Then she filled a green Depression-era relish dish with pickles, slices of apple, deviled eggs, and Ritz crackers.

I chewed my sandwich. Memory sat back in her chair and said, "You figure that out all by yourself?"

"Yeah."

"My boy, he weren't never smart or nothing, kinda ding-toed and whatnot. And he had these spells where he would fall down and rattle around on the floor. But he was always a sweet boy. And he was all I got. His daddy run off not too long after he was born, which was fine by me, 'cause Bobby Atkinson was nothing but crowbait. Don't know what I ever seen in him, 'cept he liked fat women, and he'd buy me beer even when I wasn't legal. 'Course, that was before I met Jesus."

"Doc said Robert has a brain injury?"

"The fool boy, he used to go out drinking with his buddies from the mill after work. 'Bout five years ago, he gone and crashed his car into a tree one night. Ended up like you see in there. Them doctors say he don't know anything now, and maybe he don't, but that ain't make me any less his mama. They said to put him in a home and let some strangers worry 'bout him. But that ain't what mamas do.

They take care of their babies, no matter what. You'll know what I mean one day."

I stabbed a pickle and slid it around my plate, juice leaving a green trail, like snail slime. If I had been more like Memory, my own child would be alive now. Then again, my stillbirth was probably a gift from the gods—or, as Jack said, grace. Imagine me with a kid. I'd only screw it up. "I don't think I'm cut out for the whole mothering thing."

"You say that now, but just you wait until you meet the one who scrambles your insides."

"No, not me."

"Mm-hmm. I'm fat for sure, but I see fine, and I see how you look when you get talking 'bout that buck nun Reverend Watson."

I twisted my napkin around my finger. Was it that obvious? How many other people knew? Beth hadn't been treating me any differently, but Maggie did seem a bit distant at Christmas. And Jack? I needed to play cool for a few weeks. "That's crazy," I said.

"Maybe," Memory said. "Maybe. All I'm saying is you ain't as tough as you think you are. That's a good thing, in case you was wondering. I know you been trying real hard not to get close to no one. But things ain't always up to you, and sometimes you don't got no choice in the matter.

"So, you gonna bring that fiddle of yours back next Sunday?"

I nodded because I couldn't find my voice. Memory was right; I'd gotten soft over the winter. And the only thing I hated more than Memory being right was my father.

I drove home past Granger Pond. Skaters of all ages and shapes covered the ice. Five or six boys shot hockey pucks into a makeshift goal at one end; some teenage girls stood around a barrel fire, giggling and watching the boys. Families skated together in clusters, some with matching hats and mittens. I saw Beth and Dominic, gliding hand in hand.

It had been years since I'd tried ice-skating. But each time I passed the pond, I felt the inkling to try it again. The next time I stopped into the variety store, I decided, I'd buy some skates. And I'd go late at night to use them, when no one would see me stumble and fall on my face.

chapter TWENTY-SEVEN

Memory grasped both of Robert's wrists and tugged him forward. She wriggled his rugby style shirt over his head and, before easing him back down into his pillow, covered the top half of the bed with a plastic shower curtain. Then she lifted his hips, stripped off his pants and diaper, and pushed another shower curtain under his legs. She hated to look at him undressed, all shriveled and bony, and stippled with moles. She thought of that song. *The leg bone's connected to the knee bone; the knee bone's connected to the thighbone.* Robert's bones hardly seemed connected to anything at all, loose and floppy like jellyfish tentacles. She'd never seen a live one, but as a child she took a book about sea jellies from the mobile library—a bus full of donated books that came through Jonah once a month between May and September—and she'd peed standing up for weeks, afraid one would swim up the toilet and sting her.

She remembered when she only had a plain, flat mattress, and had to lift her son's limp weight unaided. The hospital bed—a gift from Luke Petersen—made it easier to bathe Robert. Clomping around the bed, Memory kicked the pot near her feet, and warm, soapy water sloshed onto the floor. She dipped the washcloth into it, wringing it out onto her son's hair several times, until his head was wet enough to shampoo. After rinsing his hair, she gently massaged his skin clean, patted him dry, and rubbed baby lotion into his cracked elbows and knees. She stuffed towels around him, soaking up the extra water on the shower curtains. Then she rolled him onto one side and maneuvered him into his flannel pajama top, removing the wet towels and curtains before buttoning him up. She tugged his bottoms on over a clean diaper.

She bathed him twice a week, all she could manage now, and still, by the time she finished, she was wheezing and massaging the twinge behind her breastbone.

She was so tired.

Memory emptied the bathwater and refilled the pot, adding Epsom salts and five leftover Christmas peppermint candies. Sitting at the kitchen table, she stuck her feet into the hot water, soaking them until they puckered up like albino prunes. Then she got ready for bed, dragging her pillows and blankets out from the hall closet and throwing them on the couch. She hadn't slept one night in her bedroom since Robert came home from the hospital after the accident, the den the only room that could accommodate both of them. But the couch wasn't nearly wide enough for her. She slept sitting up, stacking pillows on a milk crate she used as an ottoman.

She read her Bible for a while. Then she pulled a paper sack of rag strips onto her lap, frowning at the unfinished rug. She'd been making it for Sarah, a gift for her, to take with her when she left in the spring. But it didn't seem right now, all stormy blues and grays. Sarah wasn't quite so thundery anymore.

Memory's eyes welled as she recalled Robert following Sarah's music around the room, and gave thanks again to God. She'd known her boy was still in there.

She felt another prick in her chest, and belched. A bout of indigestion, probably. Exertion immediately after eating always gave her heartburn, and bathing Robert was the most exercise she got these days. Still, each winter, when it took a little more effort to breathe, she wondered what would become of her boy if she could no longer care for him.

She shook off the thought. With Robert frail as he was, Memory was certain she'd outlive him.

chapter TWENTY-EIGHT

Other than throwing the bachelorette bash—
something Beth told me she didn't want—I didn't know
what a maid of honor did. I had one at my wedding, one of
David's cousins, but she merely showed up that day to sign
the marriage certificate and, clad in black velvet, stood next
to me in the courtroom, holding a cheap bouquet from the
gas station around the corner.

I didn't even get a party out of her.

Maggie happily took over much of the planning. She
buzzed from idea to idea, from wedding shower games to
the reception menu, her to-do list growing faster than a
field of dandelions.

"The chair covers are already sewn, with nearly three
weeks to spare," Maggie said at one of her twice-weekly
organizational meetings. Usually she, Beth, and I met for
dinner at the inn, but today she'd asked us to come in the
morning. Nine in the morning, to be more exact. My eyelids
kept falling closed, despite my three cups of coffee, and I
refused to empty my bladder, the itchy pressure forcing me
to stay awake.

Beth and Dominic would move into the inn after they were married, and Maggie wanted to prepare their new bedroom—Jack's old room, and the room she used now for her sewing and storage. Boxes needed to be moved and walls needed to be painted, and a full-sized bed from one of the inn bedrooms had to be disassembled, dragged downstairs, and put back together for the newlyweds.

Crossing number 17 off her two-page list, Maggie said, "Now, music."

"I didn't ask her yet," Beth said. They both looked me.

"No," I said.

"Please, Sarah?" Beth asked. "I wasn't going to say anything, and Patty was just going to play, but she was practicing after church and it just sounded so lonely. It would be so much better if you played along with her."

"No," I said again. "No."

"For a wedding gift? Please?"

"Oh, come on. You can't do that to me."

"I'll beg. I'll do your laundry until you leave."

I considered this. "And fold it?"

Beth nodded.

"And deliver it to me, and put it away?"

"If that means throwing it into the bottom of the closet like you do, I can manage that."

"All right, I'll play."

"Wonderful," Maggie said, scratching a line through number 23.

"I'll talk to Patty," Beth said, "and set up some time for you to practice together."

Double wonderful. "Anything else for me on that list that I don't know about?" I grumbled.

"Not that I see," Maggie said, laughing. "For now, at least."

"How's the food coming?" Beth asked.

The reception was being held at the Grange. After the ceremony, the folding tables would be set up, and guests would partake in a lasagna extravaganza, eating off disposable plates with plastic forks. Ten church ladies volunteered to each make four pans of pasta—cheap, easy to freeze, and conveniently transported when needed—while several others would be baking Italian bread, making tossed salads, and decorating wedding cupcakes. At least two hundred and fifty people were expected. Probably more.

When I'd asked Beth how many guests she planned for, she shrugged and said, "I'm not sending out invitations. Anyone who wants to come can come."

"You're going to have random crazies walking in off the street?"

"No one around here is random, Sarah."

The wedding date, she said, had been announced during Sunday services. She'd been telling people who came to eat at the diner; Dominic did the same at the gas station. Word of mouth would spread the news into each corner and crevice of the mountain. Beth didn't want to forget to invite anyone—there were so many people, she said, who'd prayed for her since before she was born, who wrote cards of encouragement after the fire, who wept with her mother. Those who sent a couple wrinkled dollars to help pay for her treatment, money they should have used to buy milk. Anyone who loved her, she said, was welcome.

And, with Beth, that was all who knew her.

Beth belonged to Jonah. Every person in the town had taken her for their own. I'd seen that the moment she declared her engagement—everyone from the lumberjacks to the nosy old women, to the children who offered to tie ribbons around the tulle baggies of Jordan almonds for wedding favors. Beth's marriage, it seemed, ended the mourning shrouding the town since the fire. She no longer needed anyone hovering over her to protect her from the sun, or the stares. She was moving on, and the people of Jonah could share her joy, give her a set of steak knives, and move on with her.

"Oh, and flowers," Maggie said. "Beth, you still need to figure your flower budget."

"Yes, drill sergeant," Beth said, saluting and giggling. "This is why I only gave you eight weeks. If you had eight months, the entire Grange would have been renovated, and you'd be serving a twelve-course meal at the reception."

"Oh, hush," Maggie said. "Are we going to paint now?"

"Yes," I said. "But after I use the bathroom."

"Wait," Beth said. "Your dress came yesterday. You have to try it on first."

She took the dress from the closet and gave it to me, the thin plastic that covered it clinging to my leg. I carried it to the bathroom and changed into it after using the toilet. A full-length mirror hung on the back of the door. I spun, and could see the outline of my panties bulging through the fabric. So I slipped them off, turned again, and made a mental note to get a slip before the wedding. The dress pulled a little across the hips; I'd been too stubborn to order the next size. I sucked in my stomach. No potatoes or bread for the next three weeks.

"I love it," Beth said when I returned to the kitchen. She'd given me a mail-order catalog and dog-eared four different styles. I chose this, a spaghetti-strapped, basil-colored chiffon with three sheer layers of skirting. Hundreds of tiny beads embellished the top, sparkling like the dancing snow on New Year's Eve.

Maggie knelt, tugged at the hem. "Do you have her shoes, Beth?"

I stepped into the silver heels, feet sticking to them because I had no hose on. Maggie gave the hem another look. "I don't think it needs to be taken up. Do you? Walk a bit."

I paced around the room, fabric cool and flowing over my legs, swishing, tickling my ankles. Maggie pinched the seams at my hips. "I can let this out a little," she said.

"It looks fine, Mom. Stop fussing," Beth said, and then turned to me, hiding her mouth behind her hand, as if she had a secret to tell in my ear, but instead spoke in a mock whisper. "She's always like that, Sarah. Ignore her. I do."

"Forgive me if I want everything perfect for your big day," Maggie said.

"I'm bloated," I lied. "You know."

The women nodded, like women do, conspirators in the monthly drudgery, and Beth wanted to know if I needed Motrin. I shook my head, and asked, "Where's your dress?"

"Oh, that," Beth said, rolling her eyes. "Another saga."

"Go get them," Maggie said. "We need Sarah's opinion."

I changed back into my jeans and sweater while Beth fetched the gowns from her room. She hung each one in front of her, bending the wire hanger so it fit over her head.

There were three dresses. One was plain and white, a simple A-line with a corseted bodice and thick, gathered straps. The second, an ivory silk with three-quarter sleeves and high neck, had a two-tone beige pattern on the skirt.

The final dress glittered with pounds of rhinestones and sequins, tag hanging from the zipper, red clearance sticker announcing *Final Sale*. The other two dresses were dirty at the bottom, seemingly from dragging across the floor.

"Not the last one," I said. "That's awful."

"That's Patty Saltzman's dress," Beth said. "She told me I could borrow it, if I wanted. She bought it a few years ago and has been saving it—"

"For Jack?"

"I think she's given up on him, since she said she planned on dying an old maid. The other two I bought through an online auction. Only used once," she said with a chuckle.

"I like the first one," I said.

"See?" Beth said to Maggie.

"I still think the ivory is more appropriate," Maggie said.

"My mother doesn't believe a bride should show that much skin in church."

"It's not that."

"Then what?"

The older woman hesitated. "Nothing."

Beth went to her. "Mom, I don't care if my scars show. The only person I'm worried about impressing is Dom, and he's going to see a lot more than my arm and shoulders that night."

"Elizabeth Grace Watson," Maggie said, choking out a laugh.

"Well, it's true," Beth said, grinning. "I'm going to take Sarah down to my room and show her how this dress looks on. We'll meet you for painting in a few minutes."

I sat on the canopied bed as Beth undressed behind the open closet door, tossing her jeans and sweatshirt onto the wing chair in the corner. Then her socks, her undershirt—the tank kind little girls wear. She came into the center of the room, holding the top of the dress. "Zip me, please?"

I did, and latched the hook-and-eye between her shoulder blades. Then I tightened the corset, the satin ribbons woefully uneven and droopy. "I hope my maid of honor duties don't include tying you into this."

"Duly noted," she said, spinning to face me. "Okay, what do you think? I know you'll be brutally honest. I . . . I need you to be."

Her left shoulder and arm looked smooth and white-chocolaty against the dress, fine, golden-brown hairs stiff with cold. On her neck and chest, Beth had several small patches of iridescent skin, and thick nodules of tissue stuck in her left elbow, her armpit, like wads of wet, chewed bubble gum. But most of the scars were waxy, snug, as if someone had melted every pink Crayola shade—salmon and carnation, razzmatazz and wild watermelon—swirling them together with a wooden spoon until creamy, then poured the molten liquid over her body, where it cooled and hardened. The Braille of agony, of healing, to be read on her wedding night by Dominic's fingers.

"I think you look beautiful," I said.

"Really?"

"Yeah. Really."

"No one has ever seen this much of me. I never wear less than a T-shirt and shorts. Long shorts. Even swimming."

"You just told Maggie you weren't worried about it."

"She's my mother, Sarah," Beth said, as if I understood how mothers and daughters interacted, what secrets were kept, what was shared. "I was thinking about showing Dom.

This. I mean, I told him that what he sees on my neck and face is all over me. I told him I don't have any—"

She wiped away a stray tear. "It seems so stupid to be crying about having no breasts when I'm alive, and there are people with so many worse things wrong with them. I just don't want him to be disappointed."

"He won't be," I said.

"I keep trying to tell myself that."

"Has he ever been with . . . you know?"

Beth shook her head. "No. Neither of us."

"Then trust me. He won't be thinking about your boobs. Or lack thereof."

She smiled a little. "Thanks."

Beth changed, hanging her dress on her closet door, so she could see it each morning when she woke, she said. Then, in the spare room, we packed up skeins of yarn, fat quarters, and Christmas decorations that hadn't made it down to the basement yet. Maggie labeled each box, and we carried them into her bedroom. After the wedding, she'd find a place for them.

We covered the wood floor with several paint-spattered canvas drop cloths. Then we taped around the moldings and ceiling; none of us wanted to cut in freehand. I pulled on a pair of white painter's overalls, and asked, "So, what color did you choose?"

"That's a good question," Beth said. She pointed to the closet, where I found fourteen cans of paint. "We couldn't get down the mountain to the hardware store, so that's what we have. Leftovers from whoever I could find to give them to me."

Six of the cans were white. There were also two shades of green, three yellows, a blue, a gray, and a full can of magenta. I pried off the lids. "What if we mix this green with some yellow and gray? I bet we'd end up with a nice mossy color."

"Sounds good," Beth said, and found a bucket for mixing.

The walls needed only one coat, so we were able to paint the walls and trim by midafternoon. I dropped my brush into the paint tray and sighed, twisting to crack my spine. "What's next?"

"I'm working dinner, so I have to clean up and go," Beth said. "Sarah, thanks for all your help. I'll let you know about practice with Patty."

"Great," I said, and she flitted off.

Maggie closed the paint cans. "I'm beat. We'll do the bed another time. Or I'll have Jack get some men to do it."

"Let me help you wash those." I gathered the paintbrushes and trays, and followed Maggie to the basement—a cellar, actually, with damp stone walls and cobwebbed beams that brushed the top of my head. Only cold water flowed from the utility sink, and I rinsed the brushes until the water ran clear through the bristles, and then went back upstairs, filled the bathroom sink with bubbles and hot water, and soaked my hands for several long minutes.

"Maggie, I'm going," I said, poking my head into her bedroom.

"Wait. I want to show you something."

She propped open her hope chest and removed a quilt, all vibrant yellow, ivory, pink, and brown. "It's a tradition in my family. Mothers make a quilt to give their daughters when they marry. I started this when Beth turned thirteen." She ran her hand over it, hugged it. "After the fire, I buried it in the mothballs, unfinished. There didn't seem any point in working on it. I wasn't sure she was going to make it, and if she did . . .

"Well, that seems like such a silly way to think, now. Anyway, I finally picked it up again about a year ago, figuring I'd give it to her when she turned twenty-one. I'm glad I don't have to wait that long."

"The wedding will be perfect," I said.

"I know. Even if everything turns out wrong, it will still be perfect, 'cause every mother wants to see her baby girl married and settled. And happy."

"I don't think they get happier than Beth," I said.

"You don't have to tell me that twice," Maggie said.

No, I didn't need to be told twice, either.

chapter TWENTY-NINE

I picked up the groceries Doc ordered each week for Ben and Rabbit, and drove to their shack. The trip took more than an hour now—each way—because of the weather. Municipal snowplows rarely found their way into Jonah until two or three days after a storm. The main streets were kept clear by the townsfolk who had their own plows attached to the front of their trucks and Jeeps. The less-traveled mountain roads were not as well maintained, and on several occasions I had to drive two or three miles in reverse because I'd hit a stretch of road blocked by snow, and there was no room to turn around. When this happened, Doc would call in a favor, and in a few days the route would be cleared so I could deliver the food. Remarkably, I had few problems driving on the small, dirt roads close to the Harrison home, as the thick pine canopy sheltered them from the elements.

Rabbit still refused to open the door for me. I'd stopped knocking and now just plopped the two paper sacks in the snowbank next to the woodpile.

On the way home, I swung into the junkyard to visit Hiram Dennison. It hurt my knuckles to knock on the glass bus door, so I kicked at the bottom of it. "Mr. Dennison, it's Sarah," I called.

The door didn't swing open as usual. I walked to the side of the bus, jumped up and down, trying to see into the high, frosty windows. Then I kicked some more. Sheets of snow slid off the roof.

Luke had kept a toolbox in his truck, behind the front seats. I'd never lugged it out, too heavy for me to bother lifting. Now I went through it to find a pry bar, jammed the metal between the bus doors, and pulled. The doors popped open. I fell backward, landing on my rear.

"Mr. Dennison?" I said, climbing inside. I could still see my breath; usually, Hiram kept the air inside the bus toasty warm. At the top of the steps I looked toward the back of the bus and saw him, stiff in his chair, eyes frozen open. His dog, Nola, lay curled around his foot. She'd torn open the bag of kibble, little brown chunks strewn across the floor, her water bowl crusted over with ice.

I'd never seen a dead body before. I gave him a couple quick jabs with the pry bar. The dog raised her head and whimpered, her tail swishing a little. I bent over to pat her head.

"I guess you're coming with me for now."

The mutt stood and shook. Yawned.

"Oh, thanks," I said, and she licked my fingers, as if apologizing.

Nola jumped into the truck, scratched the passenger seat and turned around once, twice, before settling into a ball and closing her eyes again. I drove straight to Doc's office, leaving the dog in the car. She bolted up when I slammed the truck door, and pushed her nose against the window, watching me.

Patty vacuumed the waiting area. She clicked off the machine when I entered.

"I need to see Doc," I said.

"He's not here."

"It's an emergency."

"He's still not here."

She turned the vacuum back on. I yanked the plug out of the wall, tossed it onto her pointy-toed boots. "Where is he?"

"Making a house call," she said, wrapping the cord and wheeling the vacuum back into the closet.

"You missed a spot," I said.

"And you can go now."

"I told you, I need to see Doc."

"And I told you he's not here."

She sat down behind her desk and opened the calendar. Ignoring me, she highlighted appointments in several different colors.

Patty and I had practiced together four times for the wedding. On three of those days Beth acted as referee, lightening the tension with her smile, marching up and down the Grange hall's aisle to find the right speed for the music. She practiced in her heels and ignored our verbal sparring.

The fourth time—just two days ago—Jack had listened to us, too, hovering in the door of his office. Patty sat at the keyboard, back straighter than a sheet of plywood, chest out, flicking her hair on each accent, as if she were performing at the Van Cliburn International Piano Competition, not merely the wedding march on a rickety Yamaha upright. Not to be outdone, I added slides and grace notes to Wagner's score, being unabashedly showy. In the end, mediocrity won; Patty gushed over Jack's last sermon, and invited him over for pot roast and green bean casserole that night at Ima-Louise's house. In fact, she purred, they could leave together now, and she'd drive him home after dessert—his favorite, apple cobbler.

I'd had nothing better to offer.

"Look," I told Patty, "I just found one of Doc's old guys dead. If you know whose house he's at, could you please call him there? Then I'll leave."

Huffing, she picked up the rotary phone and dialed. "Hi, Linda, this is Patty at Doc's office. Is he still there? Great, thanks . . . Doc, Sarah is here. I told her you were seeing a patient, but she insists she needs to speak with you." She held the phone out to me, dangling it between her thumb and forefinger, as if it were a grimy jock strap. "Here."

"Hello," I said.

"Sarah, what is it?" Doc asked.

"Hiram Dennison is dead."

"Are you sure?"

"I don't think people get deader than that."

He sighed. I could picture him tugging off his glasses and wiping them on the bottom of his shirt. "Okay, I'll take care of it."

"What should I do with the dog?"

"Is she still on the bus?"

"No," I said. "I have her with me."

"I'll try to find someone to take her. Can you manage her for a few days?"

"Can't you?"

"For crying out loud, Sarah. I'm asking a simple favor of you. Throw some dog food in one bowl, water in another, and let her out a few times a day. Even you can handle that."

"Fine," I said, shaking off the prick of Doc's reprimand.

"Fine," he said. "We'll talk later."

The line went dead. I gave the phone back to Patty. "See, that wasn't so hard," I said.

"What's hard is being in the same room with you for five minutes."

I blew a little snicker of air through my nose. "Get over it, Patty. Jack is never going to marry you, and that's certainly not my fault."

"Is that what you think? I'm jealous because Reverend Watson is running around trying to help you put the pieces of your sorry life back together?"

"You don't know what you're talking about," I said.

"Luke used to ask us to pray for you, because you were lost, but he was too embarrassed to give specifics. I can only imagine," she said. "Yep, the whole town knows about you, Sarah. And everyone knows that the only reason Jack Watson has taken any interest in you is because he feels like he owes your father something, because Luke saved his sister's life."

"What?"

"You heard me. Luke pulled Beth out of that fire, and now Jack's trying to keep you out of hell." Patty closed the appointment book and began filing her nails. "If you ask me, he's just wasting his time."

Patty's mug sat on the desk. I picked it up and tossed the coffee at her. It splattered over her face and neck, on the front of her white blouse. "Are you insane?" she yelled.

"If I'm going to hell, I might as well have some fun on the way there," I said.

I stomped out of the office, slamming the door hard enough to knock icicles from the roof; they clattered to the pavement, shattering. In the truck, Nola nuzzled my face.

"Get away," I said, pushing her off me. I sped down the road, but when I saw Jack's truck parked in front of the diner, I cut the wheel to the left and pulled next to him.

Beth saw me burst into the restaurant as she balanced several blue-plate specials in her arms. "Sarah, is everything all right?"

"Where's Jack?" I asked.

She jerked her head toward the back booth. "He's there."

I didn't care that patrons had stopped eating to stare at me. I sidestepped the tables, walked past the booths until I found Jack, sitting with his headphones on, Bible open, scribbling on a yellow legal pad. He sensed me next to him, looked up and turned off his cassette player. "Hey, Sarah," he said, smiling and stacking his papers to make room for me. He touched his dish. "Care to join me for the meat loaf?"

"What am I to you?" I asked.

The diner went silent. Jack said, "I'm not sure I understand."

"Am I just some charity case? You put in your five hours of dealing with me each week, and pat yourself on the back for fulfilling your duty?"

"Of course not. Where did you get an idea like that?"

"So, Luke didn't ask you to save my soul?"

"Even if I wanted to, I couldn't."

"You know what I mean. Are you supposed to be keeping an eye on me?"

Now Jack stood. He reached out and put his hand on my elbow, trying to guide me into the booth. "He did ask that. But, Sarah, it's not like—"

I twisted away from him. "Not like what? Not like you owe him your sister's life?"

He took me by the shoulders then, squeezing them. It didn't hurt, but his sharp grip got my attention. "Just sit," he said. Something in his voice—some mix of pain and exhaustion—made me listen. I slid into the padded bench, unzipped my coat, and biting the fingertips, pulled my gloves off with my teeth.

Jack left me there, alone, for a few moments. He walked to the counter; I could see him talking quietly to Beth. She nodded and filled two white mugs, adding a swirl of whipped cream to the top of each. He carried them back to the table. "Hot chocolate. I won't spill it on you this time, I promise."

"Jack, I—"

"Shh," he said. "My turn now." He looked at me, eyes brown, but not dull and mud-colored like my own; specks of amber and gold floated in them. "That night, the night of the fire, everyone was outside. It was chaos. Black smoke was pouring out into the sky, and we gathered in groups of three, five, six. Counting. Finally, someone screamed that the kids were still inside, in the basement. I remember my mother; she sank into the snow, and was sobbing, 'My baby, my baby. Lord, please don't take her, too. Please, please, no.'

"Luke was standing next to Mom. He told her he would find Beth. And he did. He ran into the building. Everyone else just stood there—stunned, frightened, I don't know. He came back out carrying her, his hair singed off, huge blisters bubbling on his hands. Some of the other men tried to get back inside then, but it was too late. The church collapsed on itself.

"So, yes, your father saved Beth. And, yes, I would do anything he asked of me. But if Beth had died in that fire,

191

I'd still be here, sitting across from you, trying to convince you that you're not just Luke's daughter to me."

"Because that's your job," I said.

"No, because I care."

"Because it's your job to care."

Jack rubbed his hand over his face, through his hair. "Obviously, we're not going to agree on this one. I'd like to remind you, however, that I know of several people who don't have 'look after argumentative, pigheaded redheads named Sarah' listed in their official job descriptions, and they happen to care about you a great deal. And believe you me, you don't make it easy."

No, I didn't. I pushed and pushed, bending people until they snapped. For all his bravado, Jack was no different than anyone else who'd breezed through in my life. He'd eventually quit trying. Everyone did.

"Your mom and Beth don't count," I said, mashing the whipped cream into my cold cocoa with the back of the spoon.

"I give up," Jack said, looking at his watch and cramming his pens and books into his messenger bag. "At least for today. But, if you wake up tomorrow and realize that you just might be worth something to someone, give me a call."

"I don't have a phone." I was being a jerk, but couldn't help needling him closer to the breaking point. I wanted him there sooner rather than later, to crush the tiny, insistent longing that whispered, *Someday, someone will stay.*

He was tenacious—there was no denying that.

But I was more so.

Jack closed his eyes, and I watched his jaw muscles expand and contract, like gills. He took a deep, impatient breath and nodded slowly. "I'm going now."

Sarah, one. Caring Reverend Jack, zero.

He slung his bag over his shoulder and walked down the aisle, but stopped and turned back to me. "Is there a dog in your truck?"

"Oh, shoot. I forgot," I said, standing and grabbing my gloves off the table.

"That looks like—"

I shook my head, eyes wide and darting around the room. Jack understood. He ground his teeth into his lip, and held the door for me.

Once outside, he asked, "When?"

"I found him this afternoon. Doc knows."

"He wasn't in church Sunday." He opened the truck and scratched Nola on each side of her head, behind her ears. "I should have gone to check on him then."

"Jack—"

"Not now," he said, closing Nola in the cab of my truck and getting into his own. His headlights flashed on, and he drove away.

I slammed my door. Nola sat up in the passenger seat, looking up at me, her head tilted to one side. "What the heck are you looking at?" I asked, and she barked.

A Closed sign hung in the variety-store window. I rattled the doorknob, but no one came to let me in. So I went back to the cabin and tossed several slices of bread onto a plate and set it on the floor. Nola gobbled it down, and slurped all the water in the bowl I put next to her.

I scrounged around the cabinets for my own dinner, finally settling on the couch with a peanut butter and potato-chip-crumb sandwich. Nola put her snout on my knee, licking her nose as I ate.

"Go away," I told her. "You're not getting any."

She stayed near me all night, following me around the kitchen, into the bathroom, her nails clicking against the wood floor. When I went to bed, she sat next to the couch—her face the same height as my own—and panted on me. I turned my head into the cushions and stuck my fingers in my ears so I wouldn't hear her whining.

I woke sometime later, unable to breathe, a crushing weight on my chest. Nola lay on me, snoring softly.

"Oh, no. Get off," I said, shoving her to the floor. She whimpered a little, dazed and half asleep.

I pulled the quilt and pillows off Luke's bed and threw them down next to the couch. "You can sleep on these."

She sniffed the pile and burrowed inside the folds of the blanket. I fell asleep listening to her breathe.

chapter THIRTY

Jack found Doc at Hiram Dennison's place, dozing in his Jeep, two wool blankets wrapped around him. When Jack tapped on the window, Doc rolled it down and started the engine, pushing all the heat levers to high, including the rear defroster. "Sarah tell you?"

Jack nodded. "How long?"

"A week, give or take. He stopped marking off his calendar last Wednesday." Doc blew into his hands, held them against the vents. "Nothing you could have done."

"Maybe," Jack said. "Are you waiting for the coroner?"

"He said he'd be here before midnight."

"I'll stay, if you want."

"You're not dressed for it," Doc said. "He was dead four or five days before the generator went out. You can't turn the heat back on in the bus. It'll thaw the body, and the smell . . ."

"Yeah," Jack said. Though, that would be a fitting end. Hiram Dennison may have had an icebox and cooking stove in his bus, but he didn't have running water. He came to church each Sunday with scent of body odor ground into his clothes, and sat in the front row, belting each hymn out in his gurgly baritone. On particularly pungent days, Jack would have one of the elders douse him in a fog of disinfectant; Hiram graciously agreed, apologizing for being unable to smell himself—"Lost the old sniffer in the war," he'd say— and would stand with outstretched arms, spinning slowly, so the spray would coat him completely.

"I'll take care of the arrangements, then," Jack said.

He only spoke with Doc when someone was sick or dead. Quite honestly, Jack didn't know what to make of the man. He kept to himself, didn't attend church or town events, and rarely accepted a dinner invitation—from anyone. But, he slaved for the people on the mountain. Jack's initial distrust had disappeared years ago, after a quick phone call to the state medical board. Doc's record was clean.

He shook Doc's hand and began the drive home, mentally listing the things he'd need to do to prepare for the memorial service. He lost four or five congregants each year, and faithfully made certain that those without immediate family left written instructions, with him or Rich Portabella, regarding the distribution of their worldly goods. He knew he would be getting several hundred magazines from Hiram, and his favorite ratchet.

Jack hadn't been concerned that Hiram wasn't in church Sunday. He missed a handful of services in the winter when his old snowmobile wouldn't start. In fact, Jack had offered up a small praise for the respite from the bitter cut-grass-and-boiled-onion smell he usually had to breathe while giving his sermon, followed by halfhearted repentance for his callous celebration.

If only Sarah had known how caring he'd been, then.

He'd wanted to smack her earlier. She exhausted him,

and each battle-weary day he swallowed down the urge to tell her, "Fine. If you want me to leave you alone, I will." He'd expected opposition, but her attacks ate at him. He took them personally now. And, despite his constant prayer, he felt as if he were running circles in the mist.

With God, nothing is impossible, he reminded himself, holding on to that promise with a child's hands, all sticky with lollipop and faith. He needed to, because his clumsy fumblings were no match for Sarah's pain, her past.

chapter THIRTY-ONE

I left Nola alone at the cabin Thursday when I went
to the variety store for dog food   I'd scrambled eggs for her
breakfast, and gave her several slices of bologna—and a leash
and collar. Earlier that morning I had learned she loved to
pounce in the snow, and expected me to jump around with
her. When I didn't, she dashed down the road and stood,
cock-eared, just within eyesight until I called her and stepped
off the porch. Then she ran around the bend. I took the truck
to find her. She jumped into the passenger seat, ice matted
in her fur, grinning and drooling.

I refused to play that game again.

I returned not an hour later with a value-priced bag of
dog chow and discovered Nola also did not like to be left
alone. She had chewed Luke's pillows and dragged them
around the cabin, scattering gray feathers everywhere, and
gouged the front door trying to tunnel through it. She also
defecated on my sleeping bag.

I fastened the new collar around her neck, dragged her
outside, tied the leash to the porch post, and kicked snow
on her. Then I went back inside to sweep up the feathers.

The broom did little more than puff the down around the room. I'd have to borrow Maggie's vacuum.

After rinsing my sleeping bag in the shower, I read the feeding instructions on the dog food bag. Nola looked to be about forty pounds. One cup twice a day. I dumped the food into a dish and went outside to get her.

The leash and collar dangled from the post. Nola frolicked in the snow fifty yards away. She saw me, barked, and ran down the road. I followed again in the truck.

I took her with me on Friday while I visited Doc's other patients. She clawed at the window until I rolled it down enough for her head to fit through, and chewed the armrest when I shut her in the truck by herself.

And it didn't matter how often I knocked her off the couch. I'd still wake four or five times each night, Nola between my legs, head resting on my hipbone. But the cabin had a certain fullness with her in it. In those murky moments between sleep and waking, even before I remembered she was there, I sensed a difference in the air—maybe it seemed warmer from two bodies instead of one, or moved with two breaths—and that fullness comforted me.

I didn't know if I wanted to kick her, or keep her.

Doc pulled his Jeep into my driveway Saturday morning as I stood there in pajamas and boots, holding Nola's leash, shaking from cold and cursing at her to hurry. She began whimpering at six, but I wouldn't take her outside until at least seven. She nipped at my feet, face bearded with snow, backside wagging up in the air. I flicked the leash, snapping it against her side. She barked and jumped around some more.

"It might help if you walked with her," Doc said.

"I can't. I'm frozen."

He took the leash from me and whistled. Nola pulled him along, tunneling through the snow like a groundhog. I went inside and dressed, for no reason other than to stay awake until the dog came in. I'd be going back to bed as soon as Doc left.

Nola burst through the door with all her early-morning canine exuberance, jumping up on me with her wet paws. I shoved her, filled her bowl with food. Doc followed, tossing a plastic grocery bag at me.

"What's this?" I asked. The handles were tied together, so I ripped open the bottom and a rumpled white shirt fell out. White, with an angry coffee splotch on the front.

"Patty expects someone to pay for that. Either you," he said, "or me, because I hired you."

"It's so hard to find good help these days." I said. "Don't you want my side of the story?"

"I think I can fill in the blanks." He picked up the shirt and handed it to me. "It's designer, I've been informed."

"Right, vagabond chic," I said, looking at the label. "She got this at Kmart. I have socks that cost more."

"Then you won't mind reimbursing her."

I tossed the shirt at Nola. She rolled onto her back, on top of it, grinding her dog scent onto it. "Whatever. It's not coming out of my wallet. That can't be the only reason you're here at this ungodly hour."

"It's not ungodly if the sun is already up."

"It is if it's before eleven."

He jiggled Nola's leash. "I've come to get the dog."

"Who's taking her?"

"No one. I'm bringing her to the county shelter."

"You were supposed to find someone to take her in."

"I'm not a pet-matching service. I asked around. No one wants her. You don't want her. I'm getting rid of her for you. What's the problem?"

"Nothing, except they kill dogs at the pound if no one adopts them."

"If I didn't know you better, I'd almost think you cared," he said. "Speaking of which, Hiram Dennison's memorial service is tomorrow at ten, if you're interested."

"I'm not."

"He would have liked you to be there."

"He won't know the difference. He's worm food."

"He was cremated."

"It's all semantics. He's still dead."

"Would it hurt you to have some decorum?"

"Probably," I said, grabbing the orange juice pitcher from the refrigerator and pouring a glass. I took a gulp and spit the fermented mouthful into the sink. "Oh, that's gross."

"Lovely," Doc said. "So, am I taking the dog?"

"Yeah." I dumped the remaining juice down the drain. "But tell them . . . tell them if no one takes her, to let you know. I'll go get her before they put her down."

"Okay."

"Oh, and tell them to call you if she's adopted. Just so I know that, you know, I'm rid of her, for good."

Doc fastened the collar around Nola's neck. She strained toward the door. "By the way," he said, "Memory told me about Robert."

"Well, don't get too excited. I've played for him every Sunday since, and he hasn't responded again, not like the first time. It must have just been some sort of coincidence."

"One man's coincidence is another man's miracle."

"Come on," I said, opening a two-liter bottle of Diet Coke. "You're not serious."

He put on his hat, the old man kind, with the flaps that covered his ears. "I've seen too much that can't be so easily explained."

I felt as if I'd lost an ally. My only ally. Doc, some kind of freaky closet Crusader? He'd betrayed me. "Just go," I said. "Your optimism is ruining my day."

"Good," he said. "Because your pessimism ruined mine."

He left with Nola, and instantly the cabin emptied of life.

chapter THIRTY-TWO

On the eve of Beth's wedding, the Grange building had been transformed into a white paper wonderland. The children in Beth's Sunday school class had snipped and strung hundreds of snowflakes, which now dangled from the ceiling, dancing each time the wind snuck in through the front door. Half of them were made from doilies with lacy, scalloped edges.

Maggie and her friends had sewn enough muslin chair covers to dress three hundred chairs—a couple hundred metal folding ones from the church, and another hundred pillaged from basements and attics across Jonah. And the chipped plaster walls were disguised with white crepe-paper streamers. Every evening of the past week, Tom Hardy had pulled out his monstrous ladder, climbed to the ceiling, and stapled the end of a streamer roll to the very top of the wall. Then he'd dropped the roll to Carl Brooks, waiting at the bottom, and Carl twisted the strand two dozen times, cut it, stapled it against the floor, and chucked the roll back up to Tom. They still had ten feet of wall left to dress.

Beth didn't want a rehearsal; she didn't want Dominic

to see her come toward him until the moment her wedding began, even if she wore her corduroys and turtleneck. She didn't want to hear the ceremonial words until she stood in front of those who came to witness her marriage. I wouldn't be walking down the aisle anyway, emerging instead from Jack's office to join Patty at the piano. So she and I practiced one last time, tucked in the corner as dozens of people scurried around us in last-minute preparation. We didn't make eye contact. Finishing, I closed my violin in its case and picked it up.

"You know, you can leave it here," Patty said. "No one will steal it."

I shook my head. Now that I had an instrument again, I needed to keep it close. Since New Year's Eve, I didn't play it while alone at the cabin, to myself, for myself. But I tucked it under the couch while I slept, and sometimes held it just to feel it in my hands, or pushed my nose between the strings to smell its belly.

"Suit yourself," she said, closing the piano. "But you better not forget it tomorrow."

I ran into Beth in Jack's kitchen, filling his refrigerator with flowers. There'd been no snow or ice storm for more than a week—a minor miracle, according to Maggie—and Beth had been able to drive an hour down the mountain to a florist. She'd bought whatever two hundred dollars would allow—lilies, mostly, but some daisies and stephanotis, as well. And pots of white poinsettias, left over from Christmas and a bit shriveled, but perfect, she said, to flank the altar.

"You're still coming over, right?" she asked.

"As long as you're making the popcorn," I told her. Beth had said she wanted one more movie night as a single woman, and invited me to stay at the inn afterward. I thought she simply wanted assurance I wouldn't oversleep and spoil her day. The ceremony began at eleven in the morning, and the hairstylist wanted to have us completely beautified by nine.

I followed Beth home, and we watched an awful remake of *The Beverly Hillbillies*. "Don't make any comments," she said. "Do you see a video store around here? I had to borrow this from the neighbors." After the movie, Beth went to spend the last night under her eyelet canopy, and I took a shower in the guest bathroom, upstairs, so I wouldn't have to get up earlier the next morning. Maggie made up a guest bedroom for me—the same one I slept in the first night I arrived in Jonah.

"Shoot," I said as I caught my pantyhose on the bottom corner of Jack's dresser. A run snaked up my leg, from ankle to the ultra tight control top. I hadn't lost as much weight as I'd wanted. "I didn't bring another pair."

"I did," Beth said. "I'm always running hose. Check my bag."

I rummaged around her pretty pink suitcase, destroying her perfectly stacked piles. I grabbed the hose—not control top, and really, why would Beth need them with her boyish hips and flat tummy?—and went into the bathroom. Jack kept nail scissors in his vanity drawer, with his comb and razor. I pulled off my ruined hose and cut the legs off, just beneath the support panty. Slowly, I slipped on the new pair, and then tugged the panty from my old pair over them. Instant liposuction. I looked five pounds thinner.

I'd overslept that morning. Beth had come into my room at eight-thirty, and when I didn't respond to her gentle shaking, she pinched me. "But I set the alarm for seven," I told her.

She checked. "For seven *p.m.* Come on, we're going to the hall now. Just throw on your shoes and grab what you need."

So I stuffed my feet, sockless, into my boots and tripped down the last three stairs while trying to zip my parka. Maggie crammed me into her Jeep, two hot trays of lasagna on my lap, burning my thighs through a bath towel and my thin flannel pajama pants. Beth had followed in her own car; she had the dresses. Beth's beautician friend would meet us at the Grange to fix our hair and makeup.

All I'd needed to remember was my violin.

"My violin," I yelled, bursting out of the bathrooms and jamming my legs back into my pants. "I left it at the inn. Beth, give me your keys."

"You can't go," the beautician, Dianne, said. "I need to do your hair now."

"Forget my hair," I snapped.

"Sarah, relax," Beth said. "I'm done. I'll find someone to run back to the inn. Where did you leave it?"

"In my room. I'm such an idiot."

"It's okay. Really. There are at least thirty women in the kitchen. I'm sure one of them isn't busy."

I sank into the chair as Beth left, and Dianne stuck a brush in my hair. She gave a tug. "Your hair is like a rat's nest," she said.

"Give me that," I said. I hated having my hair brushed by others. Some women found it relaxing; I found it annoying. And painful. Knots hurt more when someone else tried to comb them out; I'd rather torture myself.

With my hair finally smooth, Dianne used huge plastic

clips to clamp my hair into sections. "Beth wants me to curl your hair, and pull it up."

She twisted handfuls around hot rollers and then doused me with hair spray, the cheap kind that smelled like perfume-laced vodka and turned hair into a bulletproof helmet. She removed the rollers, sticking dozens of bobby pins into my scalp before holding a hand mirror in front of me and declaring, "Done." Then she grimaced. "You were supposed to wear a button-down shirt."

I plucked at the neck of my thermal top. "It will stretch."

"It won't. You'll mess your hair. We'll cut it off."

"No way."

"Fine. I'll help you, then." She grabbed the back of my collar and pulled, choking me.

"Stop it," I coughed.

"You need to pull the front."

We maneuvered the shirt over my head, and Dianne fussed with each ringlet, fluffing and spraying again. She wanted to do my makeup, too, but I said I'd take care of it. So she left, and I stood in my hose and push-up bra in Jack's dimly lit bathroom—one yellow 60-watt bulb hung, coverless, in the middle of the ceiling—squinting, face pressed to the mirrored medicine cabinet, wiping clumps of mascara off my lashes. Beth poked her head in. "Mission accomplished. Your violin will be here any minute."

I blotted my lips on some toilet paper. "Thanks."

"Can you help me into my dress? Mom ironed the ribbons, so you shouldn't have a problem."

She unzipped the plastic cover off the gown, eased it off the hanger, and untied her robe. I held the dress open for her to step into, and she did so, with pointed toe, like someone stepping into the bathtub, checking the temperature of the water. I shimmied the dress up and worked the laces of the corset, pulling, tightening, unfurling—my sweaty fingers laboring to make it perfect. "How's that? Too tight? Too loose?"

"No, it's good. How do I look?"

The dress fit perfectly now, and the soil at the hem had been scrubbed out. Beth wore her pearls, of course. "Something new," she said. "Well, new enough." Dianne had curled just the top layer of Beth's hair into corkscrewed tendrils, and kept the left side down, covering her mangled ear. The right side was pinned away from her face with a fresh lily. Beth never wore makeup and had been concerned that wearing it today, on one side of her face, would look clownish. But now a little blush colored her cheek, and a touch of ivory shadowed her left eye.

"Beautiful. Are you nervous?"

She smoothed her hands over the front of her dress. "It's funny. You always read in those romance novels about brides being all fidgety and fluttery before their weddings. Or in those cheesy made-for-TV movies. But I don't feel any of that. It just feels . . . natural, I guess. Like it's supposed to be."

I put on my dress and shoes. "Where's my slip?" I said, pawing through my knapsack. I shook everything out onto the floor.

"I think it looks okay without it," Beth said. "Put that lamp on the floor and stand in front of it." I did, and she nodded. "You're fine."

Maggie came in then, carrying Beth's flowers, three lilies with balsam boughs, stems tied in white silk ribbon. "Oh, baby, you look so beautiful," she said, nose turning red.

"Mom, stop. You promised."

"I know. I just can't help it." Maggie dabbed her eyes with a tissue. "This is one of the happiest days of my life. Right up there with my own wedding, the day the twins were born, and you, too. You were such a feisty little thing. Cried for three days straight."

"Who's crying?" Jack asked, coming out of the kitchen holding my violin case. "Not my dear, sweet mother, who swore to her only daughter she wouldn't, at least not before the ceremony."

"Hush, both of you," Maggie said. "When your babies get married, you'll understand."

"This, I believe, is yours," Jack said, giving me the instrument. "You look lovely."

"Thanks," I said, popping the latches.

"And you," Jack said to Beth, "look like an angel. I'd hug you, but I don't want to wrinkle you."

"You'd better hug me," Beth said, and Jack folded his arms around her, pressing his mouth to her ear and whispering. She nodded, blinked, tears catching in her eyelashes on one side, tumbling over her scars on the other.

"Not you, too," Jack said softly. He took a handkerchief from his pants pocket and caught the tears on her jawbone. Then he looked at his watch. "We'd better head back there."

Beth put on her snow boots—she had to walk around the outside of the building to get to the vestibule unseen. Jack took her white silk heels. Maggie draped her coat over her shoulders, gathered up the back of her gown. "Ready?" she asked.

"More than ready," Beth said.

The three of them left me there, alone, holding my violin. They were family, and I watched them like a child

211

at Christmastime, staring through the front window at the toy store, watching the trains puff around the track, looking at the dolls and balls and video games, and knowing I'd be getting only one gift under the tree—a sweater or an atlas, or some other dull, practical item.

I went out into the hall. Patty sat at the piano, and she looked at me, all smug and cheerful. "Like Reverend Watson has nothing better to do than clean up your messes."

"Shut up," I said, pushing in front of her to pick out an A, her nose in my armpit.

She grunted, scooted to the other side of the bench. I tuned my violin, and she banged out a few noisy chords. The guests scrambled to their seats. There were more people than chairs; some shared, some stood behind the last row. A woman wearing faded plaid stirrup pants, slouch socks, and high-top sneakers sat next to another dressed in her best Sunday blouse, rayon with a wild ivy print, who sat next to another in a skirt stitched together from hand-me-downs. There were men with cruddy dungarees next to men with ironed chinos, next to men in jogging suits. Greasy baseball caps and polyester ties and polished shoes. They were all here. All together.

Patty and I started to play, and the mothers were escorted in. Mrs. Draven, a doughy, potato-faced woman, waddled to the front, then Maggie, wearing a navy brocade suit she'd ordered from the Macy's catalog. As soon as she was seated, Patty transitioned to the "Wedding March," and Beth, her arm hooked though Jack's, stepped from the vestibule. Right foot. Left foot. She walked toward Dominic, who stood at the altar, his gray suit too short in the sleeves, hairy wrists sticking out beneath the cuffs of his white shirt. He couldn't take his eyes off her.

Jack gave Beth a kiss on the forehead. He took her hand and Dominic's hand, and joined them together, holding his hands around theirs for several moments. He spoke to Dominic, who nodded vigorously. Jack slapped him on the back and stepped behind them, facing the crowd. I left my violin on top of the piano and stood near Beth, taking her bouquet from her.

"Friends," Jack said, "we are all here today to celebrate with Dominic and Beth as their hearts and lives are united in love. The essence of any marriage relationship is love, both the couple's love for Christ, and their love for each other. But much of what we call love—the warm, fuzzy glow, the excitement and romance—will never be an adequate foundation for marriage. Love, by its very nature, is active and giving, not self-centered and self-serving.

"Jesus Christ is our example of true love, and He has commanded us to love one another as He loves us. And how does He love us? First, He gives all for our sake, without hesitation or concern for himself. He laid down His life for us.

"Next, from Christ's example, we see that love shares all. There are no secret compartments, no hidden rooms, no locked closets in a successful love relationship. There is only openness and, as a result, trust when a husband and wife truly love each other.

"Finally, the Lord Jesus teaches us that love provides all. It provides security, it seeks to develop ability, and it shares the common purpose of obtaining what is best for the one loved. Such love is not merely impossible—it is supernatural. Only Jesus Christ can love this way, and our love for one another can resemble this only if we submit to Him and depend on His Spirit to love through us."

Memory hoisted herself from her seat in the first row. She

plucked the rubber bands off her Bible. One of them caught her finger, stretched, and shot into the crowd. "Guess I should have gone done that 'fore getting up here," she said, flipping through the pages, pulling out a sheet of lined paper. "This here's what Paul says 'bout love, and he's bunches smarter than any of us, so we better listen up.

"Love is patient. Love is kind. It don't want anything that belongs to other folk. It don't brag. It ain't proud. It ain't rude. It don't look out for its own concerns. It don't get angry too easy. It don't keep track of other folk's mistakes. Love ain't happy with evil. But it's all joyful when the truth is spoke. It keeps on protecting. It keeps on trusting. It keeps on hoping. It ain't never giving up. . . ."

I could add a few more to the list. Love doesn't hurl full mugs of steaming coffee at someone's head. It doesn't purposely leave the gas tank on empty, or party all night, without a phone call, and come home at breakfast reeking of other men.

My marriage to David had no chance of taking—two years drinking together, two months sleeping together, and two hours of meaningful conversation the entire time we'd known each other. He'd tended bar at a club I frequented. I told him about the pregnancy in the club's bathroom, stale urine in the bowl, splashed on the cracked tile floor.

"I have three more of these at home, if you want to see them," I said, waving the stick with the boastful pink line in the window.

"You getting rid of it?"

"I guess. I hadn't really gotten that far yet."

"Marry me," David said, and he held the pregnancy test so gently between his thumb and forefinger, as if at any moment it would sprout legs and arms, and start crying "Dada."

"You're crazy."

"I've always wanted kids."

I'd thought of my grandmother then, how devastated she'd be to learn I'd gotten knocked up out of wedlock. She had no illusions of my purity, but the flashing neon sign of a pregnant belly couldn't be hidden as easily as the half-empty pack of birth control pills she found tucked between my mattresses when I was fifteen. I had despised the tiny part of me that still believed I could, somehow, earn her love. I'd show her, I thought. Let all her pious cronies know that she had a whore for a daughter *and* a granddaughter.

"Let's do it," I'd told David.

After Beth and Dominic exchanged vows, the best man—I didn't know him—took the rings from his pocket. Dominic's hands shook, unable to get Beth's plain gold band over her knuckle. She pushed it on the rest of the way and then gracefully slipped Dominic's ring onto his finger.

"Dominic and Beth, I now pronounce you husband and wife. May God give you enough tears to keep you tender, enough hurts to keep you compassionate, enough of failure to keep your hands clenched tightly in His, and enough blessings to make certain you walk with Him. May you never take each other's love for granted, but always experience that wonder that exclaims, 'Out of all this world you have chosen me.' When life is done, may you be found then as now, hand in hand, still thanking God for each other. May you ever serve Him happily, faithfully, together until you return to glory or until at last one shall lay the other into His arms. And we pray all this in the name of Jesus Christ our Lord. Amen.

"I now introduce to you Mr. and Mrs. Dominic Draven. What God has joined, let no man put asunder."

Everyone stood and applauded, and Beth said to Jack, "Can we kiss now?"

Jack grinned, reddening slightly. "I forgot that part. Of course you can kiss. You're married."

The newlyweds brought their faces close, noses bumping, laughing as they tilted their heads in the same direction several times before their lips met sweetly, awkwardly. The clapping grew louder, punctuated by whistles and camera flashes. I wondered if this was their first kiss, not as man and wife, but ever.

Beth took her flowers, and she and Dominic made their way to the back of the hall. Patty and I played until the crowd swarmed to greet them and no one listened to us anymore. I stashed my violin in Jack's office and wandered into the kitchen. Pans of lasagna—stacked four or five high and wrapped in blankets—lined the counter. Several women gathered plates and cups and brought them into the main hall. I grabbed a few boxes of plastic forks and followed.

Already the men had the tables set up and covered with white paper tablecloths. Guests pulled their chairs around the tables and sat. Maggie, Adele, and others carted the hot pasta to the food table, and soon people were serving themselves, eating and gabbing.

"Over here, girl," Memory called to me. She sat on two chairs, and wore her favorite yellow sweat suit, all blond and pink-faced, a banana pudding pie with a juicy Maraschino cherry on top. "I got a place for you."

"If the whole town is here, who's with Robert?" I asked.

"Doc White said he'd sit with him. He ain't the celebrating type. Seems he got the sadness stuck all over him, and is hankering to keep it there." She said it like that. The Sadness. As if it were a disease. "You got your speech ready?"

"What speech?"

"You're the maid of honor. They always give a speech 'bout how special the bride is and all that whatnot."

"You mean the toast."

"If that's what you fancy folk call it. To me, toast ain't nothing but some crunchy bread. With butter, yes, ma'am. And that raspberry jelly Aggie Standing makes. Mmm-mmm."

I excused myself as our table went to fill their plates. I wouldn't be eating today, not if I wanted my dress to continue fitting.

Not everyone could sit at the same time, so people hovered, holding cups of soda, some waiting for a place to sit, others snapping photos and shaking hands with the bride and groom. Music trickled through the room. I didn't recognize the song, but Beth and Dominic danced together. He stood a head taller than her, and she fit under his chin. She swayed against him with her eyes closed, trusting him to lead, a tiny, contented grin glossing her lips.

Near the end of the song, other couples joined Beth and Dominic. Husbands and wives. Fathers and daughters. I saw Jack and Patty; she tugged on his arm, motioning to the dance area. He shook his head. She persisted, red nails bright against his navy jacket. But Jack removed her hand, said something to her. She smiled and nodded, watching him walk away.

Take that.

Patty turned, as if she felt my eyes, my thoughts. Her face pinched together as I smirked and waggled my fingers at her, a snooty wave. She flipped her hair behind her, and trotted off to her mother.

I needed air. My coat still in Jack's office, I grabbed Beth's parka from the vestibule and went outside, leaned against the porch railing. The frigid afternoon peeked up my dress, and wet, thick snow tumbled from the sky.

"If you're out here hiding from the toast, don't worry. Beth won't make you do it," Jack said, closing the heavy wood door behind him. He joined me on the railing.

"I'm not hiding," I said. "And you're not dancing. Poor Patty."

"You saw."

"She's nothing if not persistent."

"It's complicated," he said, cupping his hands to catch the falling snow. "Patty and I, we dated, you know. All through high school. It was always assumed we'd end up together. By her, by everyone."

"By you?"

"I suppose, yes."

"But?" I prodded.

He shrugged, spread his fingers. The snow plopped to the ground. "We tried for a little while, after I came back from seminary. But I wasn't the same person. I knew it wouldn't work."

"You didn't love her anymore."

"I didn't say that."

"Then you did love her."

"What is this? Twenty questions?" He sighed, rolled the bottom of his tie, then let it go. "I don't think I ever loved Patty the way a husband should love a wife. I mean, we were kids. What did we know?"

"So, have you ever?"

"Ever what?"

"Don't play games with me, Jack Watson."

"I would never dare be anything but up-front and honest with you," he said, and laughed. "Now, what was the question again?"

I jabbed him with my elbow, knocking him against the side of the building. Snow slid off the roof and, with Jack safely tucked beneath the overhang, fell onto my open-toed shoes. I danced out of the pile. "Oh, sh— sugar. That's cold."

"Sugar? Okay, where'd you hide the real Sarah Graham?"

"Memory's taken to smacking me with a wooden spoon anytime I, as she puts it, cuss around her."

Jack laughed again. "I think I'd pay to see that."

"And I think I'd like an answer."

His smile flickered, faded. "I was in love. Once."

"With who? What happened?"

"Someone I met during seminary," he said. "It didn't work out."

My jealousy wanted to probe, to learn more about the memory of the woman who could steal Jack's crooked grin. He stared out toward the field, where the footprints and sledding tracks filled slowly with new snow, regret darkening his beautiful, long-lashed, amber-streaked eyes.

I put my hand on his arm. He looked at it, startled to be touched, I think, as if it had been a long time. Then he covered my hand with his own, his warm fingers wrapping under and squeezing.

"So, how about you?" he asked. "Have you ever?"

Yeah. Right now. "Of course," I said. "More times than I can count."

"That's not what I mean, Sarah."

"Like you would know, Reverend."

He took his hand away, suddenly realizing who—what—his skin touched. My hand, protected for a few moments from the snow and wind, froze again. I stuck it in my pocket. Jack turned around, his back against the rail now. "You know, Sarah, you really know how to—"

The door opened. Jack and I jumped away from each other. It was Maggie. Her forehead wrinkled, and she said, "Beth's about to cut her cake."

"We were just coming in," Jack said.

He went inside first. Maggie followed closely, protectively. She didn't hold the door for me; I stuck my foot in to stop it from closing, bashing my knee against the sharp edge. Still wearing Beth's coat, I backed into a corner and willed myself to disappear into the wall.

If I had a way to get home, I would have left then. I'd been there only for Beth, and she was too busy, too happy—too loved—to notice my absence. But with my truck parked at the inn, I'd need to find someone to take me to it. Not Maggie, though. The woman might like me, but not nearly enough to want me breathing the same air as her son.

chapter THIRTY-THREE

Both the wedding and the cake sat poorly in my stomach. The former dredged up memories I'd worked years to bury, the latter wound through my intestines as if I'd swallowed tacks. I woke from nightmares—David and Jack volleying me between them in a game of hot potato, neither of them wanting to keep me; rows of gray-skinned babies, dressed in pink buntings and lying silently in hospital incubators; Maggie, ten feet tall and waggling her index finger at me, grinning maliciously with vampiric fangs—all dazed and clammy. And with cramps that forced me to the bathroom every two hours.

Midmorning, I abandoned my attempt at sleep and decided to make my way over to the inn. I still had Beth's wedding gift, and I wanted to speak with Maggie. I needed to convince her I had no interest in her precious son. Even if I did.

Plus, I had no clean underwear. I couldn't wait three days for Beth to return from her honeymoon and do my wash.

I gathered my dirty laundry in a plastic garbage bag and drove to the inn. "Maggie?" I called. When she didn't answer,

221

I lugged my clothes to the washing machine, in a tiny closet under the staircase. I loved nooks like this, and had spent more than one afternoon in here, lying across the tops of the washer and dryer, one of Maggie's clean, honey-scented towels folded beneath my head, knees bent, lulled to sleep by the sloshing and thumping, and the warmth.

Starting my whites, I tossed in socks—some balled up, some inside out—panties, bras, and thermal long johns. The bleach splashed on my navy sweatshirt, leaving milky blotches across my chest and sleeve.

"Maggie?" I walked down the hallway to Beth's room. It still smelled of fresh paint. An antique brass bed stood in the center of the room, headboard under the window, and Maggie had covered it with Beth's wedding quilt and several throw pillows. I propped a card against them.

I hadn't known what to get for a gift. Because Beth and Dominic were moving into the inn, they didn't need shower curtain hooks or potholders, or any of those newlywed things. So I gave money—a check for one thousand dollars. I'd never be that generous with my own cash, but right now it still belonged to Luke. And I loved spending money that wasn't mine.

Across the hall, Maggie's door was cracked. I knocked and pushed my head through, into the empty room. The hope chest open, baby clothes hung over the lid. I went to look at them—two sailor-style rompers and a long gauzy gown embroidered with pink and lilac rosettes.

Something creaked outside the room. "Maggie?" I turned to look and noticed some letters on the bed—five or six, tied with a burgundy ribbon. When I picked them up, a photograph slipped from between the envelopes, fluttering to the floor, landing face up. Maggie gazed at me from the picture, arms around a red-haired man in a baggy cable-knit sweater, brown leather buttons down the front.

I yanked one end of the ribbon. It fell away, and I spread the envelopes in a row across the bed. Closing my eyes, I chose one, opened it. The paper smelled of cedar.

> M&M. You have waited long enough. Forgive me. I do love you. L.

The words blurred as I stared beyond them, tracing the wrinkles on the blue-lined notebook paper with my eyes. I wadded the page in my fist, squeezing until my fingernails cut into my palm.

"Sarah? Are you here? I thought I heard—"

Maggie stopped in the doorway. She wore a sweater, the one she had on the first night I came to Jonah, the sleeves cuffed three times, patched on the elbows. And leather buttons. I knelt, slowly, picked up the dropped photo. "It's his sweater," I said.

"Sarah, I—"

"What had you waited long enough for?"

"Maybe we should sit down. I'll put on water for tea and—"

I threw the crumpled note at her. "What had you waited long enough for?"

She caught the paper, flattened it, smoothing it against her chest with her hands. And kept it there, pressed against her heart. "For Luke to ask me to marry him."

I swallowed. "You wanted him to."

"Yes. Very much."

"Why?"

"I loved him," Maggie said.

All my emotions collapsed in on themselves, compressing to a dense iron marble rolling around and around the pit of my stomach. "He killed my mother," I said softly.

"I know."

"But you didn't care."

"You think Luke was some sort of monster. But he wasn't. He was kind and generous, and decent."

"And he fixed shutters, and pulled children out of fires, and leapt tall buildings in a single bound."

She stood there, shoulder against the door's inner molding, cocooned in that shabby sweater. I wondered how many weeks, months, had it taken for Luke to fade from the worsted yarn, how many mornings Maggie woke and buried her nose in the collar, searching for the last remnant of his cologne. Did she take out his letters every day, or only when loneliness overwhelmed her?

Did she still cry over him?

I wasn't certain of the reasons, or the precise date and time, but in my distraction I'd allowed my anger, my life-blood, to dissipate. It happened somewhere between the brumal mountain nights, the pot-roast dinners with the Watsons, the so-called *softening* Memory spoke of, and the afternoons with Zuriel. But now, the thought of Maggie—of anyone—mourning the loss of my father melted my indifference, and a viscid warmth radiated from my gut, seeping into my extremities. My toes and fingers tingled with heat. Ah, this was hate. I closed my eyes, savoring the broken-in fit.

Maggie cleared her throat. "Sarah, I know you're hurting, but—"

"You don't know anything."

"Then tell me."

"What, Luke didn't fill you in?" I asked, eyes on her now.

Maggie turned her head away; her mouth trembled. "He didn't, did he? He never told you anything about me."

"He—" She swallowed, massaged her knuckles. "Luke didn't talk much about the . . . past."

"And there wasn't much to remember, was there? Just his dead wife. And his only daughter. But he didn't need any of that. He had his new family."

"It wasn't like that—"

"Stop defending him," I shouted. "He doesn't deserve it."

"He loved you, Sarah. I know he did."

Her words pierced me, and I deflated, sinking crookedly onto the bed, one hip on the mattress, leg tucked under me, the other foot flat on the floor. With one finger, I traced a path around the remaining letters. It was my bowing hand—no tough, callused skin on my fingertips—and I felt the bitty, hand-quilted stitches in the calico. "No one has ever loved me."

Maggie shocked me then by laughing. "Don't be silly. Even if that was true in the past, it sure isn't now. If you'd just let us help you—"

"I don't need help. I don't need you and your friendly stepmother routine. And I don't need him," I said, raking Luke's letters into a pile. "Any part of him."

The envelopes were thin, light. They couldn't have had more than one sheet of paper in each. I held them before Maggie and, with an exaggerated motion, tore them in half. I stacked the halves together and tried to rip them again, but couldn't. The paper was too thick now.

With a disgusted snort, I flicked the pieces toward the door, toward Maggie. "He's all yours," I said, watching her ease down to the floor to retrieve them. I stepped over her.

I drove all the way back to the cabin before remembering my laundry. But I wasn't going back. For the next couple of days, I'd rinse out the underpants and bra I had on in the sink, and hang them to dry overnight. Like the pioneers, I thought. Self-sufficient. Resourceful.

Nope, I didn't need anyone at all.

chapter THIRTY-FOUR

Maggie couldn't get up.

She could still move her legs, though, and she kicked the door. It bounced off the wall, swinging into the room far enough that she could slide her toe beneath it and pull it toward her until it bumped her hip. She stretched her arm up to the doorknob, grabbing it and straining with moth-eaten muscles to pull herself to her feet. Her hand slipped off the metal and one of her fingernails bent backward. She cried out, squeezing the injured finger inside her fist until the initial sting subsided, then pulled off the broken nail and dropped it down the heating grate, half an arm's length from where she sat, trapped, tailbone grinding into the hardwood floor.

Her spine had stiffened already, and she felt a cold numbness filling her legs. She considered rocking to one side, falling over onto the floor so she could roll onto her hands and knees, and stand from there. But she feared she'd still not be able to move, and then would be trapped, with her face against the hallway floor. At least now she could reach the phone; it was behind her on the nightstand. She flailed around above her head until she felt it and gave it a shove. It clattered to the floor, receiver off the hook, dial tone taunting her. She listened to it until it turned to the ear-splitting *whah-whah-whah*, then grabbed the cord and reeled it into her lap.

After one more unsuccessful attempt to stand, she dialed Jack.

"Hello," he said. "Hello?"

Maggie scrunched her eyes closed.

"Anyone there?" Jack asked.

"Jack."

"Mom, what's wrong?"

"I just . . . I'm stuck."

"I'm coming now."

The pieces of Luke's letters no longer lay scattered around her. She'd managed to collect them before stiffening—all except the one that she'd watched slip beneath the linen closet door across the hall—and tuck them in her pocket. She ran her fingers over the ragged edges as she prayed for her son to arrive quickly, and for her anger toward Sarah to leave her just as fast.

Jack barged into the house; she heard him push open the pocket doors and clomp into the kitchen without removing his wet boots. "Mom? Where are you?"

"My bedroom," she called to him.

He found her and bent down to her. She clasped her arms around his neck, and her body unfolded as he lifted. She didn't let go of him.

"My feet fell asleep," she said. "I can't stand on them."

Jack swept his arm behind the back of her knees and carried her to the bed. "What ever possessed you to sit on the floor?"

"I was picking something up."

"You see—this is why you can't be alone. I'm staying here until Beth gets back."

"And who invited you?"

"This isn't a joke, Mother."

"I'm not joking. I don't need you here."

"You don't have a choice," he snapped.

Maggie winced, both from her son's tone and the pins and needles collecting in her feet. Not the tickling kind, but sharp, as if thousands of tiny electrodes stuck to her feet, shocking the blood back into them. She leaned forward to remove her Keds, but couldn't reach past her knees. Jack saw this—had seen it many times before—and after he untied her tennis sneakers, he massaged her toes through her socks.

"I'm sorry," he said. "Do you want some tea?"

She nodded. "And could you bring me the Scotch tape?"

While he was in the kitchen, Maggie folded the comforter over herself, and listened to her son clatter and bang through the drawers, the cupboards and pantry. Graceful, he was not.

Jack returned with the tea and some cookies, a magazine, a bag of pretzels, and the tape. "I thought you might be hungry. And I know how you like some salt after something sweet."

"Thanks, hon. Just put everything on the nightstand."

"Are you okay for me to leave? I'll only be gone an hour or so."

"I'm fine, really. I'll probably have supper ready by the time you get here."

"Don't cook. I'll bring in something from the diner for us."

"Jack—"

"Indulge me. Just this once," he said.

She nodded, and Jack kissed the top of her head before leaving.

Maggie emptied her pockets of the letter pieces, matching each half to its partner, then taping them together—first the sheets of paper within, then the envelopes. She read each one again.

She missed Luke more than she missed her husband. Perhaps she should have been ashamed of that, but she wasn't. She'd had twenty-two years with John, and all those treasured moments before they were married—from the day he shoved her in the mud puddle when she was seven, to the time in sixth grade when he helped her find all her scattered jacks after some bully kicked them across the playground, to their first kiss at the senior dance. She'd known him all her life.

With Luke, there just weren't enough times like that. Nearly seven years he lived in Jonah, and it had taken almost as long for Maggie to halfway understand him. And, almost as long for her to ask about his wife. She'd spent weeks mustering the courage, preparing for some violent, Poe-like tale of dismemberment or revenge.

Instead, Luke spoke plainly. "I was young and stupid, and sinful," he said. "I'm still sinful, but I'm not young anymore, and not nearly as stupid. I hope, anyway. And I'm forgiven. That, I know."

"I'm not saying you're not," she'd said.

"And I'm not saying you're saying I'm not. I'm reminding myself," he said with a short laugh. "If you want the gory details, I'll tell you."

She didn't. She'd fallen in love with him by then.

After that, Luke would talk about Helena often. Little things, recollections mostly, about how she always sneezed when first stepping outside on bright sunny days, or how she could flip pancakes to the ceiling, catching them perfectly in the skillet. Maggie fought stabs of jealousy, and then she'd do something special for Luke—cook his favorite meal, or go to the cabin and scrub his shower—to prove she was as worthy of his love as Helena.

But he'd rarely mentioned Sarah. He'd bring her up in prayer meetings occasionally, with vague references to her struggles. Or, he'd begin sentences with, "When Sarah was—" and stop, shaking his head with a quiet, "Never mind." Maggie had seen that, for all his brave talk of forgiveness, Luke carried his sins against his daughter with him always, a millstone dangling around his neck, and scourged himself for his inability to change the past.

Maggie stretched, stood. She retrieved the last piece of letter from the closet, taped it, and returned all the envelopes to her hope chest. Had some Sarah-like stranger happened upon the inn, all sandpaper and swearwords and defensiveness, Maggie would have handed her a bill the following morning and not thought of her again, except perhaps to laugh with some of the ladies about the obnoxious city girl who'd spent the night. She wouldn't have offered her a bag of breakfast to take with her, nor taken five minutes to wonder where the girl was headed. And she certainly wouldn't have spent the last three months praying for her every night. Earnestly praying. Not merely dropping her name into a list of toothaches, sore bunions, and noisy furnaces needing to get through one more winter.

She cared for Sarah, yes—but only because of Luke.

If anything, Maggie should have been ashamed of that.

chapter THIRTY-FIVE

My hair looked like pumpkin-colored straw.

I'd run out of conditioner in the week before Beth's wedding, and given all the commotion, only remembered I had none after I was in the shower, soaked and groping for the bottle while rinsing the last suds of shampoo from my eyes. Today, my to-do list consisted of two things: buying skates and conditioner. I'd visited all Doc's patients earlier in the week.

The variety store sold two brands of conditioner, both costing less than two dollars. I dropped the more expensive bottle into my shopping basket. I'd tried the seventy-nine-cent bargain stuff first because it was unscented, but it made me look as if I wore a wig of dank, orange seaweed. With the dollar ninety-nine bottle, at least, my hair wasn't greasy, even though I smelled like my eighty-seven-year-old great-aunt Penelope's sock drawer sachets—rose and clove and artificial orange.

A jar of dry shampoo hunched between the conditioner and hair spray. The label read *No water necessary*. Thinking of Rabbit and her ponytails, I picked it up, along with a soft-bristled brush. Then I searched the back wall for ice skates. Only two pairs remained—both men's, and neither of them my size. On the way to the counter, I snagged a jumbo bag of potato chips, a box of Devil Dogs, and a half-dozen packages of chicken-flavored ramen noodles.

"Are you getting any more skates in?" I asked Nancy Brooks as she rang up my purchase.

She shook her head.

"Is there any other place around here I can get them?"

"Bethel Baptist Church has a thrift store. Sometimes they have skates."

"And that is?"

"In Bethel."

"I figured that one out," I said. "Where's that?"

"It's t-two towns over. East. No, west. No, wait. Now I'm not sure," she said, absentmindedly plucking the lint balls from the cuff of her sweater. "I'm sorry. I'm no g-good with directions. I can get Carl—"

"I'll find it."

She nodded and folded the top of my bag, stuck the brown paper in the stapler and pressed. Nothing happened. She tried again. "I think I'm out of staples."

"It's fine." I snatched the bag and looked at her, gummy and shrunken-headed under her prodigious hair. Normally, I enjoyed how she slunk away from me, eyeballs jittering back and forth, waiting for me to pounce. But today there was no pleasure in it. "Look, I'm sorry I snapped at you. Really."

Nancy pulled her thin, brown lips into a smile of sorts, and said, "Oh, that's okay. We all have our bad days now and again, don't we?"

Some of us more than others. "Isn't that the truth?"

"Here, why don't you go ahead and take this map with

you," she said. "And just you keep it now. It fits nice in your glove box. I got one in my own. Not that I'm so good at reading it."

"Thanks."

"And maybe you can make your way over to the house for supper some night soon. Carl and me, we hardly had any time to get to know you, and Luke, he—" She stopped, shoulders all twitchy again, remembering, no doubt, our first encounter.

"He helped you when your husband was sick," I finished for her.

She smiled wider now, dentures straight and brown from too much coffee. "That he did. Well, then, you just come on over any time. There's always enough for one more."

I nodded.

In the truck, I unfolded the map and found Bethel. It was west, and I needed to drive by the Jonah Inn to get there.

I hadn't spoken with Maggie since the blowup, four days earlier. I was still angry with her, but I didn't want to be. What did loved people—those who'd never had a moment in their lives when someone, somewhere, didn't love them— know about going without? They couldn't fathom that there were others like me in the world, the hapless forsaken who didn't share in their blissful ignorance. Others like me who understood too well that love didn't come to all.

It came to my father, though. More than once. More than it should have, after all he'd done.

Truth and I, we weren't well acquainted. But it had been creeping up on me, like a shiny, black cockroach—one that scurried under the basement door when the lights came on, disappearing too quickly for me to smash under my heel, and lurked, waiting to feast on the unswept crumbs as soon as the dark came again.

I knew lies. I spoke them, loved them. They kept me out of trouble, and got me into it. They comforted me and hid me, and felt more real than any truth I'd known. I lied now out of habit, even when a simple, honest answer would cause fewer headaches and far less complications.

But each day it became more difficult to deceive myself— too much time spent alone, stagnant, without the distraction of my usual mind-numbing activities. And the truth was, I wished I'd known my father.

Oh, I hated him. I did. I had to. But the pigtailed little girl in me wanted to reach my hands to the ceiling and have him grab me under the arms and toss me into the air so, for a second, I could fly. Or have him dance with me, my white stocking feet standing on his shoes.

He'd called me only once. I know Aunt Ruth told him I didn't want to see him, but if he had loved me, as Maggie insisted he did, why hadn't he tried again? Why hadn't he called every day, or inundated me with letters, or come pounding on the door of my shoddy 176th Street apartment at midnight until I let him in so the neighbor wouldn't call the police because of the noise?

Because he didn't need his inconvenient daughter to remind him of the past while embarking on his new beginning with the happy Watson clan. I couldn't compete with Reverend Jack and Saint Beth, and Maggie's deep-dish cherry pie.

I approached the inn, slowing, then speeding up, then slowing again, and when I saw Beth's car wasn't in the driveway, I drove past. I would have had an excuse to stop if she were home. Yesterday, she'd returned my laundry, all folded and ironed, and lavender-scented. I'd been out visiting Doc's patients, so she left the piles on the porch in thick, green plastic bags, a handmade card taped to the top so I'd find it. The note thanked me for the money and all I did for the wedding. She wrote she'd stop by soon, making no mention of my argument with her mother.

The village of Bethel seemed more downtrodden than Jonah, if that was possible. It didn't have a main street, only several clusters of two-story houses, painted white and gray—and a putrid green that somehow always made an appearance in towns of this sort. Even with the map, I got lost. I couldn't find a single street sign or an open business I could stop at to ask for directions. I knocked on a few doors, but no one answered; they peeked out from behind bed-sheet curtains, suspicious faces dropping from sight when I looked toward them.

All this trouble for a stupid pair of skates.

Finally, I spotted a soggy flap of cardboard box nailed to a corner telephone pole, the sign for the church with a streaky black marker arrow pointing to the left.

The thrift store was in the basement, and it smelled like moldy gym clothes. Nearly thirty people hunted and pecked through stacks of jeans, plastic laundry baskets crammed full of shoes, shelves of mismatched dishes.

Ice skates lined the stone windowsills. I took the only pair in my size—jaundiced and creased, with blades so rusty they stained my hand. One boot had no laces, the other, half a tongue.

"Well, if it ain't Miss Sarah Graham, coming to grub through somebody else's castoffs."

"Well, if it *isn't* Memory Jones, who's certainly not a miss, and is better at grubbing than anyone I know," I said.

"Then you don't know no one," she said, laughing. "Girl, seeing your sourpuss gone done tickled my toes. And, you know, you take a bit of steel wool to them skates, they'll be right as rainbows."

"I'll remember that. Who's with Robert?"

"Beatrice Rawlings. She sits with my boy when I gotta stock up on these here shirts," she said, grinning and lifting her overstuffed grocery bag up for me to see, proud as a hunter who's shot a prize-winning fowl.

"I would have watched him, if you needed me to."

"Then you wouldn't be here," she said. "And while I got you here, you better be picking out some colors for that rag rug of yours."

"What rug?"

"The one I'm making for you. Now, go get some."

She pushed me into the crowd of clothing vultures pawing through the hand-me-downs, the *screech* of hangers against the metal racks echoing in the tiny space. I tugged a forest-colored T-shirt out from between the others, holding it with the tips of three fingers. "Is this good?"

"They wash 'em first, you know. Got a machine just over there," she said, draping the shirt over her shoulder. "And you're gonna need eight, ten more. So, just dive on in there."

I found several other green shirts in varying shades, and chose a few earth-toned ones, and a couple muted blues. "Okay, I'm done."

"What about that yellow one?"

"What yellow one?" I asked, though I knew.

"That one there, that you keep picking at and putting back."

"It's too bright." And it was—a vibrant sun color that seemed alien in the dim basement. Out of place, like me. But I couldn't stop looking at it.

"No, it ain't," Memory said. She yanked it from the rack, hanger flipping around the metal bar before it clattered to the stone floor. "See. Perfect. These colors, they be more suiting to your insides."

"If you say so. You're the expert."

"Expert! Ha! Me, Memory Jones, an expert at something. I like that." She hunkered down to pick up the hanger, and squashed my shirts in with her own. "I gotta get home to my boy. But I'll be seeing you Sunday."

She plodded to the counter to pay. I threw a dollar down for my skates and hurried after her. "Wait," I said. "Let me follow you. I don't know if I'll be able to find my way back, especially in the dark."

"Well, well. I'm fat for sure, but my ears work fine, and I just heard you asking for help. Ain't never thought I'd hear that, no, ma'am. Not never."

"I didn't ask," I said. "I told. Ordered, really. Demanded."

"Mmm-hmm."

"Never mind. Just go. I'm perfectly capable of getting there myself."

Memory swung her bag onto the passenger side, then dropped in the driver's seat, feet still dangling outside, the car sinking a good three or four inches beneath her weight. She slid one thigh under the steering wheel, then the other, inching her bulk around to face forward. "You know, the trouble with stiff-necked folks is they can't turn their heads from side to side to see what's coming up behind them," she said, face flushed, chest heaving. "Close the door, will ya?"

I did, and went to my truck. Memory circled the parking lot, pulling next to me. I rolled down my window. "What now?"

"I forgot to tell ya, I ain't so good at turning my head neither. And I ain't never got 'round to gluing my rearview mirror back on after it fell off last winter. So, if somebody got the hankering to follow me, I wouldn't know it at all."

She drove away, making a left turn out of the lot. I waited five minutes, counting each blink of the colon on the dashboard's digital clock. Then I took a left and drove down the road, slowing behind a car at the corner, idling at the stop sign with its hazard lights flashing.

Memory's car.

Her hazards went dead, and her right directional glinted on, off, on, off, in the dwindling daylight. I considered going the opposite way, but being lost in the dark mountains held even less appeal than admitting to Memory that I needed her help to find my way home. So I pushed my hair behind my ears, clicked my right blinker on, and followed.

chapter THIRTY-SIX

I'd left the dry shampoo and brush I bought in the truck so I wouldn't forget them when I went to the Harrison home. They were for Rabbit. A peace offering.

The drive up the mountain had become routine to me. My body leaned into the familiarity of each bend, my hands knew when to turn the steering wheel, my foot knew when to press the gas, or let off it. Instead of focusing on the road, I let the steady white hum of the engine lull my mind to sleep. Some days, I'd start on Mountain Drive, two roads north of my father's cabin, and only snap out of my trance when I bounced into the giant pothole just before the Harrison's turnoff—nearly an hour's drive—and not remember a single minute between.

I wasn't paying attention when I whipped around the second-to-last curve before the shack. A deer stood in the road, frozen, its liquid eyes fixed on my truck. I jammed down on the brake with both feet and screamed. The doe bounded into the woods; I saw her white hindquarters flash through the tree trunks as I lurched to a stop, unharmed.

My pulse drummed behind my cheekbones, in my groin.

I sat, staring, gulping for breath. When my heart rate slowed to a near-normal pace, I took my feet off the brake pedal. The truck crawled forward, and I drove the last hundred yards without the speedometer crossing ten miles an hour.

Without knocking, I left the grocery bags near Ben and Rabbit's door, the shampoo and brush tucked under a carton of eggs, a box of powdered milk. Then I drove—slowly, stiffly, eyes scanning each dark nook between the trees—to see Zuriel.

She was in bed when I arrived, still in her nightgown—a plain ecru cotton, worn sheer—knitted shawl draped over her shoulders. Her Bible flopped open on her legs.

"I can't see the words, but the weight gives me comfort," she said.

"Are you sick, Zuriel? Should I get Doc?"

"I'm ninety-nine years old, and today I feel like it. Doc can't fix that."

She looked gray, lumpy, like a bowl of oatmeal left overnight in the sink. Her eyes were runnier than usual, and her tear sacs bulged purple. I took a Kleenex from the box beside the bed, gave it to her. She blotted the discharge. "Have you eaten?" I asked, concerned. Hiram Dennison dying was one thing, but Zuriel was the grandmother every child wanted, the one in the bedtime stories who kissed bruised knees and made everything better. The grandmother I wished I'd had, the one I eventually stopped praying for when, year after year, my prayers went ignored.

I didn't want her to die.

She coughed. "Some hot water would be nice."

"Just hot water?"

"I know, old women are supposed to sit around, knitting and drinking tea. I do enjoy the knitting. The tea? Not so much."

"I'll be back in a minute."

Zuriel's kitchen had a freestanding utility sink, a wood-burning cookstove, a Hoosier cabinet, and a small table with a microwave oven perched on it—a gift, Zuriel said, from her great-grandson five years ago, when she lost her sight. In another corner, a claw-foot tub and a curtained toilet. This was the only room with plumbing. Zuriel told me when she was a child—before the house had running water, before several of the additions had been built—they kept the tub outside, in the backyard, because there was no other place for it. Her brothers and father would carry it in and out each Saturday, bath day.

I found a chipped teacup hanging on the wall—a line of eyehooks under the window held a dozen of them, mismatched, crazed but clean—and filled it with water, then stuck it in the microwave for forty-five seconds. Stacked on a corner shelf near the cups were plates of different sizes. I found a saucer and brought the water to Zuriel.

"Thank you, dear. I have a chill on the inside, and no amount of blankets will help."

"I know it; I'm always cold when my neck is bare," I said, wrapping my own scarf around her. "I don't have to stay if you're too tired."

"Please. I wait all week for your visit. And I believe Miss Marple was about to unmask the villain."

"I can read your Bible to you, instead, if you want."

Zuriel smiled. "How wonderful." She gave me the Bible, then clasped her hands together and closed her pus-filled eyes.

"Where should I start?"

"Anywhere is fine."

I bent the soft cover with my thumb, quickly flipping through the whispery pages. Then I turned to Jack's passage, the one he mentioned on Christmas, the beginning of John, chapter nine.

The story of the man born blind so that Jesus could perform his miracle. I continued reading, how the man went to the temple after he was healed and the religious leaders scoffed at him, accusing him of fraud. When the man's parents testified that their son was indeed born blind, the Pharisees again interrogated the man, trying to scare him into recanting, and finally forced him from the temple.

I closed the book. I couldn't take anymore. But Zuriel said, "That is one of my favorite passages. Now I have a story to tell you. About that piano."

I looked at it, hunkered in the shadows, thick-legged and dull with dust. "I've wondered about it."

"When I begin to forget what it looks like, I run my hands over it, all those carvings and dimples. I think of my mother. She would let the babies bang on the keys, and it always sounded beautiful to her.

"I've told you my grandmother was a slave."

I nodded, and then said, "Yes," because she couldn't see my head move.

"Her parents worked a plantation in Virginia, and she was taken from them when she was nine or ten, sold somewhere a bit more south. One of the Carolinas, I believe. My grandmother thought she'd die of lonesome and fear, but the mistress of the plantation took a liking to her. Her own daughter had died just months before my grandmother came to work there, and they were the same age. It's easier, I suppose, to love a stranger when she's the same size and shape as the hole in your own heart, even if she happens to be a little slave girl.

"The mistress taught Grandmother to read and write. She gave her nice dresses and sang to her sometimes. The other house slaves were quite jealous. They sometimes stole my grandmother's clothes when the mistress let her take a bath, or fed her supper to the dogs. Once, they beat her with spoons. It was the only beating she ever received, at the hands of her own. When the mistress found out, she ordered five lashes for all the women involved, but my grandmother pleaded for mercy, and the mistress relented.

"When my grandmother was sixteen, she married my grandfather. He was a field slave. They jumped over a broom and were married, just like that. The plantation master turned up dead soon after, drowned in his whisky and vomit. The farm was sold, and the mistress called my grandmother into her parlor and said to her, 'Do you want a new master?'

" 'No ma'am,' " my grandmother said.

" 'Nor I,' the mistress said. 'I'm going north. Come with me.'

"My grandmother said she couldn't go without Grandfather, and the mistress told her to bring him, too."

Zuriel took a sip of her water, cold now, trembling hand bringing the cup to her mouth. "It took four grown men to load that piano on the wagon. The mistress wouldn't leave without it. She took some clothes, a few baubles, and the piano. It was just months before the war began, and they rode all the way to New York, where the mistress had kin. She became ill during the trip, and was dying. She gave Grandmother and Grandfather their free papers.

"But my grandmother loved that woman; she stayed and took care of her. When the mistress died, she left my grandmother five acres of land, some wilderness that her husband had won in a gambling game. This land. And the piano."

She smiled at the memory. "The story is, my grandfather used a mule and some logs to get that piano up this mountain, cussing all the way. It's been in that same spot since then. One day it's going to fall through the floor. Even when they were starving, when we were starving, no one ever thought of selling that piano. My sister learned to one-finger 'Amazing Grace,' and we would all stand around it and sing as loud as we could. But it hasn't been played proper since it came here.

"The mistress, her name was Sarah, too. Sarah Chappell. My grandparents took her family name because they didn't have one of their own.

"Could you do something for me, child?"

"Of course. Anything," I said.

"Next time you come here, could you bring some furniture polish and a cloth, and maybe just clean that piano off a little?" she asked. "It certainly deserves a bit of pampering, a regal instrument like that. And it doesn't need my smeary fingerprints all over it."

"I will."

"Ah, well, I think I'll have my nap now." She scooted down under the blankets, head sinking into the down pillow. "You know, the scarf did help. I'm much warmer."

"Then it's yours. I have a bunch more at home. Sometimes I wear two," I said, and before I tucked Zuriel's hands under the stained blanket, she was asleep.

I drove straight to Doc's office to find Patty Saltzman, boots on the desk, polishing her claws. "Stay away from me," she said.

"I need a favor." And, man, did it hurt to ask.

"Yeah, right." She sniffed, shaking her hands through the air, blowing on her nails.

"Really. I'll pay you."

Her head popped up. "For what and how much?"

"Thirty bucks if you come with me when I visit one of Doc's patients, and play the piano for her."

She gingerly screwed on the polish cap. "When?"

"Tuesday."

"Fifty, and I'll do it."

Greedy wench. "Fine."

chapter THIRTY-SEVEN

I waited until ten-thirty to go to the skating pond—
late enough, I figured, that anyone under twelve would be
tucked in bed, and anyone over twelve would have better
sense than to venture out on a moonless night to glide around
a sheet of frozen water.

The air was mild, as mild as Jonah got in mid March, in
the low twenties, no wind. Even in the darkness, my eyes
could make out the blanket of clouds above, several subtle
shades of gray patchworked together. The bright days, when
sunlight painted every surface with gold, and the perfect
starry nights, those were the most frigid—no clouds to hold
the heat against the earth.

Still, I wore tights and two pair of thermals under my
clothes, gloves inside my mittens, and two scarves. I couldn't
double up on my socks; my feet didn't fit inside the skates
with more than one layer.

I parked as close to the pond as I could without driving on the ice, turned the cab light on, and fastened my
skates as tightly as possible. Memory had helped me clean
the blades last Sunday. Actually, she scoured both of them

with steel wool until she could see herself in them. I had tried to scrub one blade, but the thin steel filaments hurt my hands, and I complained with each prick. Memory got tired of my whining, grabbed the steel wool, and told me to restring the laces. I also scrubbed the leather boots until they were a nice French vanilla color.

My ankles bent in and out as I walked to the rink. I sat down on one of the logs that had been strategically pushed around the pond for benches and pulled the laces taut enough to cut off my circulation in hopes of stabilizing my wobbly ankles. Then I stepped out onto the ice and lost my balance, jamming my wrists as I tried to break my fall.

I flopped over onto my knees and, digging the toe picks into the ice, struggled upright. I held my arms out and inched across the blackness. The blade caught on something, and I fell again, this time forward, chin kissing the ice.

Skating in the dark was, I decided, a bad idea, despite all the romantic notions I'd attached to it.

I half-crawled, half-wormed along the frozen surface until my hands touched snow. As I tried again to stand, I saw my shadow, at first a squatty pygmy near my feet, then stretching into an anorexic giant, all arms and legs, as a light swelled behind me. I turned my head; two headlights ogled me, yellow-white rectangles about fifty feet off in the distance.

And I fell.

"Sarah? Is that you?"

I cupped my mitten over my eyes, squinted into the severe brightness. "Jack?"

"Yeah," he said. "What are you doing here?"

"Skating," I said, but made no move to get off my butt.

I didn't want to look like an utter fool in front of him. Again.

"That usually requires standing."

"I was fine until you came. And why are you here?"

He dropped his hockey skates—the ones that had been hanging over his shoulder, laces tied together—onto the ice. "To skate."

"Now? In the dark?"

"You're here."

"Yeah, but you're normal."

He laughed. "I like to skate alone. It gives me time to think and pray. To shake off the day, so to speak. This is the only time I can do that. But I'm smart enough to keep my lights on. Only had my battery go dead on me once."

"So, I'm interrupting?"

"I guess, technically, I'm interrupting," he said, and pulled me up, steadying me as I tottered against him. "You were here first."

"You can stay. I mean, the pond's big enough for both of us, right?"

"I'd be afraid to leave. You might trip and split your skull open, and some poor kids would find you after school tomorrow, bleeding and unconscious."

"Funny," I said, shoving him, flailing as I lost my balance. He grabbed the front of my jacket.

"Not really," he said. "Think of those poor, traumatized kids."

He sat down on the ice, took off his boots. He wore striped socks, lime green and red and violet.

"Talk about trauma," I said, pointing to his feet.

"They were a gift from a lovely elderly lady in my congregation. She's worn glasses since 1926, and they don't come much thicker than hers." Jack tied on his skates, kicked his boots to the side of the pond, and looped around me. "So, are you going to stand there all night?"

Knees locked, I slid one leg forward from my hip, then the other, like scissors. My blades moved back and forth, cutting deeper into the ice.

"I'm not going anywhere," I said. "And the ice looks like it's bending. I don't want to fall through."

"Green ice. It bounces like rubber, but don't worry, it's solid." Jack came up behind me, wrapping his arm around my waist and taking my mitten in his glove. "Now," he said, his words hot in my ear, "you have to bend your knees. And you can't just move your blades in a straight line. Push off a little, to the outside."

I did, taking short, choppy steps. Jack moved with me, held me. "Now, lengthen your stride," he told me.

We looped the pond two, three times, picking up speed. I heard only our jackets rubbing against one another, and our breathing—mine raw and labored, his smooth, comfortable. His touch lightened; I barely felt him.

"Let go," I said, and he did.

My blades grated over the ice, making a *sha-sha-sha* sound. I listened more closely, and the scratching metamorphosed into my name. *Sarah.* I moved my feet faster. *Sarah.* Faster. *Sarah-Sarah-Sarah.* It chased me around the pond, the masked fiend in a bloody slasher flick. I couldn't escape it. I couldn't escape myself.

The wind brushed over me. I took off my mittens and gloves, my two scarves, my hat, flinging them into the snow. Then I sailed from one end of the pond to the other, blades still, soundless, arms spread, fingers combing the air. I cut through the headlights, tilting my head back, up toward the bearded sky, and slowed to a standstill.

Jack sprinted past me, and as he approached the snowbank, he turned his hips and skidded, stopping on his edges. He crossed back to the other side. And again, and again—at least twenty times. Then he took a plastic five-gallon bucket and hockey stick from his truck. He set it on its side, mouth toward him, and dropped a puck onto the ice. I watched him slap the puck into the bucket, which clattered upright from the force.

"He shoots. He scores," Jack said, raising the stick over his head.

I laughed, and he made several more goals from different areas of the pond. He'd taken off his hat and gloves, too, and his coat. He looked good in a fitted, black turtleneck sweater, his hair dark and feral.

I skated more, avoiding the whizzing pucks. I grew confident, daring, making wide figure eights and sharp turns, and bunny-hopping a couple inches off the ice.

"Not bad," Jack said. "Want to take a few shots?"

"No, I want to do that sideways stop thing you do."

"I don't think you're ready for that yet."

"Have you seen me flying around here? Tell me how."

"You have to build up some speed, then quickly twist your blades and dig into the ice."

"Piece of cake," I said, and started skating to the far side of the pond. About six feet from the edge, I tried to stop. My feet twisted together and I hurtled into the snowbank, shouting unintelligibly at the frigid wetness against my hands, down my collar.

Jack slid gracefully to a stop next to me, spraying me with a thin glaze of shaved ice.

"Show-off," I said. "Go ahead, say it."

"I told you so," he said, laughing, reaching to pull me up.

"I can do it." I shook off his hand and flailed around, trying to turn over. Instead, I kicked Jack's legs out from under him. He fell, hard, next to me.

"Oops," I said, now my turn to laugh. "Sorry."

"I bet you are."

Our faces were close; his Doublemint breath melted my frozen cheek. My hair fanned out over the snow, rivulets of lava in the otherwise unblemished whiteness. I closed my eyes and leaned into him, toward his face, his lips.

Suddenly, I felt myself yanked up by both arms. I opened my eyes and saw Jack skating off, collecting my abandoned woolens and stuffing them into my hat. "Your hands are freezing," he said. "Come on. The diner's open. Let's get something to warm up with. My treat."

I shook the snow from my hair and glided toward Jack, running my hand slowly up the front of my jacket to my neck, to the metal zipper, and pulling it down. "The rest of me isn't cold," I said.

My body moved instinctively—chest out, stomach in, a bit more sway in the hips—but my mind churned in protest. I felt as if I'd been sliced in two, the woman in the magic show whom the illusionist lays in the box and saws through, the halves placed side by side so her feet wiggle next to her head. For the first time in a long time, I didn't want an empty fling. But I didn't know how to stop.

Jack did. He skated away, picked up the hockey stick and bucket. "You can come or not. It's up to you."

"Why don't we go to your place?" I purred.

"We could go to the inn. Mom's always up late. I'm

sure she'd be glad to see you. It's been—what? A couple weeks?"

"I was just hoping we could, you know, talk. Alone."

He tugged on his hat and gloves. "About what?" he asked, zipping and snapping his coat closed. A message to me. *Don't touch.*

"About Luke."

My answer was ninety percent manipulation, designed to stall Jack, to force him into giving me more of his time. It worked. He sat on the log, untied his skates and put on his boots. "What do you want to know?"

I sat on the log, too, at the other end. "What was he like?"

"Quiet."

"Not like me."

Jack laughed, just a bit, more of a sniffle. "We played chess together, almost every day. He was terrible. Four, five moves and I'd have him in check. We used to talk theology during the game, and I think that distracted him. He'd be the first to admit, he couldn't do two things at once."

"What else?"

"You really want to know?"

I nodded. The nonmanipulative ten percent did, honestly, want to know.

"He loved books. He'd read anything, from John Calvin to Stephen King. And he'd do anything for anyone. He was great with his hands, always fixing something, building something. Always had time for a friend. Or a stranger."

I snorted a little. "So, you think he was a saint."

"I think he was a man who tried to serve God the best way he knew." Jack stood, stomped his feet on the ground.

"I'm cold now. But that offer for cocoa at the diner still stands."

"I think I'll stay."

"I'll see you, then, I guess," he said, and he walked across the ice to his truck, dumping his hockey gear in the back.

"Hey," I called. My voice echoed around me. "What if he just did all that good stuff to make up for what he did—you know, like trying to balance the scale? Karma or whatever. He wouldn't be such a great guy then, huh?"

A shadow passed over Jack's face, and for a moment, I thought my question had angered him. He kicked some sooty icicles from the underside of his truck, blinked his eyes a few times, and slowly shook his head. "No," he said. "I don't think Luke was like that."

He left, taking the light with him. And I stepped back onto the pond, and skated, snuggled against the dark.

chapter THIRTY-EIGHT

Jack opened his freezer and spotted the box of waffles crushed under two pizzas and a gallon ice cream tub filled with turkey soup. He grabbed the box and shook it, open end down. Two pale waffle squares tumbled onto the kitchen counter, glued together with frost and age. He tried to twist them apart. Couldn't. So he took a butter knife from the draining rack and jammed it between them. The waffles split, one falling onto the floor. He picked it up, wiped it on his T-shirt, and stuck it in the toaster with the other.

He tried to remember the last time he skipped breakfast at the diner on a weekday. It had to be two years. But he'd slept terribly the night before—if tossing and pacing and brooding could be called sleep—and wasn't in the mood to deal with people this morning. He told himself that even Jesus retreated from the crowds to be alone. Of course, Jesus spent that time in prayer, not moping in his pj's hoping no one would bother him until noon, at least.

The waffles popped up from the toaster. Jack sprinkled powdered sugar on them, folded them in half, and ate them standing over the sink. Usually, he liked them with syrup, the artificial kind, like Aunt Jemima—much to the horror of his mother and dozens of his congregants who tapped the maples yearly during sugaring season—but he didn't want to dirty a plate, or knife and fork, for that matter, because, quite honestly, he hated touching the leftover food on used dishes. And he refused gloves. Every time he saw someone wearing that squeaky yellow rubber, he remembered how his brother had teased him because he said he'd only get near chewed-up food with gloves on. Timothy called him a wimp.

Maybe he'd been right.

For once, Jack wished he had a television, so he could simply plop in front of it and let the box do the thinking for him, distracting him with images of toothpaste, luxury automobiles, and sugared breakfast cereals. He didn't want to use his brain at all this morning, and even the most mindless activity he could engage in—those time-devouring computer games like Minesweeper or Hearts—still required some effort on his part.

He was angry with himself about how he'd acted last night at the skating pond with Sarah. Or wanted to act. After they'd fallen in the snow, as Sarah's face inched closer to his own, he thought about kissing her seeking lips. More than considered. Longed for it. And that longing stayed with him as the sun poured into the night sky, like cream in a cup of black coffee, blanching it.

He tried to convince himself that the kiss would have been for Sarah; he'd simply be speaking her language, telling her in a way she could understand that, yes, he did care for her. But Jack had never been good at self-deception. He knew darn well that he missed feeling a woman's body beside him. His own fault. People couldn't miss what they didn't know.

And he knew.

Sometimes, in tired, wobbly moments when shame wrenched his gaze from heaven to earth, he wondered if he would be alone until he died—his punishment for prior indiscretions. Then he'd take out his Bible, as he did right now, opening to the back cover where he'd taped a list of verses nearly seven years prior. Verses for these times.

Though your sins are like scarlet, they shall be as white as snow.

Therefore, if anyone is in Christ, he is a new creation; the old has gone, the new has come.

Jack looked up each one, twenty-five of them, even though he'd committed them all to memory a long time ago. He repeated them, prayed them, trusted in their truth. Then he'd remind himself, yet again, that God didn't whack his children with a giant flyswatter each time they sinned. That was what grace was for.

chapter THIRTY-NINE

The truck skidded through the trees, snow crunching under the tires. I gripped the steering wheel, leaning forward to wipe the condensation from the windshield. Patty clung to the armrest.

"Careful, you might break a nail, holding on like that," I told her.

"You drive like a maniac," she said.

"It's not me; it's the ice."

I parked close to Zuriel's house. Patty pulled on the door handle.

"That door sticks," I said, getting out. It had been that way since my crash into the ditch on Christmas. Dominic said he could fix it, for two hundred bucks. I passed; no one used that door. Except today. "I have to open it from the outside."

I yanked on the passenger door, and Patty nearly tumbled into the snowbank. I didn't tell her about the rotted second step. She put her foot through it, the broken boards scraping at her leg. "Ouch. My pants ripped. Shoot, look at this, I'm bleeding. If I get tetanus, you're paying the bill."

Ignoring her, I went inside. "Zuriel, I'm here," I shouted over her radio.

The music stopped. "Sarah, did you bring the polish?"

"That, and better," I said, walking into her room, Patty limping behind me. "This is Patty, and she's here to play your piano."

The old woman's heathered eyebrows quivered with delight, and she clapped her hands, once, needles clinking together. She stood, set her yarn on the seat of the rocker, and shuffled to me, fumbling over my arms before taking both my hands. "Child, child, you do have the perfect name."

I squeezed back quickly, pulled away. "I'm just going to run this cloth over the piano. Then we'll have a little concert."

Patty watched as I sprayed Endust over the thirsty wood. "That's a square grand," she said.

"A what?" I asked.

"A square grand piano. That's what it's called. They stopped making these over a hundred years ago."

"You've played one before?" Zuriel asked.

"No. I've only seen pictures," Patty said. "It's supposed to sound like a harp, sort of. May I?"

"Oh, yes. Please," Zuriel said.

Patty opened the keyboard—it was offset, more to the left than right—and played several chords. "It's wonderful. And only a little out of tune. Amazing."

I tilted the polish can toward her, coating her fingers with the lemon-scented foam. "Oops. Sorry," I said.

She glared at me, and glad Zuriel couldn't see a thing, I squatted and wiped the leaf carvings on the legs, twisting the corner of the cloth to fit into each crevice.

"These pianos were very popular during the Victorian

era," Patty went on. "When the regular grands and uprights were made, no one liked them at first. They thought they sounded too harsh because they were so used to these and melodeons."

Show-off. "How do you know?" I asked.

"I can read," she said. "Is there a bench?"

"It broke years ago. When I was five, I think," Zuriel said. "Sarah, get your friend a chair from the kitchen."

I did, and Patty sat, testing the pedals and cracking the knuckles in each finger beneath her thumbs. "So, what would you like to hear?"

" 'Amazing Grace,' " I said. "If you know it."

"Of course I know it. It's one of Reverend Watson's favorites," she said, and began to play.

Zuriel sat in the rocker next to the piano, her palm resting on the top, feeling the vibrations. "Do you sing?" she asked.

"Not me," I said.

"I will," Patty said, and added words to the music. She had a strong, clear voice—nothing remarkable, but on key and pleasant. Zuriel joined in, her harmony patinaed with years, a verdigris of time and wisdom.

> Amazing grace! How sweet the sound
> That saved a wretch like me!
> I once was lost, but now am found;
> Was blind, but now I see.

> 'Twas grace that taught my heart to fear,
> And grace my fears relieved;
> How precious did that grace appear
> The hour I first believed!

Through many dangers, toils and snares,
I have already come;
'Tis grace hath brought me safe thus far,
And grace will lead me home.

The Lord has promised good to me,
His Word my hope secures;
He will my Shield and Portion be,
As long as life endures.

Yea, when this flesh and heart shall fail,
And mortal life shall cease,
I shall possess, within the veil,
A life of joy and peace.

The earth shall soon dissolve like snow,
The sun forbear to shine;
But God, Who called me here below,
Will be forever mine.

When we've been there ten thousand years,
Bright shining as the sun,
We've no less days to sing God's praise
Than when we'd first begun.

They finished, and Patty asked, "What's next?"

Zuriel exhaled, the satisfied sigh of someone who had just breathed in the top of her freshly bathed baby's head, smelling tearless shampoo and talc and innocence. "That's more than I could have hoped for," she said. "Thank you. Both of you."

She was spent, weary from the singing and the joy it brought her. I said I'd see her next week. She embraced

Patty, touched her cheek. "You keep playing like that. For God," she said.

"I will," Patty assured her.

We drove back to Jonah in silence. We'd come that way, too, but this silence felt different. Full. I sensed Patty's thoughts swashing behind her brow bone; what she thought about, I hadn't any idea. Her head listed to one side as she stared ahead, eyes empty, tapping her index finger against her thigh. I watched it. There was no rhythm, no pattern that I could tell. Just the soft, soundless beat of flesh against stonewashed denim.

And my thoughts—I was afraid Zuriel would die that night.

During the song, after the song, she'd had this glow in her face, like a Madonna statue, all bathed in golden light and peaceful. As if she could go to sleep and, content in having heard her favorite song on the prized piano one last time, simply decide she was done being old, and blind, and not good for much of anything.

If Patty hadn't been there, I would have told Zuriel— No, I wouldn't have said anything. But I was counting the hours until I could check on her.

Stopping in front of Patty's house, I handed her a white envelope. "Here's your money," I said. "I'll get the door." I left the engine grumbling and ran outside, around the truck.

My gloves slipped from the door handle. I took them off and pulled with both hands. Patty pushed on the window from the inside. The door flung open.

"Well, thanks," I said.

She nodded. "If you ever want me to go play again, just let me know."

"Right. You'll do anything for fifty bucks."

"Just about," she said, her tone not sarcastic, but sober, pensive.

I jumped back into the warm truck. Patty had left the money on the seat. I stretched across the armrest and cranked down the passenger-side window. Far too much exertion for someone I couldn't stand, I thought, as I waved the envelope in the waning daylight. "Hey. Your money," I shouted.

She heard me; I know she did, because she looked at me from the front stoop of her trailer. Then she turned, unlocked the metal door, and went inside.

chapter FORTY

I went to see Zuriel the next day, and the next—
every day for a week. She chuckled at my concern. "You
don't have to worry about me. The Lord has my days num-
bered. Your coming here isn't going to hasten or lengthen
my time on earth," she said. "I do enjoy your company,
though."

I started to believe she'd outlive me.

Several days later, Doc asked me to take double groceries to Ben and Rabbit. A huge storm approached so I might
not be able to get there again for two, maybe three weeks.
I packed the extra food in the truck and drove the winding
mountain roads, anxiously expecting a deer—or worse yet,
a moose—to dash in front of me.

The heater seemed not to be working properly. I cranked
it up as hot as possible, and still I couldn't stop shivering.
It hurt to move my eyes, too, and felt as if I had a kitchen
grater on the underside of each eyelid, zesting my corneas
with each blink.

Finally there, I managed to lug all five bags out of the
truck at one time, squeezing them against my chest. But I

couldn't see over them and tripped on a log that had fallen off the woodpile. I fell, packages of sausage and heads of lettuce cartwheeling into the snow.

Dropping to my knees, I dug around for the food and, since Memory wasn't in earshot, used every variation of all the indecorous words I knew.

"Need help there?" Rabbit asked. She stood in the doorway, snuff-colored hair shiny and loose around her.

"I think I found everything."

She came outside, a pair of too-big men's work boots on her skinny legs, unlaced, flopping as she picked up three of the bags and went into the cabin, leaving the door open. I followed her with the rest of the groceries.

I latched the door and stood against it, wind knifing through the rough, gray wood. The entire shed shifted, groaned. Rabbit separated the food—meat in one bag, vegetables in another. She stacked the jars and boxes on a shelf.

Ben slept on the mattress. I heard snoring under the blankets, saw his bandaged foot propped up on a stack of clothes.

"Want some coffee?" Rabbit asked. She pointed to an enamel pot on the stove. "Made it fresh this morning. It's chicory."

"I really should go. There's a storm—"

"I smell it. It'll be here in two, three days."

"Well, I won't be back until the roads clear," I said. "Maybe a couple weeks. But there should be enough food for you both until then."

"Hold up." She took two jars off another shelf, pickles and some strange fuchsia chunks floating in syrup. "Doc said them hair things, they was from you. I don't take no charity, so that's to pay for thems."

"Sounds fair," I said.

She nodded. "See you, then. Next time."

I couldn't open my eyes. At first, I thought I was caught in the tail end of a dream, those last moments before consciousness, when I wanted to move my arms, to sit up, but my body refused to obey my brain. Finally I realized I was awake and brought my hands to my face and felt my eyelashes crusted together with sinus drainage.

This had happened to me once before, as a child. I remember my grandmother pressing a damp, warm washcloth over my eyes until the mucus loosened. I kicked out of the sleeping bag and rolled off the couch, onto my hands and knees. I crawled in the direction of the bathroom, one arm flapping in front of me, until I bumped into the wall. Then I stood up and inched to the bathroom door.

I yanked a hand towel off the bar, drenched it under hot water, and put it over my face. After several minutes, I rubbed the towel over my left eye until it came unglued. I looked at my reflection, right eye coated with yellow crud, and pinched my upper lid between two fingers. Pulled. It opened with a jellied snap.

My throat felt itchy, sore, probably from sleeping with my mouth open in the dry heat. I said, "Ah," and tried to peer down it in the mirror, but saw only the back of my tongue, bumpy and smeared with thick, white fuzz. My head hurt, too, a deep drumming pain. I wanted to go back to sleep, but it was Sunday; Memory expected me. So I swallowed a few dry Tylenol, got dressed, and drove to her house.

I pounded on Memory's door. She opened it. "When you gonna quit that knocking, girl?"

Shrugging, I butted past her. "I forgot my violin."

"That ain't all you forgot," she said. "You're white as a blizzard in a snowstorm."

"That's not how—" I leaned against the wall, took a deep breath. "Everything's spinning."

My knees buckled, and I fell forward. Memory caught me, throwing one of my arms over her shoulders, behind her neck. "I'm putting you to bed," she said, dragging me to her bedroom, to a mattress and box spring on a black metal frame. No headboard. No footboard. One window the size of a shoebox. She turned down the covers. "Get in."

"I can't stay here."

"You ain't going nowhere." She nudged me onto the bed, untied my boots, took off my coat, and tucked the blankets around me.

"My stomach," I said. "I think I'm going to—"

I puked down the front of my sweater, on the blankets. It stunk like the can of tuna fish I ate for dinner the night before. Memory stripped off the soiled coverlet and worked my sweater over my head without smearing the vomit in my hair. She wiped my chin and neck, dressed me in one of Robert's shirts, and put two clean quilts on the bed. Then she left the room with the dirty laundry, returning with a glass of water and a batter bowl. "You go 'head and swish that water 'round your mouth, then spit right in this," she said, jamming the bowl under my chin.

I did, and flopped back on the pillow. "Memory . . ."

"Ain't you know when to shut that piehole of yours? You just rest up."

I stayed in that bed for a week. Memory shoved broth in my mouth every hour, and forced me to sip sulfury, luke-warm water. I vomited several more times and peed myself once, the second day. Dizziness came over me every time I stood, and Memory had to help me—I refused the bed-pan—to the bathroom. But on this occasion she didn't get me there quick enough, and the urine spilled over my legs as we shuffled down the hallway together, leaving a trail from the bedroom, like Hansel's crumbs of bread. I was so sick and feverish I didn't care that Memory stripped me down, sat me on the tile floor, and turned on the shower. I did swear at her, though, for the too-cold water; she wouldn't smack an invalid.

Doc came with his thermometer and stethoscope, peering and prodding, and declaring I had one nasty virus.

"I could have told you that," I said, teeth chattering with my temperature of one hundred and three. "Can't you give me something?"

"Other than Tylenol for your fever and general achiness, there's nothing to give," he said.

"Zuriel—"

"Is fine. As is everyone else. You just need to rest."

Beth came every day, and I anticipated each visit as a child waits for summer and all it encompasses—swimming, vacation, Mr. Ding-a-ling's ice-cream truck. Since the wed-ding, our time together had become much less frequent, perhaps once a week, and I missed her. Usually, I sidestepped those I met, arms pinned to my sides, never touching them. Never letting them touch me. Beth, however, had wedged herself into my tiny corner of the universe during the time we spent practicing for the pageant and planning her wedding, and as she dislodged to become more of a wife and less of a girl friend, I found I missed her. But marriage suited her. She moved like a woman now, spoke with newfound maturity, and told me she'd quit her job at the diner. Dominic asked her to.

"How archaic," I said.

"I think it's sweet that he wants to provide for me," she said, twisting her wedding band around her finger. "Maybe if I had an important job, I would have put up some sort of fuss. But I was only carrying around plates of food. And not even very good food at that."

I asked what she did all day now—unable to imagine anyone filling so many hours with mere domestic duties, wondering if she ironed Dominic's pants to perfect creases down the front and cooked his favorite dinner each night, having the meal on the table just as he stepped foot through the door. She told me she made breads and pies and soups for the needy people around town, did some baby-sitting for the single mothers when they needed a couple hours alone to reclaim their sanity, and helped several elderly couples with their errands or housekeeping.

"My mom always gave like that, in little ways. She still does, but I know it's getting real hard for her, with her arthritis," Beth said. "And speaking of Mom, she was wondering if she could come see you."

"I've been meaning to get over there," I lied.

So Maggie came, and stood small and awkward in the bedroom door until I said, "I'm not contagious." Still, I sensed she was afraid to say anything about our argument. I was, too. I didn't think my queasy stomach—now able to keep down dry toast and crackers, but not much more—could handle looking at Maggie as she spoke of Luke, her eyes all lovey-dovey, her face pinched with sorrow.

And Jack stopped by once. Memory told me he was waiting in the den and wanted to make sure I was decent before coming into the bedroom.

"Decent," I squawked. "I haven't washed my hair in days, and do you see this zit on my cheek? It's practically my twin. Tell him I'm sleeping."

"I ain't gonna lie," she said, and I heard her tell Jack, "She's a wee bit sen-see-tive 'bout her looks right now."

"Great, Memory. Thanks a lot," I shouted from the bedroom when I heard Jack leave.

"You be welcome," she yelled back.

Memory. I'd figured she sat around all day eating cookies and caring for Robert. But the woman kept busy. She had people over every day for lunch, and sometimes dinner, too. No one I knew—mostly women she met at the thrift store or families from the church, and all poorer than her. Memory paraded them through the bedroom to make introductions, as she thought it rude not to, and I saw the sunken, toothless mouths, the shoulders—young and old—stooped with the weight of mountain living, the puffiness of too many potato dinners. I smelled their unwashed clothes, their kids' rancid diapers. Memory treated them all like royal dignitaries, and they feasted on macaroni and cheese loaf sandwiches—yes, the pasta was actually pressed into some sort of pork by-product luncheon meat, I found out—pickled beets, and hot water chocolate cake.

In the evenings, Memory sat making rag rugs. She tried to teach me, when I could finally sit up without pain rushing to my head, but soon declared me all thumbs.

"I don't know how you play that fiddle the way you do,

with hands as clumsy as cows full up with moonshine," she said, and started coughing, dry, crumbly coughs that shook her stout back.

"You're not getting sick now, too, are you?"

"Nah," she said, pulling a lozenge tin from the pocket of her flannel shirt. "Nothing these here horehounds won't cure. It's that ol' poison wind. Comes in from the east every year. Makes me hack like a ninny."

The jolt of concern I felt for her startled me. I was still getting accustomed to these intrusively bizarre feelings. They came often now—weekly, sometimes daily. I tried to fight them. They made me mushy, translucent, like onions sautéed in butter. I'd let people too close, and they could see through me.

Especially Jack.

He knew how I felt about him. He had to. I'd been slowly losing my chameleon skin, and each time I saw him my heart beat more rapidly, my desire seeping from my pores as I swayed between aloof and flirtatious, searching for the slightest indication he might be interested in me, too. But Jack remained a stranger.

I didn't understand him at all.

I understood Maggie, and the lumberjacks, dour old Ima-Louise Saltzman, even sweet, simple Beth. They fit. If Grandma Moses painted this place, they would be on the canvas chopping trees, scrubbing pots, or picking tomatoes in the summer. But Jack, he wasn't made of the same stuff as the others. I hoped he wasn't. I didn't want him to be.

I just wanted him.

"Memory, can I ask you something?"

"Sure thing. But don't be expecting any sort of answer."

"That first day I played my violin for Robert, and you were talking about children, and . . . Jack. Do you think—"

"Nope."

"Aren't you going to let me finish?"

"Nope. You be staying away from Reverend Watson."

"You don't think I'm good enough for him?"

"Ain't nothing to do with good or bad. You just ain't whole enough yet."

"I don't follow."

"Say there be two little girls, both pretty as pumpkin pies, and they both got these real nice dolls. The fancy kind, with the eyes that open and shut. Now, one of them girls busts up her doll. Not on purpose or nothing. Maybe it just fell off the table and broke. You think that little girl with the busted-up doll is still happy for the other girl with the doll that ain't broke? No, she ain't happy, no, no. She wants to break that other girl's doll, too, so they both can be sad together."

"What are you talking about?"

"Girl, my grandmamma always told me that God gave folks two ears and one mouth, so they gotta listen twice as much as they talk. If you stop yapping, I'll tell you my point. And that's that you ain't got no clue how to love nobody. Not like that way I read at Beth's wedding. But that's 'cause you ain't never been taught."

"Oh, really? Are you volunteering?"

"No, ma'am. Not me. Only Jesus can teach you something like that."

I rolled my eyes and snorted, Jesus' last name slipping out of my mouth.

Memory took a melamine dish off the bedside table—my dinner plate, I'd had a dry ham sandwich—and smacked me with it, hard, on the top of my head. I howled in pain.

"If you're well enough to take the Lord's name in vain, then you're well enough to get whacked," she said. "I gotta go feed my boy. You need something else?"

"A personal injury lawyer," I said, rubbing the berry-sized lump in my hair.

"Ha! You ain't need no lawyer. Anything I got, you're welcome to. G'night."

She left, and I heard her in the den, speaking to Robert in hushed, gentle words.

I stared at the dark-paneled walls, hunting for pictures in the grain. I'd found dozens this week—a penguin with a fedora, several trees, a giraffe head, a shoe-shaped house, fish, snails, and a submarine. Now I spotted another, a heart with a harpoon protruding from it.

I switched off the bedside lamp. What did Memory know? I only needed to get Jack alone in a warm, dry place. Then he wouldn't be able to resist me. No man ever had, and Jack put his pants on one leg at a time, just like the others. I figured he took them off the same way, too.

chapter FORTY-ONE

I could smell freedom.

Three weeks until my imprisonment ended. Three weeks until I could leave this cabin, this town, and take my money anywhere but here. I had plans, too. A week's stay someplace tropical, in a posh resort with a king-sized bed, a sauna, and room service all hours of the night. On the beach, of course, with hundreds of hard, well-oiled male bodies available for my perusal—or more. I hadn't lived six straight entirely celibate months in the past ten years.

Jack had been making himself unavailable to me. I went to the Grange three times since the skating debacle—and all three times he ran out the door as I slogged up the driveway toward his apartment door, tugging on his gloves and apologizing for having somewhere else to be right at that very moment. "But you can meet me for breakfast any time," he'd said. "I'm buying."

No thanks.

I shook off twinges of sadness when I thought about Beth, or Memory. There were stamps, right? And telephones? And, honestly, they'd go back to their lives, and I to mine, and in six months we'd all be lucky to remember to send a Christmas card.

Maggie had invited me for dinner, and I drove to the inn through a mid-April snow shower. The flakes, satiny and flat, whorled through the air with the swoops and dives of Kamikaze pilots, crashing to the ground, disappearing in the pavement's dampness. After all the storms this winter, I'd begun to learn how to read snow. This squall wouldn't last, and there'd be no accumulation; already the clouds thinned in the evening sky.

I smelled gravy as I entered the inn's kitchen, the small room warm with baking pie and roasting chicken. Maggie handed me a wooden spoon and a cup of chopped scallions, asking me to add them to the rice, along with a little butter. I dropped my parka on a chair and cut a hunk of butter from the stick on the counter.

"Dom's running late tonight," Beth said, bursting into the kitchen and shaking the snow off her cute navy beret. "He said not to wait." She swiped a carrot from the salad bowl, and Maggie slapped her hand.

"Go wash those fingers of yours," Maggie said.

Beth tossed her coat on the kitchen chair and pumped some dish soap onto her hands. She lathered them in the kitchen sink, drying them on the blue plaid dish towel stuck through the cabinet handle. Then she took a slice of pepper, crunched it. "Did you tell Sarah the good news?"

"Tell me, what?" I asked.

Maggie frowned, giving Beth a long, scathing look, shrill with disapproval.

"Mom," Beth said. "Stop."

"You're a married woman now, and you can do as you

like," Maggie said, tearing the lettuce in pieces. "It don't seem to matter what I think."

"What am I missing here?" I asked again.

"I'm pregnant," Beth said.

"Already?"

She took a stack of dishes off the counter and set the table. "Six weeks."

"Well, congratulations. That's wonderful," I said. "I think."

"Don't mind Mom. She's just being a worrywart."

"Elizabeth Grace, you'd be worrying, too, if you'd gone through what I did," Maggie said, grabbing the kitchen towel. She wiped her hands in it, squeezing until I heard one knuckle, then another, crack. "When you have a miscarriage, and everyone is asking you how far along you are, and if you're having morning sickness, and you have to explain over and over and over again that you lost the baby, then you'll understand."

"*When* I have a miscarriage?"

Maggie's face sagged. "I didn't mean it like that."

"Yes, you did," Beth said, her eyes darkening in a way I never thought possible for her. "You'd love to be right on this one, wouldn't you?"

"Beth—"

"No, Mother. I don't want to hear anymore." She dropped the napkins she'd been folding, stomped down the hallway, and I heard a door slam.

I stood there in stunned disbelief. The Watsons—fighting? It had to be some twisted mistake, a *Twilight Zone* episode where the universe split in two, and life turned inside out.

Maggie picked up the cutting board and threw it in the sink, knife clattering against the porcelain, celery tops and pepper stems bouncing onto the counter, the floor. She slumped into a chair, hiding her face in her hand. She wore no rings, her joints like walnuts. Beth had told me Maggie had to have her wedding band cut off six years ago.

"I just want to protect her," she said.

"I know," I said.

"That's what mothers do."

Yes, it was what mothers were supposed to do, hungry lionesses ready to rip apart any threat to their young. But it wasn't what I did. Not me.

Not me.

For nearly seven months I'd carried my baby inside me—indifferent on the best days, loathe-filled on the worst. I never rested a protective hand on my belly, never pulled up my shirt to watch a foot poke against my expanding flesh. I didn't keep my first and only clinic appointment for a pre-natal checkup, and never returned the phone calls asking me to reschedule.

David had loved the baby. We would lie in bed, and he'd press his ear to my stomach, listening for gurgles or hic-cups, for the sloshing of amniotic fluid. He bought a home monitor, so he could listen for the heartbeat, and strapped it on me night after night, the *woosha-woosha-woosha* filling our bedroom before he kissed my navel and fell asleep. If he could have married my torso and carted it around in a stroller until the baby was born, I think he would have.

The cramps began at twenty-seven weeks, blunt and easily ignored. Four days later, it felt as if rats were gnaw-ing on my uterus. But I had the rehearsal for an important performance—a chamber ensemble with an intimate and renowned guest list—so I downed eight Advil and hopped the number 1 train to practice. I never made it there, fainting instead in a puddle of blood on the 66th Street platform.

I woke hours later, in a post-operation recovery room after an emergency cesarean section. I'd had a placental abruption. My baby was dead. She. A little girl. They kept her warm while I slept, and a grief counselor who looked no older than me said I should hold her; it would help me heal. So I kicked David out of the room and cradled the blanketed bundle against my chest. She weighed two pounds, had shiny pink fingernails, and a subway system map of veins beneath her skin. And red hair.

I loved her.

Now I wanted her, when it was too late. When I'd spent the last six months thinking of her as some maggoty parasite, an unwanted intruder in my life. Now I'd give anything to have used my cigarette money—I didn't think two or three secret smokes a day could affect the pregnancy—to pay for a cab to the hospital when the discomfort first began, and David told me he thought she was moving less.

She was a real baby. We had to choose a name for the birth certificate, for the headstone. David and I still hadn't decided on one. He wanted Zoë or Chloë, or Daisy, after his childhood *Dukes of Hazard* fantasy, but spelled with the umlaut. Daisë. I told him to pick something for the paperwork, and he went with Brenda Susan, in honor of his grandmothers, not wanting to waste one of his precious other names on a corpse.

But in my mind she was Allegra—the name I'd chosen when I first found out I was pregnant; the name I hadn't told a soul about.

I quit smoking the day she was buried. I dropped out of Juilliard the next week.

Three months later, David wanted to try again. I snubbed him, first by sleeping on the couch, then moving to other men's beds. And did anything, everything I could, to forget that, like my father, I was a taker of life.

I left Maggie in the kitchen—she'd finally gotten up from the table to take her pecan pie from the oven—telling her I'd call Beth to eat, and knocked on the bedroom door. Beth didn't answer, so I went in and saw her lying on the bed, headphones on her ears and shirt pulled up to the bottom of her rib cage. She stroked her stomach softly, distractedly, like someone petting a cat while reading. I knocked louder, and she looked up, clicked off her cassette player.

"Dinner," I said.

"I'm not hungry."

"You're eating for two."

"Did Mom send you down here?"

"If there's one thing you should know about me by now, it's that I'm no diplomat." I made some ridiculous fencing motion, waggling my invisible épée toward her, quoting some fragment of Bible verse dredged up from Sunday school classes long ago. "I come not to bring peace, but the sword."

She sat up, chuckled a little. "You don't have to tell me twice."

I leaned against the armoire. I did my best talking while standing—conditioning, I think, from all my years on my feet with violin in hand. "Listen, Beth. Maggie—"

"Uh-huh."

"—is really trying to look out for you."

"Mmm."

"And, no, she didn't tell me to say this." I took a guarded breath, pressure building between my ears. I hadn't mentioned this, aloud, in more than five years. "I'm speaking from experience."

Beth squinted, shook her head a little. "What do you mean?"

"I lost a baby once."

"Sarah, I'm sorry."

"Yeah, well, sh— garbage happens, right? Anyway, my point is, for months, whenever I ran into someone who knew I'd been pregnant, they'd ask me where the baby was, how she was doing. Just like Maggie said. And I had to relive the whole thing all over again. Whether or not you agree with your mother, and whether or not she's speaking from fear, so what? She just wants to save you some of the pain she went through."

"I know," Beth said, pulling the headphones off her neck and, with a flick of her wrist, pitching them across the bed. "It's just harder than I thought. Being married and here, at the inn, still living with Mom. There's no . . . break. From her, I mean. I still feel like a kid, not a woman with a husband to care for, and a baby on the way. I think I'm trying too hard to flaunt my independence."

"A little late for the teenage rebellion thing."

"I won't be twenty until September."

"Then I guess you have five months to get it out of your system. You've got the door slamming down. And the back talk. Try a couple midnight joyrides with a twelve-pack."

She smiled wistfully, with only one side of her mouth. "Sarah, I'm really going to miss you."

"Shut up," I said, "and go hug your mother."

chapter FORTY-TWO

Beth stood, naked, in front of the full-length mirror on her closet door, watching her reflection rub oil over her hips, waist, tummy, a blend of sweet almond and vitamin E, with calendula and carrot extract. Aggie Standing mixed it especially for her. Most of the pregnant women in town used Aggie as their midwife, but the scars concerned Beth. She worried there'd be problems with her skin stretching properly and planned to see an obstetrician as soon as the weather broke. Until then, she'd try to keep her stomach supple and elastic with the oil.

"Need any help?" Dominic asked from the bed.

"No, I'm done."

She scrunched her nightgown so she could pull it over her head, but Dominic said, "Why don't you leave that off?" and folded down the quilt on her side of the bed. She slid beneath the chilly sheets and scooted against him, the ardor in his skin still unexpected, and they made love quietly. Beth knew her mother wore earplugs at night now—she'd seen them on her nightstand, the gummy, neon foam kind—but even if Maggie couldn't hear them, two doors away was still too close for privacy. Dominic suggested moving their bedroom upstairs, as if fifty paces instead of five would make a difference.

She doubted it.

Beth didn't consider herself a ponderer, shucking the husk off each thought that roamed through her mind. Lately, however, as the disquiet grew between her and Maggie, she had been examining their relationship more closely. She partly blamed hormones for her sudden oversensitivity to her mother's hovering, but it was more than that. In those early months after the fire, Beth depended on Maggie for everything from pureeing her meals to emptying her catheter bag. As time progressed and Beth's wounds healed, her mother continued to shelter her, to straighten her bedroom and pack her schoolbooks each night. To do all those things she could now do for herself. She knew her mother found purpose in helping her, and Beth, under the weight of the debt she felt she owed Maggie for all she'd done, never figured out a way to say she didn't need that help anymore.

She kept telling herself the awkwardness between them, while they tried to figure out their new roles, their new relationships to each other, would settle eventually. Until then, she prayed she didn't say something she'd regret.

Dominic snored in his sleep, one arm under her neck, stretching across the bed, the other leaden on her rib cage. She wriggled out from beneath it and put on her nightgown. She got cold sleeping without clothes. Then she settled back into bed, tucking herself under her husband's arm again. He stirred, snorted, and pulled her close.

Her hands roamed over her stomach, to the plateau between her hipbones. She couldn't keep from imagining the tiny life inside her. A miracle. She knew her baby wasn't any different, any more special, than any other six-week-old fetus—bean-sized with its own heartbeat now. The miracle was that she was alive to have this baby. She remembered times when she wished Luke had left her to die in the flames, those painful days of bandages and surgeries, and physical therapy. And yet the Lord had carried her out of Egypt and through the desert, to a Promised Land more glorious than she imagined.

Beth didn't worry about being a good mother. Not too much, anyway. Maggie wouldn't be timid about giving advice, and any mistakes she made—many, she was certain—would be covered by God's grace. His plans couldn't be thwarted by an imperfect, bumbling, first-time mommy.

But her face—

She touched her reconstructed cheek, pinched it. It felt like Silly Putty, rubbery and too smooth. She wondered how long it would be before her baby understood that Beth didn't look like other parents. Certainly by grade school, when children sang taunts about anything peculiar, about the outcasts. She'd heard them, even made up some of her own. *Greg, Greg, smells like rotten eggs, and he doesn't wash his legs. Boogerhead Michele picks her nose and eats it, cooks her snot in a pot, and pours it on her biscuits.* She could easily imagine what might be said about her own face.

Her worst fear, however, was that her baby would be afraid of her.

Not at first, of course. But later, when little ones learned to fear monsters under the bed and the noises of creaky old houses. Then, perhaps, it would be Beth's face her child saw in his nightmares, chasing him through the darkness.

Dominic told her she was being ridiculous, and Beth prayed he was right.

chapter FORTY-THREE

I noticed the air first, warmer than it had been since I arrived in Jonah, and with a spicy, green scent. A spring smell, though Maggie had warned not to be too optimistic; it wasn't uncommon to have snowstorms in June.

Then I noticed the birds. Crows. Huge, black, and dead still on the fallen tree.

Aunt Ruth had dabbled in augury—she'd dabbled in just about anything that would make my grandmother drop to her knees in fervent prayer for her last living child's soul— divining omens using eggs and stars and onion sprouts. Her favorite, though, was auspice, and when I was in grade school we'd recite an old counting-crows rhyme together every time we saw the ink-eyed birds preening on telephone wires or rooftops: "One for sadness, two for mirth; Three for marriage, four for birth; Five for laughing, six for crying; Seven for sickness, eight for dying; Nine for silver, ten for gold; Eleven a secret that will never be told."

I didn't believe that bunk, but I tallied the birds anyway. Eight.

Picking a stone up from the driveway, I chucked it toward

them, hitting one. It cawed, and they all scattered, shiny black confetti falling up into the sky. I pushed my sleeve away from my watch; Memory would be late to church again, because of me. Still, I drove slowly, just in case those crows decided to turn around and fly through my windshield to exact a bit of revenge. I'd watched *The Birds* enough times that images of a screaming, bloody Tippi Hedren spontaneously entered my head anytime I saw several feathered beasts flocking together.

At Memory's, I parked the truck and took the terraced steps in twos, surprised she wasn't standing on the porch waiting for me. I banged at the door. Nothing. I knocked again, glancing through the dirty front window. I saw Robert in bed, uncovered, his sheet and blankets in a heap on the floor.

A heap with toes poking out of it.

"Memory," I shouted, barging inside and falling to my knees beside the bed. Pawing through the blankets, I found her, face pressed against the hard floor. I grabbed her and rolled her onto her back. Shook her. Her eyes were open. "Memory. Memory, come on. Get up."

She didn't move.

I stood, flapping my arms as I turned this way and that, looking for a phone until I remembered she didn't have one. "What's wrong with you?" I shouted. "How can you not have a phone? How can you not—" and I kicked her.

"—have—" Another kick.

"—a phone?"

I sprinted to the truck and sped to Doc's office. It was Sunday. Closed. I drove to his house and pounded with both palms on his door.

"Sarah, what's wrong?" he asked, coming to the door dressed but wearing slippers.

"It's Memory. She's . . . she's not moving. I don't know what's wrong with her."

"You drive," he said. He didn't put on shoes, just grabbed his old-fashioned black medical bag near the coatrack and followed me. I fumbled with the keys, dropped them under the truck, in a slushy puddle. Doc fished them out, wiped them on his corduroy pants, the wide wale worn flat at the knees. "Never mind, I'll drive."

He put his seat belt on. I tried to, but my hands shook too much, so I just held the armrest as Doc swerved sharply around the corners.

"Is she breathing?" he asked.

"I don't know," I said.

"Pulse?"

"I don't know! I don't know."

I tried to get out of the truck before it stopped in front of the house, forgetting the passenger door didn't open from the inside. I crawled out the driver's side, wriggling past Doc, and ran back to Memory. Doc found me on the floor, grabbing at the front of her shirt, shaking her. "Sarah," he said, hand on my shoulder.

"Why are you just standing there? Get down here. Do something."

"Sarah, stop."

"Do something," I pleaded.

"She's gone."

"No." *No. No. No.* "Please," I whispered. To whom, I didn't know.

Doc crouched beside me, and I fell into him, sobbing. I mashed my face against his shoulder, vaguely aware of his arms moving around me, his hands resting on my head, my hair. My body shook, and I cried until I coughed up mouthfuls of snot, and my throat tasted raw. I felt Doc wipe my face with something rough, a paper towel I think he took from his back pocket. He lifted me to my feet, sat me in a chair, and I watched him examine Robert, checking his heart, his temperature and blood pressure, his incision. "He's dehydrated. I need to feed him."

I nodded. My vision blurred with pain. Everything in the room looked distorted, fuzzy. Except Memory. Her pale face shone against a blue and purple rag rug, the moon in Van Gogh's midnight sky. Doc noticed me staring, transfixed. He gently covered her face with the blanket.

"I need to make some phone calls. Are you okay here? I'm just going down the road a bit to the neighbor's. I won't be long. Twenty, thirty minutes."

I managed to nod. I heard the truck spray pebbles across the pavement as it pulled away. And then my chin fell into my chest and I closed my eyes. A low hum filled my head, rising to the top of my skull, swimming, digging, whirling like a dentist's drill. I wrapped my arms over my knees and sat there, motionless, listening to the noise in my brain. Focusing on it, really, so that no other thought could worm its way inside, until Doc returned with Iris Finn. She would stay with Robert tonight, and wait for the coroner.

Doc grabbed my elbow, propelled me out the door. I staggered to the truck, zombie-like, booted feet scraping across the soft earth, lacerating it with each step. My hand wandered to my neck, and I pulled at my skin, pinched it, kneaded it. But I felt nothing. Doc helped me into the passenger seat and buckled my belt for me. Then he slid behind the wheel, squeezed it with both hands.

"Sarah—"

"I knew she was dead," I said, voice flat.

"You shouldn't be alone. Let me take you to the inn."

"I want to be alone."

He didn't argue. He drove me to the cabin, saying something about returning my truck later.

I fell into the couch without removing my boots or coat, and clamped my forearm down over my eyes. I wanted to sleep but soon grew hot. My head began to clear, the white noise dissipating, and snippets of conversations I'd had with Memory fidgeted around in there, urging me to reminisce. I needed to do something, anything, to make it stop.

Flinging off my coat, I turned on the light in the kitchen and scoured the cabinets. Flour, sugar, cocoa powder. I found measuring cups and spoons, a chipped Pyrex bowl, a cake pan. Memory's hot water cake recipe was taped to the refrigerator. I grabbed it, along with a couple of eggs, breaking them into the bowl, fishing out a broken shell. Then I measured the flour without scraping the top to level it. Just dumped it in, along with the sugar and cocoa. And poured in the water.

I didn't have an electric mixer but found a whisk at the back of the utensil drawer. I stuck it in the batter without rinsing off the dust and twisted it around the soupy chocolate with short, hysterical strokes.

"How could you leave me?" I threw the whisk against the wall, and swept my arm across the counter, knocking the bowl to the floor. It shattered, spraying glass and batter over my toes, the tile, everywhere.

I collapsed in the puddle, glass crunching under my knees, batter soaking into my pants. Sobbing, I wiped my eyes and nose with the back of my wrist, smearing chocolate on my face. The dense, churlish smell made me retch, and I vomited bile onto my hair, between my fingers.

I stayed there until my knees ached and my feet went numb, and the batter dried and cracked on my skin, cocoa lizard scales. After showering, I dug through the cold remedies I'd bought when I first decided to stay in Jonah, almost six months ago. I found the nighttime cough medicine and guzzled half the syrup straight from the bottle, leaving the rest of it on the coffee table, right next to the couch, in case I woke during the night.

chapter FORTY-FOUR

I would still be asleep if Beth hadn't come to bring me to the service. She lifted all the shades and started the shower for me, then hauled me into a sitting position. "You need to get ready," she said.

"I'm not going."

"Yes, you are, and I'll drag you into the shower with your clothes on if you don't get up now. Don't think I can't."

I ignored her. So she grabbed my ankles and pulled until my hips slid off the cushions, my legs suspended in the air, a bridge across the coffee table.

"Fine," I said, and she dropped my feet. The back of my heels slammed onto the table. "Ouch."

"There's a dress for you in the bathroom, hanging on the hook behind the door."

I washed and dried my hair, and shaved my legs because the dress Beth brought, a simple navy cotton with white embroidery at the collar and cuffs, hung only midcalf. A new package of pantyhose lay next to the sink.

I found Beth in the kitchen, washing cake batter off the walls, floor already clean. A plate of scrambled eggs sat on the counter. "I didn't know if you were hungry," she said. "You don't have much to eat around here."

"I'm not."

Beth covered the plate with a napkin and put it in the refrigerator. She looked lovely in the same dress she wore at the Christmas recital and her pearls around her neck, her face rouged with that fabled pregnant glow, tummy still flat. "Do you need shoes?" she asked, pulling several pairs from a plastic grocery bag.

"I have some," I said, and I rummaged through the closet until I found my Mary Janes.

"Listen, Sarah. Mom thought you might want to play something to—"

"No." I zipped on my coat. "Are we going?"

My truck was back in the driveway. Beth asked if I wanted to ride with her or go by myself. I chose alone, and followed her to the Grange, trying my best to ignore the cheerful weather.

Death should never come on sunny days.

I remembered my grandmother driving past a cemetery one Saturday while taking me to violin lessons. The rain poured down, mourners huddling under a small, white canopy, their smart black shoes coated with freshly turned earth. "What terrible weather for a funeral," she had said, and I thought, *No, what perfect weather for a funeral.*

But today, the sun blazed with springtime. Only a few wispy clouds stretched over the sky, and I noticed, for the first time, the young red tree branches spotted with buds. Despite this, a foot of snow hid the ground in some places along the sides of the roads, where the plows had piled it during the winter months.

There wouldn't be an actual funeral this morning. The

ground was still frozen, and it cost too much to call in a bull-dozer to dig a Memory-sized hole. Instead, she was stuffed in the morgue icebox until June, and we'd have some sort of memorial service—a celebration of a life, Maggie called it.

What bull.

It had been three days since I'd found the body. I spent Monday and Tuesday in an over-the-counter medicinal stupor. People—Doc, Maggie, Beth—came by to check on me. I'd forgotten to lock the door, so they walked in and poked at me until they were satisfied I still breathed. I managed a few strangled grunts from beneath my pillow. Jack had come, too. Every few hours, it seemed. Or perhaps I had dreamed him, sitting on the coffee table, stroking my hair and whispering beautiful, unintelligible things.

Jack approached me as soon as I walked into the Grange. He looked at me as if I would crumble at the slightest touch, and jammed his hands into his pockets. But his eyes pored over me. "How are you?" he asked, then shook his head with an embarrassed sniff. "Sorry. Dumb question."

"Yeah," I said.

"We were waiting for you; didn't want to start without you."

I looked around, the hall filled with almost as many people as during the pageant. At the front of the building, a small card table held a vase of yellow flowers and a framed picture of Memory—both perched on a rag rug of gold, scarlet, and purple.

Beth sat close to the front, with Maggie and Dominic; she saved a seat for me. My legs moved down the aisle as if on their own accord. I tripped over Dominic's work boots as I shimmied past him and to the empty metal folding chair, noticing the cold, hollow *thunk* as I slumped into it.

At the piano, Patty played a few measures and everyone began singing. Maggie gave me a hymnal, opened to page 103—"Nothing But the Blood of Jesus." I didn't pretend to follow along.

The song ended, and Jack walked to the podium. "Amen," he said, garnering a chorus of "Praise Jesus" and "Hallelujah" from the crowd.

"We gather here today," he continued, "on a day that many in the world would face with sadness. But we come full of joy, because our dear friend and sister in Christ, Memory Jones, has entered into the glory of her Lord. And anyone who knew her and loved her as we did could have no doubt that she heard His voice say, 'Well done, my good and faithful servant.'"

I gazed out the window, Jack's voice fading to background noise. I had no use for any of that imbecilic God stuff today. All these people could delude themselves, wave to Memory up in the sky, and have themselves a good night's sleep. The only things that kept her from rotting into oblivion were my memories of her, and I hadn't decided if I would keep those or not.

I knew how to forget.

People got up and down, and talked. I closed my eyes and counted the number of days until I could leave. Nine. The number of steps to Memory's house. The number of months it took for a child to leave its mother's womb.

The number of times I wished these fools would shut up.

Patty played another hymn. Everyone stood to sing, except me. Then the chairs were pushed against the walls. The men opened several tables in the center of the floor, the women covered them with yellow paper tablecloths, foil-wrapped casseroles, plastic forks, and various desserts. Rich the Mushroom and Shelley cornered me. Too tired to fight, I stood there while they made small talk and offered to get me plates of food. I said I'd get my own, and instead went to hide in Jack's office. I took an afghan off the back of the desk chair, curled up in the corner of his sofa, and, breathing in the musky scent of leather, dozed off.

When I woke, Jack sat at his desk, his back to me, typing on the computer. I stretched, yawned, and he turned around.

"Is it over out there?" I asked.

"Just about. There are a few folks left, and the ladies are just starting to clean up. Give it another hour, and you should be able to sneak out completely unnoticed."

"I won't stay that long."

"You're welcome to," he said, "if you want. If not, I think I have some sort of disguise you can put on." He dug around in his bottom desk drawer and pulled out a dark blue ski mask, the kind bank robbers wear in the movies, with the eyes and mouth cut out. "Here you go. It even matches your dress."

I laughed a little, and Jack said, "It's good to see you smile." He smiled too, this tender, lopsided grin that made my palms prickle with sweat.

"Did you come sit with me the past few days? I think I remember you . . . sitting there," I said.

"That was me. I was worried about you. I still am."

I shrugged a little, dismissing his concern. "It's fine. Nothing that won't be cured next Friday."

He raked his teeth over his lower lip, pulling off a bit of skin. "If you say so," he said, turning back to the computer.

I looked down into my lap, eyes tracing the color pattern of the afghan, fingers stuck through the crocheted holes. "Is Iris Finn still staying with Robert?"

"No," he said, eyes still on the monitor. "Doc's been there, mostly. I know he's been seeing patients there. Someone from the church will sit with Robert for a little while if he has to go out. But it's only for a couple more days."

"What do you mean? Then what?"

"Doc called in a favor and got Robert into a hospital a couple hours from here."

I blinked. "You mean an institution."

He stopped typing. "Yes."

"No." I shook my head, swallowing hard. I pictured Memory doting over her son, gently combing his hair and brushing his teeth. Tucking the blanket around him. Kissing him good-night. "There has to be another option. Maybe someone, someone could—"

"Most of the people around here can hardly afford to feed their own families," Jack interrupted. "Are you going to take care of him?"

Quietly, I said, "I just meant she wouldn't want that for him."

In one quick, bewildering motion, Jack swiveled to face me. "No, Sarah, she wouldn't have wanted that," he said in a tone I'd never heard from him before, jagged, ugly, like something I would say. It troubled me, coming from him. "But life isn't always about what we want, is it? If you stepped away from your own personal pity party for two minutes, maybe you'd see that other people have had some pretty terrible things happen to them, too. But they're not sitting around, hating the world and everyone in it.

"Do you think Beth wanted to be burned half past

recognition, or that my mother wanted Dad and Tim to die? Do you think Memory wanted an invalid for a son? Huh? Do you think I wanted to—"

He stopped, his angry cheeks turning white, as if someone had jabbed a straw in the top of his skull and sucked out all the blood.

I grabbed a cross-stitched throw pillow, clutched it to my chest and huddled deeper into the corner of the couch, crying. Not the loud, hiccupping sobs of the past few days, but shocked and silent. Jack pounded the arm of the chair with the fleshy part of his fist. Then he came over to the couch, sat down and pulled me into him. "Sarah, I'm sorry."

"No," I said. And I meant, *No, don't apologize.* Because he was right. My tears were not for Memory or Robert. They were for me.

I sniffled, aware of the weight of Jack's arm across my shoulder, the scent of his deodorant. This was where I had wanted to be since our first breakfast at the diner. Another feeling rose to the surface like curdled milk. Not quite lust— oh, yes, I knew that well—but something warmer and more vulnerable. I tightened my grip on the pillow. It might as well have been made of cellophane.

"I didn't want to come back to Jonah," Jack said, voice muffled against the top of my head. "After seminary, God forgive me, I didn't want to come back. I had such big plans. There was so much need in the city. In all my youthful idealism, I thought I could make a difference.

"And there was Allison."

"That girl in college," I said.

Jack disentangled himself from me and paced across the room once, twice. He leaned against the dining table, nodded. "I loved her. I thought I loved her. She got pregnant," he said. "I told you I wasn't perfect."

I watched him, light blue dress shirt unbuttoned and untucked, hanging loose over his white undershirt, looking perfectly imperfect, and my initial shock dissolved into relief. He wasn't immune to pleasure, to base human instinct. His confession made him all the more accessible.

He was no better than me.

"By then," Jack continued, "the summer after graduation, everyone was wondering why I wasn't home yet. I gave dozens of excuses, told dozens of lies. The guilt ate ulcers into my stomach. I couldn't sleep. My hair started falling out. I kept picturing the look I would get when people—all those people who had put me up on the stupid pedestal for so long—found out what I'd done."

"You fell in love."

"Maybe in your world, Sarah, but not mine. I was a fornicator having a child out of wedlock. Godly, Christian men don't do things like that. Pastors don't. And Jack Watson sure as heck didn't."

"You didn't have to come back here."

"That's what I tried to tell myself. Every day of that year Allison and I were together. But, in the end, I knew this is where the Lord wanted me. I'd known since I was eight. So I asked Allison to marry me. Obviously, she said no. She didn't want to be some backwoods pastor's wife. She had her big plans, too."

"And the baby?"

Jack withered into himself, head slumping forward, arms crossing stiffly against his chest. "She had an abortion. I didn't do anything to stop her. Some part of me thought it would make things easier. No one would ever know what I did.

"Except me. I wake up every day knowing."

I went to him, stood in front of him and reached out to take his hand. My fingers brushed against his wrist instead.

His jaw tightened. "I've never told anyone this."

I nodded slightly and, heart thudding in my ears, kissed his cheek.

Jack's mouth found mine, and we fell against each other. It felt so good to be touching someone. Him. He rubbed his thumb over the button at the nape of my neck, the only button on my dress, but didn't open it. I pulled his T-shirt from his pants and slid my hands up his back.

"No," he said, and he shoved me away. "That's enough."

I slapped him.

The blow surprised both of us, whipping across his cheek with force enough to turn his head, my palm print red in his skin. I recovered first, and raised my arm to hit him again, but he caught me, his grip an iron shackle on my wrist. My other hand tightened to a fist, and I hammered Jack's chest until he restrained that, too. We stood there, panting, staring at each other, bodies rigid with adrenaline. I twisted from his grasp, stepped back.

"Sarah—"

"Don't. Just don't."

I left the office, stunned, face itchy with humiliation. I'd never been refused before, not like that, with a man staring back at me, his eyes dark with disgust. And I don't think I'd ever wanted to be wanted more. I didn't know how to handle it.

I stumbled around the hall, searching for my coat, finding it finally hanging on the vestibule coatrack. I opened the front door just enough to squeeze outside, and ran into Adele on the front steps, puffing on a cigarette.

"I know how much you miss her, honey," she said, smoke corkscrewing between her lips.

"It's not that," I said.

"What is it?"

I hesitated, feeling like a character in a cartoon with a haloed cherub perched on one shoulder and a pitchforked devil on the other. I could eat my embarrassment, keep my mouth shut, and go home. But I was the little girl in Memory's story, the one who broke her doll, and I wanted Jack to hurt as much as I did. I wanted him to pay for not loving me.

"I-I'm not sure I should say, but I need to tell someone. Promise this will stay just between us?"

"Of course, honey. You go 'head, just get it off your chest."

So I told her what Jack told me, about Allison. About the baby. When I finished, I clutched her arm with both my hands, feigning urgent secrecy. "You can't tell anyone," I said.

She bobbed her head up and down like a Pez dispenser. "You have my word."

I trudged back to the truck, a fizzy concoction of shame and satisfaction sloshing around my gut. By tomorrow night, the whole town would know.

chapter FORTY-FIVE

Jack could hear the congregants gathering in the Grange hall; they were louder than other mornings. Then again, usually he was rushing around at this time, ten minutes before the service, either shaving his week-old stubble or washing cream cheese off his tie. So maybe he just had never noticed all the commotion outside his door. Today he'd been on his knees since before sunrise, praying for wisdom, for words.

His mother had called him Thursday morning; she'd heard this awful rumor from Aggie, who said she'd found out from Editha, who said Sarah told Adele the day before. Of course it couldn't be true. When Jack didn't deny it, Maggie hung up with a smothered, "How could you?" Moments later, the phone rang again. Ephraim Joseph assumed it was merely gossip, but still, did Jack know anything about this? After that, he'd taken the phone off the hook, stuffing the receiver under the couch cushion until it stopped buzzing.

He wasn't angry with Sarah. Not anymore. But he had been, the sting of betrayal poured, like rubbing alcohol, into his own guilty conscience. More than once he resisted the

305

temptation to go to Luke's cabin and confront her, until he realized his indignation stemmed not from Sarah's tongue, but the glaring white spotlight on him, burning the skin of a man who'd been hidden in the dark too long.

He had no more secrets now.

Standing at the door, head against the painted wood, hand hesitant on the knob, he felt the speculation, the scandal buzzing on the other side, vibrating up his arm, in his ears. " 'But as for you, you meant evil against me; but God meant it for good, in order to bring it about as it is this day,' " he whispered. "Help me, Father."

He stepped out into the hall. Mouths snapped closed, people sat, and the silence blossomed into murmurs and clucks. Patty began playing the first hymn, but Jack touched her arm. "Not today," he said.

The podium, only ten feet from where he stood, seemed miles away. He counted the steps, eyes focused on the glass of water waiting for him, liquid quivering with each footfall. Finally there, he took three gulps of water and gripped the sides of the pulpit.

"I'd like to ask the Sunday school teachers to take the children to their classes now. We're going to have the sermon first this morning."

Several women stood, motioning to their students, gathering them in like mother geese and ushering them to the two upstairs classrooms. Jack finished his water, rubbed his mouth. He felt a scab on his bottom lip; it fell off in his hand, and he tasted blood.

"I don't know what you've heard, or haven't heard. But we all know that gossip gets around this town like children playing a game of telephone; starting at one end of the line with 'Jack had fish for supper last night and didn't brush his teeth' and, after whispering in the ear of twelve giggling little girls, ending up with 'Jack has a fishy mother peeling sprouts in his sneakers.' "

The congregation tittered in that nervous Cheshire-cat way, each person seeming to recall his or her own contribution to the rumor parade, and Jack continued. "But it doesn't really matter to me what you know, or think you know, or who you told or didn't tell. In the book of James we're told to confess our sins to one another. So that's what I'm going to do.

"Yes, when I was in seminary, my girlfriend got pregnant and had an abortion. And, no, I didn't try to stop her."

The murmuring crescendoed again, and Jack let it ebb away on its own, wishing for another glass of water. "I think for many of us who have grown up in the church, in small towns where not much of anything happens, we can overlook the fact that, yes, we too can be tempted. I'd allowed myself to forget that. So, when temptation struck, instead of saying to myself, 'Even Jesus was tempted,' I ran away from God, because I was ashamed that I, Jack Watson, could be struggling with such sins. And I fell. I fell hard.

"I'm here before all of you now, asking your forgiveness. For lying to you about why it took me so long to come back here, and for thinking that I was somehow above being tempted. But I also am asking you to forgive me for being a rather pitiful shepherd.

"I've stood here, week in and week out, preaching from this pulpit that Christ's blood is sufficient to cover all sins. That His blood is all we need, and in believing on Him, we are forgiven. Salvation is His gift to us, and we can do nothing to earn it. But I didn't live my life like that. For the past seven years, I've been trying to prove to God that I am worthy of His forgiveness. And that's pure pride, too, thinking that my sin is too big for God's mercy."

Jack stopped, looked out over the crowd, harsh fluorescent casting a yellowish veneer on everyone's pasty winter skin. "I'm sorry. I'm so sorry."

No one whispered, and most people stared at their hands or the floor, or at the huge crack in the plaster on the wall behind him, just above his head. "So, I guess that's it," he said, and turned to leave the podium. Then he stopped, faced the congregation. "No, wait. While I'm here, I have one more thing to confess. Clara, I need to tell you, I hate deviled eggs."

The small, white-haired woman sat next to her husband, and she leaned on Ephraim Joseph's shoulder as she rose to her feet. "Reverend, I don't think there's ever been something easier to forgive, and more welcome to hear, because I hate making them."

There was laughter then, and like driving through fog, the tension, thick one minute, was suddenly gone. People poured from their seats to the pulpit, to Jack, his mother first in line to wrap her thin arms around him. Jack squeezed back and said, "I'm sorry I tried to be perfect."

Maggie touched his face. "I'm sorry I wanted you to be."

Through the crowd, he thought he saw a flicker of orange in the vestibule, where one of the double doors was propped open with a cinder block. He shook some more hands, accepting apologies from those who had helped spread the rumor, and watched until he saw it again. Red hair.

Sarah's hair.

He motioned to Beth. She looked toward the door and nodded, then made her way to the back of the room.

Jack knew he would have to face Sarah soon. But not today. For the first time in a long time, he felt clean. He wanted to delight in that for a while, and—God forgive him—he didn't want Sarah to ruin that for him right now.

chapter FORTY-SIX

He saw me.

I had come early and parked on the road, waiting until everyone clamored into the Grange for the morning service. There were few stragglers—due, no doubt, to the brouhaha I began. By ten the doors shut tight, and as I snuck up the front stairs I wondered if they were locked.

They weren't.

Creeping into the vestibule, I hid behind the one closed inner door and listened, concerned Jack would be ousted from his pastoral position and publicly humiliated, or perhaps something more antediluvian, like stoning. I had no clue what overzealous Bible-thumpers did to their prodigals.

But, as I'd listened, Jack seemed focused—not quite relaxed, but not apprehensive, either—and lighthearted, almost, as if he was relieved he no longer carried his secret. And the congregation responded warmly to his confession, giving hugs and handshakes. When his head turned in my direction, I jumped back behind the door, but my stubborn hair didn't follow. I should have worn a ponytail.

Moments later, Beth tapped me on the shoulder. "You've been spotted."

"Obviously."

"It's not a private meeting or anything. Why don't you come on in?"

"No. I just wanted to, you know, make sure your brother was . . . okay."

"Just go talk to him. He's not even mad."

Why wasn't he angry? I forsook his trust, dangling his sins—well, he considered them sins; I thought it nothing more than living life—across the clothesline, all his unmentionables flapping in the wind. If Jack had done such a thing to me, with all the feelings I had, the desires to please him, to touch him and be close to him, a betrayal of this magnitude would have destroyed me. I'd want blood.

Jack, however, seemed unaffected.

"He doesn't need to talk to me," I said.

"Sarah—"

"Just leave me alone, okay?"

I climbed into my truck and maneuvered through the throng of vehicles, the mirror on the passenger door scraping along the side of some white van, fingernails on a chalkboard. I drove blindly, thinking of Jack. He rebuffed me the other day because he didn't love me. Not the way I wanted—no, needed—him to. How stupid I was to think he could. The stains left on me by my parents went deep. Too deep to be scrubbed out by a six-month stay with good Christian folk and a handful of charitable deeds. I'd never change. My grandmother raised me to, at the very least, remember that.

She had told me never to go into the parlor. That was what she called it. *The Parlor.* And, really, how ridiculous to call it that, a small room in the basement of an aluminum-sided, vinyl-shuttered ranch in a suburb of Trenton, New Jersey. But my grandmother decorated it in burgundy and navy, all brocades and velvets, with gold rope tassels on the drapes and a faux-mahogany sideboard she found in a yard sale for forty-five dollars. She sipped tea there with her Holy Roller pals every Wednesday afternoon.

In my six-year-old head, I called it the Jesus room. Grandmother had thirteen different Jesus figurines posed on the furniture—some ceramic, some glass, and one cheap plastic statue with the decals peeling off its face. I remember the day I counted them all, peering in from the hallway, toes on the seam between the plush wine-colored carpet and the scratched linoleum. One Jesus, on the end table closest to the door, wore a robin's-egg-blue robe and held a lamb in the crook of his arm. The orange light from the table lamp glinted off his serene, milky face. I wondered if this was the same Jesus my grandmother always talked about, the one who could see me being naughty, who would send me to Hell for sneaking sugar cubes from the bowl or for saying I'd brushed my teeth when I'd only swirled a blob of toothpaste around my mouth and spit it in the sink. This Jesus looked so nice, and I wanted him with me, to protect me from the mean Jesus my grandmother knew.

I didn't actually disobey. My feet never crossed the threshold of the parlor. I clung to the molding around the door and swung my body toward the table, willing my arm to grow, and knocked down Shepherd Jesus. He rolled to the edge of the lace doily, and I grabbed him before he fell off the table. Then I took him to my room and hid him under my pillow, sleeping with one hand curled around him.

She found out, of course. Three days later she clomped

into my room and demanded to know what I had done with her statue. I pulled him out from beneath my Strawberry Shortcake pillowcase and held him gently in both hands.

" 'Foolishness is bound in the heart of a child; but the rod of correction shall drive it far from him,' " she said, and she meant, *Pull down your pants.*

"I didn't hurt him," I said, crying as I unbuttoned my dungarees. "I just wanted to look at him some more."

"You'll look at him," she said. She stood the figurine on the bed and bent me over so my face was inches from the shiny blue eyes. Then she paddled my bare backside with a yardstick, and the Jesus I thought looked so nice stared at me, painted pink lips smiling, and did nothing to help.

It's because I'm bad, I thought. *I'm too bad for him to love me.*

And I wanted that Jesus to love me. I wanted my grandmother to love me, too. On Grandparents' Day at school, I saw the rosy-cheeked Mrs. Claus-like grandmothers, and the ostrich-legged grandmothers, and the clanky grandmothers with canes and oxygen tanks. They all hugged and kissed their granddaughters, and ruffled their grandsons' hair, and carried Dentyne gum in their purses.

My grandmother didn't come.

I set out to be the best granddaughter ever. For six years I tried to obey the first time I was asked to do something, tried to remember to say "Yes, ma'am" and "No, ma'am." At lunchtime, I tucked my napkin in the collar of my blouse to keep peanut butter off it. Each night I ate all my soggy canned vegetables, even though Mary Ann Treaker had shared with me her parent-proof way of hiding them in her pocket, and flushing them down the toilet before bed. I flossed four times a day. I kept my church shoes polished.

And I kept a flashlight hidden at the back of my closet, so I could read my Bible under the blankets at bedtime.

Nothing I did mattered. I couldn't figure out why, until I was twelve and Aunt Ruth got sick of seeing me grovel like a mutt at my grandmother's feet. She told me the truth about my father, my mother; I always believed they'd died in a car accident when I was a toddler.

Then I understood. How could my grandmother love me? Look who my parents were, what they did. From then on, I stopped trying to please anyone. It wouldn't do one bit of good.

By the time I returned to the cabin, my entire body throbbed with the black-and-blueness of the past. I shivered, opened the woodstove. The ash lay crumbled in cold, achromatic mounds. I'd let the fire go out overnight, having only one thick wedge of log left to burn. I figured I would save it should the weather turn frigid once more; I wasn't buying more wood for five lousy days. Now I tossed a couple of rolls of toilet paper into the stove, trying to take the chill from the air.

I began packing my things, stuffing my clean clothes into the duffel bag, the dirty clothes into a trash bag, moving with long, dogged strides. On liberation day, I'd only have to load the truck, stick my toothbrush in my back pocket, and drive away. I inventoried the kitchen cabinets: two cans of SpaghettiOs, a box of instant white rice, a package of ramen noodles, and five Hershey bars. I could live on that, having no plans to leave the cabin until my appointment at Rich the Mushroom's office Friday morning.

I was done with this place.

Switching on the television, I went back into the kitchen for some chocolate and a soda. I heard a truck engine rumble, and I bent back the corner of the shade, hoping to see Jack parked in front of the cabin. And hoping not to see him there. An empty driveway stared back at me as the motor sound came again, louder, from the TV. A Toyota commercial.

I sprawled on the couch, my violin case poking my leg. I left it there, not enjoying the discomfort, but wanting to continue to feel it, focusing on it instead of the nagging disappointment that Jack hadn't chased after me. He had no reason to come. And, even if he did, what would I say to him? *I'm sorry I tried to destroy your life? I only did it for spite, because I want you to love me, and you don't?*

But I didn't love him either, did I? I wasn't patient or kind, and I certainly didn't want what was best for him. If I had the inclination to pull out the Bible that Jack had given me and search through the tissue-paper pages until I found the love list sandwiched somewhere in the epistles, I was quite sure I'd have none of the required attributes. But, like Memory said, I'd never had anyone to teach me. That wasn't my fault.

It was my father's fault.

My violin case—no, Luke's violin case—seemed to swell, growing sharp edges, digging into my leg. I pushed back against it, hard enough for the discomfort to become pain. Of all the instruments I could have chosen to play, I picked his. I looked like him. I probably smelled like him, baneful and sour.

My hate for my father had faded during the past several months, despite me. I had clung to it, but like handfuls of sand, the tighter I squeezed, the faster it had fallen away. Now it erupted as I counted my losses. Because of him, I never knew my mother, never fought with her over boyfriends, never made her a red felt valentine or a clay pinch pot for her birthday. He went off to prison, and dumped me with my grandmother.

He ruined me.

I shoved my hair behind my ears, grabbed the case by the handle and swung it into the closet, slamming the door as it bounced to the floor. Still cold, I boiled water and drank it hot enough to scald my tongue. Checked the stove. I saw the remnants of the cardboard toilet-paper tubes, black and chewed by fire. I hefted the log into my arms and, a knife-like pain shooting into my palm, dropped it again. "Sugar," I said, stressing the *shhh*, enjoying the familiar sound on my tongue. A sliver protruded beneath my thumb. I pinched it out, sucked the wound.

I felt a small, subversive tickle as my eyes fell on the bookshelves, not only in a Guy Montag way, but because Luke loved his books, and I decided then to destroy a piece of him. I went to the cases on the right side of the front door and piled a half-dozen hardcovers in my arms. The corners poked my ribs. I stuffed them into the stove, stacking them one on another; the white pages grinned back at me before igniting.

I pulled another armload of books off the shelf, but the stove was still full, so I threw them across the room. They skidded over the wood floor. I grabbed more and more, slinging them over my shoulder, listening to them bounce off the couch, the coffee table, the walls, until I emptied the bookcase.

Sitting beside the open stove door, I made neat piles for later, for the remaining week. *The Collected Works of Alfred Lord Tennyson* lay spread eagle, cover up, near my foot. I grabbed one corner; something fluttered to the floor. A newspaper clipping. I picked it up, and seeing a partial weather forecast from 1978 on the back of the paper, turned it over.

Petersen Pleads Guilty, the headline read.

Three grainy black-and-white photos flanked the article. My father, looking grizzled and shell-shocked in his mug shot. My mother, Helena, her hair loose around her face, eyes crinkling with laughter. And, beneath her, a picture of Luke's second victim, my mother's lover.

Dr. Crandall White.

I drew a sharp breath, tied on my boots, thrust my arms into my coat and drove to Memory's house. Doc's Jeep wasn't there. I looked in the front window and saw Robert's bed—empty. So I went to Doc's place and waited for him, sitting in my truck, reading and rereading the article as the sky clouded over and a cold drizzle pattered on my windshield.

I must have fallen asleep, because I woke, head kinked against my shoulder, startled by a tapping sound near my ear.

"Sarah." Doc said, voice blurry through the glass.

I twisted my stiff neck. "Where have you been?"

"I went to get Robert settled in at Wildwood. What are you doing here?"

The clipping had slipped off my lap while I slept, into a shallow puddle under the gas pedal. I bent to retrieve it. The bottom part of the newsprint tore, the words smearing into one another. But the headline—and the photos—were clear. I pressed it against the window; it stuck there from the dampness, obscuring Doc's face. I saw his breath fog around the edges of the paper, and he said, "You'd better come inside."

He walked through the front door with his head down and

heels dragging, hanging his jacket on the rack. He changed into his slippers, put on a sweater—the beginning strains of "Won't You Be My Neighbor" played in my mind—and said, "Coat?"

"I'm keeping it on."

He went into the living room and switched on a lone floor lamp in the corner. The room, full of heavy, dark furniture and Oriental rugs, seemed incompatible with Doc's ideology, with Jonah itself. "And all this on a salary of magazines and pennies," I said.

"My parents collected antiques."

"They had money."

"Yes," he said. "It seemed a waste to let all this sit in storage." Uncorking a decanter of Scotch that sat on the table beside a cushioned wing chair, he filled an amber-tinted glass about a quarter full, and downed the alcohol in a single swallow. Then he poured another glass and plunked in several ice cubes. "Need a drink?"

"I need answers."

"Answers." He sighed, dropping into his chair like a stone falling into the river, heavy and lifeless.

When I looked at him now, I saw two faces blended into one, the photo of young, handsome Dr. Crandall White transposed over old Doc.

"I was there when you were born, you know," he said. "Your mother, she was so hardheaded. Got it into her mind to take the train from Westchester to Manhattan when she was eight-and-a-half months pregnant. To go shopping, of all things. She ended up in my hospital." He took off his glasses. "I delivered you."

I sat down in a chair that matched his, this one pushed close to the fire, which smoldered stingily in the hearth.

Reaching down, I threw in another log, sending embers tumbling onto the brick. "Tell me."

"I met your parents in '78. They'd just moved from upstate to Westchester because of Luke's job. Helena was pregnant. They seemed happy, started coming to the church I also attended. It didn't take long for your mother to decide it wasn't right for me to be single, and she started playing matchmaker. Almost every Sunday, she invited me to dinner after church, and there was another pretty young woman to meet.

"I don't know how it happened, but I fell in love with her. I didn't realize it until I stood in that delivery room wishing Helena was mine, that you were mine. Then Luke showed up with his violin and played for you." He sighed, a short, disgusted puff. "I stood there, a successful, rich doctor, jealous of a drywaller.

"I knew your parents were having some problems before you were born. Luke had gotten a promotion, was working a ton of hours and had stopped coming to church. After you were born, your mother just . . . faded away. I hardly saw her. And then, after about six months, I decided I couldn't stand not seeing her. I bought some Chinese takeout and went to her house. She answered the door looking tired and thin, and beautiful. She didn't want to be alone anymore, and neither did I.

"And that's how it started between us.

"For five months I saw Helena almost every night. And you. Then she got tired of sneaking around. I asked her to come away with me, and she was going to take you and leave Luke. And that's when he found us, that last day when she had everything packed and we were so excited that we were careless. Neither of us expected Luke to show up at home, and while we were waiting for you to wake up from your nap, we—" Doc chewed his ice. "Anyway, Luke walked in on us.

"I'll never forget how he looked when he saw us together. Like a mother whose baby had been stillborn. And I just told him that I loved Helena, and he turned and left the room. Then we heard a gunshot.

"It was an accident. Your mother and I ran to the study and found a shattered window and Luke with a gun to his head, and I wrestled with him, trying to take the gun away. It went off two more times. The last bullet caught me in the shoulder, went right through. And when I pulled away, I saw Helena, bleeding on the floor. She'd been hit twice. Once in the thigh, once in the neck. She bled out before I could do anything for her.

"Afterwards, when I was in the hospital, the police came to question me. But it was just a formality. Luke had already told police he'd found Helena and I together and, in a rage, shot us. He'd agreed to a second-degree murder plea and would be sentenced to twenty years, out in seventeen with good behavior. And that was that."

I heard only the clock ticking, and the flames, consuming the birch logs in the hearth with relish. Night rubbed against the windows. I shifted in the chair, back stiff, spine crackling as I recrossed my legs.

Doc stared into his glass, clutched it, as if it had some sort of redeeming power. I'd sat in questionless silence during his story, my tongue glued to the roof of my mouth. I wiggled it around, running it over my teeth and gums. "You didn't tell them it was an accident." My voice sounded wooly, uneven.

"No." He unscrewed the bourbon cap, filling a clean glass

halfway, no ice this time, and stood leaning on the mantel. "I'm a coward."

"He didn't tell them it was an accident," I said. "Why didn't he tell them? He let them put him in jail, and made me believe—I mean, we could have been . . . I could have had a father. He didn't even think about me."

"He wasn't thinking clearly, Sarah. About anything," Doc said.

"And didn't you care about what would happen to me?"

"Sarah—" Doc stopped, turned away. "I cared. More than you could know. The guilt, it made Luke and I both do irrational things. Stupid things."

He splashed the last sips of liquor into the fireplace, onto the burning logs; the flames flared for a second, then retreated. My anger did the same. I tried to find the words to shout at him; there were none there. I felt wrung out, twisted like a dishrag, all my rage squeezed down the drain by Doc's confession. And I found, incredibly, I didn't want to be angry with him. I was tired of it all. "How'd you end up here?" I asked.

"After everything, I quit my hospital job, packed up, and went to Mexico. I traveled between clinics, searching for atonement. All I found was dust and poverty, and desperate parents who'd do anything to get their kid a shot of penicillin. I hid down there nineteen years, until the parole board letter finally caught up with me, informing me that Luke had been released. It had been forwarded at least ten times.

"So here I am. I didn't intend to stay. I thought I'd beg Luke's forgiveness and disappear again. But when I got here, I couldn't go to him. I started my practice and settled in. I'm sure he knew I was in Jonah, but he didn't seek me out, either. It took five months before our paths crossed. He was walking down the sidewalk in one direction, I was walking in the other. I remember he was with Maggie Watson, and she was chattering on and on. He kept his eyes on me the whole time, and I . . . I had to look away. The sidewalk was narrow enough that our shoulders brushed as we passed."

He sat again, picked up the bourbon, but set the bottle back down on the tray with an uncertain hand. Put his glasses on. "People always think they're going to have more time than they ever do. Maggie called me one day, just about a year and a half ago. She'd found Luke at his cabin, and he wasn't moving. I thought he was dead. Turns out, he'd had a stroke. He was almost completely paralyzed. Couldn't talk, but there was nothing wrong with his mind.

"Maggie refused to let him be put into a nursing home, which was what I recommended. She brought him back to the inn, and the first day he was home, I went to see him. I'd been rehearsing what I'd say to him for twenty-five years. But when I got there, I just knelt beside his bed and wept against his hand.

"He died a few days later."

I poured myself a drink now—seltzer water—and swished it around in my mouth before swallowing. The tasteless bubbles grazed the back of my throat, and I coughed, choking on my disappointment. The story ended there, without any of the answers I needed. "You don't know if he forgave you, then."

"No. I just hope he did."

After dropping his glass on the mantel, Doc opened the closet and kicked a stool into it. He reached for the top shelf, moving luggage and file folders before pulling down a cardboard boot box. He opened it—I saw his name printed on the cover in thick magic marker—and, dust scattering, removed a metal lockbox, key taped to the top. "He left this for you."

He gave me the lockbox, scratching at the corner of the tape and peeling the key off, but I covered the lock with my hand. "Wait."

I fished through my coat pocket and removed the little gold key Rich gave me, still attached to the ring with the others. I held it against Doc's key.

They matched.

"I need to do this alone," I said.

He nodded and left the room.

Apprehensively, I slid the key—my key—into the lock, twisted it. The lid opened, only a crack. I thought for a moment—what did I expect to find? Nothing inside the box could change the past twenty-seven years. I had long ago stopped believing in magic wands and happy endings.

Still, I wanted *something*.

I lifted the lid and saw handprints. My handprints, in white paint on blue construction paper. I'd made that in nursery school, when I was four. Under my hands, a poem read:

> Sometimes you get discouraged
> Because I am so small
> And always leave my fingerprints
> On furniture and walls
>
> But every day I'm growing—
> I'll be grown some day
> And all those tiny handprints
> Will surely fade away

So here's a little handprint
Just so you can recall
Exactly how my fingers looked
When I was very small

Sifting through the other papers, I removed crayon draw-
ings of ponies and rainbows, and four-fingered people with
square bodies and noodle legs. There were tempera paintings
and seasonal crafts. Handwriting worksheets and various
tests—math, spelling, history—from different grades.

I found orchestra programs from junior high, my name
underlined in the list of participants, or circled when I'd
had a solo. There were newspaper clippings. One indicated
I'd made state orchestra, another lauding my acceptance to
Juilliard, and yet another—a tiny square—announcing my
marriage, because David's parents insisted on putting it in
the local paper.

And photos, at least a hundred of them. School pictures of me, sitting in front of a blue background, wearing
hand-smocked calico dresses when I was younger, teased
hair and too much eye shadow as a teen. Photos of me at
awards assemblies and orchestral performances. The prom.
And various candid shots—in the bath as a toddler, on the
swings, at Christmas with bows stuck in my hair, at birth-
days and building snowmen. *Sarah, age 5, getting off the bus
after her first day of school,* Aunt Ruth wrote on the back in her
loopy, girlish cursive, or *Sarah, age 11, playing summer tennis.*
There was one with more creases and fingerprints than the
others, a black-and-white photo taken for the all-state orchestra program. Fourteen, gawky, my face not yet grown into my
nose and lips, I cradled my violin against my stomach, the
way a child holds her favorite teddy bear, and gazed beyond

the camera, trying to look disinterested and sophisticated all at once.

I crammed the papers back into the lockbox and, suddenly drained, watched the box slide down my outstretched legs, bouncing over my knees and to the floor. I felt like a pumpkin that had its pulpy innards scraped out. Empty. All the emotions that had ruled me for so long evaporated from my goose-pimpled skin, and there was nothing left of me. And, in that instant, I was frightened. Without the hatred, the thirst for revenge, the bitterness, I didn't recognize myself.

What would fill me now?

Doc returned some time later—an hour? Two? I didn't know—with a steaming mug. Coffee. I could smell it. I sat on the floral-print rug, chin on one knee, my other leg tucked under me, organizing the ephemera into tidy, chronological piles.

"I figured you might need this." He gave me the mug. "The floor can be drafty."

My reflection shuddered in the black liquid. My face. My father's face. "There's nothing here," I said.

"There's twenty-five years there."

"Of me. All of me. There's nothing of him. I thought there would be a letter, at least."

"Maybe he hoped he would have the opportunity to tell you in person. Maybe he simply ran out of time," Doc said. "But he got you here, didn't he?"

"So what?"

"This town, the people, they're his letter to you."

"Well, then, why did he waste seventeen years in prison? Why didn't he do everything he could to . . . to be with me? No one here can tell me what I want to know."

"No, they can't. But there isn't a soul in Jonah who

wouldn't give you hours—days—of his life to tell you about Luke. About what he did for them. Who he was. If there's one thing I do know, it's that your father was good for this town, and everyone in it was good for him. And you. They were good for you."

"You have no idea what you're talking about."

"I saw you when you got here. I see you now," Doc said.

"It's not enough."

"Sometimes not enough has to be enough."

I bent over and scooped up the paper stacks and relocked them in the box. "I'm leaving on Friday. That's five days away. You could have given me this the first week I was here—" I stopped, looked at him through squinted eyes. "Why do you have this, anyway?"

"Maggie found it in the cabin, saw my name on it."

"But why you, I mean."

"I know what you mean. And I can't tell you I know, though I imagine Luke thought this would be fitting penance, for me to confess it all to you."

I picked up the lockbox by the thin wire handle. "If I hadn't found that clipping, would you have told me?"

"Probably not," he said, taking off his glasses, folding the arms and sticking them in his shirt pocket. He scratched the bridge of his nose with his index finger. "I told you, I'm a coward, Sarah. Fortunately for both of us, the decision wasn't mine."

"One of your miracles, I suppose?"

Doc let out a long, tired breath. "You tell me."

I left Doc's house, drove to the skating pond, and sat there with my headlights on, staring at the melting ice, my body numb from the neck down, my mind grappling with all I'd learned. I couldn't stop thinking about what Doc said to me after Hiram Dennison died. *"One man's coincidence is another man's miracle."* How many coincidences had it taken for me to be here, right here, contemplating popping the gearshift into neutral and letting the truck roll into the pond. Not to hurt myself, but so I could feel something. Cold. Wet. So I could focus on those familiar, finite things instead of the strange rumblings in my head.

What if my car hadn't been stolen? What if I had successfully seduced Rich the Mushroom into giving me my inheritance early? What if Memory hadn't died, and Jack never told me about Allison after the memorial service, and Adele hadn't been smoking on the Grange hall steps as I walked out of the building?

What if I pulled the books off the shelves on the left, instead of the right?

Something snapped inside me and, exploding like a shaken bottle of Diet Coke, childhood recollections fizzed in my brain—scraps of Bible verses, catechism, lessons from Sunday school classes—things I probably couldn't remember if I wanted to, and wouldn't have wanted to, even if I could. But they were there, mishmashed and haphazardly stacked one on another, and I wasn't able to stop thinking of them.

I went to the inn, charged through the front door, into Maggie's living room, through the kitchen and down the hall, to Beth's bedroom. Hesitating only a second, I knocked and heard rustling from within. Dominic opened the door, eyes thick with sleep. "Sarah? It's past midnight."

"I know. I'm sorry. But I really need to talk to Beth."

He closed the door, and after some murmuring Beth appeared. "Sarah, are you okay?"

"Yeah," I said. "No."

"What's wrong?"

"I need to know. How can you tell if something is just a coincidence, or if it's—" I swallowed once, twice. "Or if it's more?"

"More? Sarah, I don't—"

"God." The word sounded almost heretical in my voice. But I said it again. "Or if it's God."

Beth's lower lip trembled, and her eyes welled with tears. Then she laughed, hugging me. I stood there, straight as a stick bug, wondering if I should sting or play dead, if I should scamper away or, finally, relent.

"This might take awhile," she said. "How about some tea?"

I nodded and turned to follow her to the kitchen. Maggie waited in her bedroom doorway, crying silently. She reached out, her cool hand against the back of my neck, pulling me close so our foreheads touched and our noses pressed together, her tears dampening my cheeks.

"Go on," she said, wiping her eyes and giving me a little push down the hall. "The Lord's waiting on you."

chapter FORTY-SEVEN

Like Jonah in the belly of the great fish, I stayed at the inn three days, asking, seeking, knocking. Beth sat with me the entire time, answering each one of my questions, sometimes three or four different ways, never tiring of my green persistence. Maggie hovered over us while we studied. She'd give her opinion on rare occasions, but mostly contented herself with attending to us—making us grilled cheese sandwiches and tomato soup for lunch, baking brownies for snack, and keeping us hydrated. In the evenings, Dominic would join us in the living room, reading mechanic's manuals in the wing chair while Beth and I sat on the couch, feet on Maggie's coffee table, Bibles open across our thighs. But he went to bed each night at nine; Beth said he couldn't sleep past sunrise, even with the thick bedroom drapes hiding the morning. Then she and I would be alone again until our eyes burned from too much reading and too little light.

Beth wanted to call Jack, to have him come and join our discussions, insisting he would be able to offer more complete explanations and, unlike her, wouldn't have to fumble through the concordance to find reference verses. "I think he has the entire Bible memorized," she said.

"I'm just not ready to see him yet," I said.

Occasionally Beth jumped up from the table and darted down the hallway to the bathroom, one hand pressed over her mouth, the other on her stomach. I'd hear retching, flushing, running water, and Beth would return to the kitchen with an apology.

"Comes with the territory," I said after one of those trips.

"Did you—" she began, then stopped. "Uh, where were we?"

"You were asking if I ever had morning sickness."

"Sarah, I'm sorry. I didn't mean to—"

"It's fine. Yeah, I got sick every day, starting at nine weeks, until I was about five or so months along. Be thankful you have a nice clean toilet to puke into. Most days I had my face in a garbage can in the New York City subway. You can't imagine the disgusting stuff I saw."

"I don't want to," she said. "Do you . . . I mean, did you know if you were having a boy or a girl?"

"No. We both thought it was a girl, though. David and I. My ex-husband, that is. And it was."

"Can I ask what her name was?"

"Allegra," I said.

"That's pretty," Beth said. "Dom and I aren't going to find out. We want to be surprised. But we already have our names picked."

"You two work faster than any couple I've ever met."

She giggled. "I guess it's easy when you know what you want. If it's a boy, he'll be John Luke. Both our fathers are named John. And Luke. . . Well, you know."

"Yeah."

"And, if it's a girl, we're naming her Sarah. Sarah Danielle."

"Stop," I said, sniffling. "It's not fair. I've cried more the past two weeks than I have my entire life."

"You'll get used to it."

"I don't think so."

By lunchtime Wednesday, my brain was saturated with chapters and verses, doctrine and doubts. I told Beth I felt like Nicodemus, hiding on the roof in the darkness, utterly confused.

"You may not understand it all now," she said, "but where was Nicodemus after Jesus died?"

Still, I had to stretch my legs, get some new air in my lungs—the inn air had gone stale with my searching. I also needed to make several last visits. I promised to have one more supper with Beth and her mother the next evening, then drove to Memory's home.

The door was unlocked, of course.

Another family would be moving in soon. I didn't know who, or when. Memory would have wanted someone to get use out of the small house, but people being as proud as they were around here, no one would take it for nothing. So it would be sold well below market value—five thousand dollars, I think Maggie said—and that little money would be put in trust for her son. Doc, however, told me he didn't anticipate Robert living much longer; since Memory's death, his organs had begun to shut down, and no life-saving measures would be taken. Doc thought the problem stemmed from the several days Robert went without food, but I knew better. He was dying from a broken heart.

The empty hospital bed seemed so much colder, more clinical, without Robert's cozy blankets draped over the shiny chrome rails. Otherwise, the house looked just as Memory had left it, except for the filmy layer of dust collecting on everything. Memory wouldn't have stood for that. She had wiped her rag, damp with olive oil and lemon juice, over her furniture each day, and used a feather duster on every other solid surface. I told her once that all she did with those bright purple feathers was sweep the dust into the air, where it floated around until landing on something else, and she'd just have to get rid of it again tomorrow. She remained unconvinced. "My mama used 'em, my grandmamma used 'em, and any-which-way, they wouldn't make 'em if they didn't work," she'd said.

It still hurt to think of Memory. Not the blinding, all-encompassing pain I'd had immediately after her death. This was a subtle bittersweetness, a skirmish between all the pleasant recollections of her, and the sad realization I didn't have her here on earth, with me, anymore. I couldn't say I absolutely knew she was in heaven, but I could almost *hope* she went there. I chuckled each time I pictured it, Memory's fat body wrapped in a white sheet, like a cherub—tiny wings glued to her back, flapping frantically to lift her bulk off the clouds—despite Beth's assurance that humans did not turn into angels when they died.

I wanted to take some rag rugs to Rabbit. I knew Memory wouldn't have minded, so I stacked a dozen on the coffee table—all different sizes, round and oblong and square—rolling the smaller ones inside the larger. I reached down next to the sofa, where Memory kept her rags, to find a strip with which I could tie the rug bundle together. Instead, I found another rug, and as I pulled, it unfurled over the arm of the couch.

It was my rug; I recognized the greens and browns, the yellow I hesitated to take. But Memory hadn't simply wound the cloth in a spiral design, the way she'd shown me, the way she'd made all the others. She wove a picture into this rug, like a tapestry. Three lofty evergreens grew from the lower right corner, a mountain towered in the distance behind them, and the sun   that vibrancy, that life I'd been so afraid of—shone down from a multihued blue sky.

I refused to cry again. I grabbed a handful of rags and found one long piece to tie Rabbit's rugs together. Then I rolled my own and, gathering all of them in my arms, went to leave, listening to each croak of the plywood beneath my boots. But I stopped with my hand on the front doorknob, taking one last look around the house.

"I won't forget," I said.

The Harrisons were both outside when I arrived. Ben hunkered on the ground, back against the woodpile, whistling, his rifle aimed toward the treetops. Rabbit had cleared any remaining snow from her garden area; she tilled the soil—half ice, half mud—her bare, stringy arms bulging with each forkful.

I got out of the truck and slammed the door. The trees shook above my head, and I watched several squirrels dart and cheep through the branches. Ben aimed, fired. When nothing fell to the ground dead, he picked up a small log and chucked it at me.

"You scared thems all away with all your racket," he

said. "If theys don't be back, my woman and I have to eat slop for supper."

"He means something from one of them cans you be bringing us," Rabbit said. "He don't like nothing, 'cept it be fresh."

"And the Doc says it be two more weeks 'fore I can get out there and walk on this here foot. I keep telling him it don't even hurt no more," Ben said.

"You sees he's been feeling much better. Can't keep from carping 'bout nothing," Rabbit said. She stabbed her hoe into the ground. "Doc says you going back to that city of yours real soon."

"Yeah. Two days."

"Good," Ben said. "Then you won't be coming 'round here, spooking off my chow."

"Hush up, you old coot," Rabbit said. "Pay him no mind. He's got a tad bit of cabin fever."

"I know the feeling," I said. "It's been a long winter."

"It ain't over, don't think," she said. "This old mountain, she got one or two storms left in her. But you ain't come to talk snow, did you, now?"

"I wanted to bring you these." I hoisted the rug bundle from the back of the truck. Rabbit opened her mouth to protest, but I said, "They're a gift. A friend of mine made them, but she— She doesn't need them anymore, and I thought you could find a use for them."

"You mind if I be giving somes to a few others 'round these here parts?"

"As long as you promise to keep at least one for yourself."

She took the rugs, nodded. "You be safe getting back home."

I returned her nod, and drove away.

Zuriel sat in her favorite chair, knitting and rocking, rocking and knitting. Making baby hats, she said. The Bethel Baptist Church, where her great-granddaughter attended, planned to send boxfuls to a crisis pregnancy center in Buffalo.

"As long as I breathe," she said, "I can still be useful somehow."

"I'm here to say good-bye," I said.

She put down the hat, sighed. "I knew it was coming. I didn't want to think about it, though. Are you rushing off right now?"

"No. I can sit, for a little while."

I dropped into the chair next to her, and we rocked without speaking and in unison—I concentrated on keeping time with Zuriel. She resuming her knitting, her needles dancing in the bright blue yarn.

"I'll send you letters. On tape, so you can listen to them," I said.

"You don't have to take the trouble to do that. Your friend Patty asked Doc if she could visit, perhaps come play the piano. She can read your letters to me."

"She's not my friend," I mumbled, possessiveness clogging every one of my pores.

Zuriel chuckled. "Ah. I see. I knew a woman, once, years ago, who wasn't my friend like that. Her name was Selma Jackson. And his name was Ezekiel Carver."

"I don't . . . I mean, how—"

"When two women dislike each other, a man is most often the reason."

"Carver, huh? I guess Selma Jackson won that fight."

"It was more like a scuffle. And, no, no one won, thank the Lord. Ezekiel Carver went to California with just the clothes on his back, and he ended up marrying and deserting several women along the way. Selma found a lovely husband, and I had my Thomas, and we were both better off. We became quite good friends, too. She was at the birth of each one of my babies. All eight of them. So, you see, there's hope for the both of you, yet."

"Maybe," I said. *But I hope not.* "Or maybe I just won't have any kids."

"Sarah, Sarah," Zuriel said with an amused sigh, shaking her head. "Patty also told me you play the violin. Quite well, in fact."

"She said that?"

"I believe 'breathtaking' was the word she used. I don't suppose I'll have the honor of hearing your music before you leave."

"I would, really, but my violin . . . It's out of commission right now." Two tuning pegs had cracked when I threw the case into the closet, and the soundpost—the soul of the violin—was jarred out of position. The instrument couldn't be played until a competent luthier made the necessary repairs.

"Well, then, I wouldn't mind a recording of that. Perhaps, when you're able."

"I promise. One violin rendition of 'Amazing Grace.' "

"How about something called *Chaconne*?" She pronounced it, improperly, *cha-cone*. "Do you know that?"

"There are quite a few chaconnes out there."

"This one is by Bach, if my memory serves me correctly."

"Yeah, he wrote one," I said slowly, surprised not only that Zuriel knew any classical music, but that she knew *my* piece, the one I'd heard on the five-cent record when I was a child. I remembered the album sleeve—yellow and held together with crumbly masking tape, Heifetz's name written in script across the cover, just above a small drawing of a violin. There had been two Bach compositions on the recording, but an ugly scratch ran through the first—his Sonata No. 1—and I was angry that I wasted my nickel. I pressed my index finger against my thumb and flicked it forward, bumping the needle to the next track, Partita in D Minor. At first, I could only listen, but as the German baroque dance suite progressed, I placed my hands on either side of the record player and felt the *basso ostinato*, the obstinate bass note pattern rippling up and down my arms. It would be years before I learned terms like *theme* and *variation*, but I had understood then that I was listening to the same four-bar phrase over and over again, played in different ways.

This was how lives were made, a string of people and happenings and emotions—scattered across a staff; written sometimes in a bright major key, other times in a somber minor mode. I realized now, as I sat there rocking back on each inhale, forward on each exhale, toes light upon the creaky floor, that these weren't variations on a life I should have had—they were my chaconne, the pinnacle of my repertoire, working together to bring me here, to this place. For good, or for bad.

I glanced at Zuriel. "Are you some sort of closet classical music buff?"

"Oh, my. No." The old woman laughed. "I heard it once, in a movie. *The Beast with Five Fingers*. It was the first moving picture I'd ever seen, and my first time in a theater, too. That was . . . 1946. Yes, that's right. It was my fortieth birthday, and I remember I wanted to see a romance, *Never Say Goodbye*, with Errol Flynn. My husband convinced me to see the scary one. I think he simply wanted me to cuddle up close to him in the dark."

"And someone played the Bach chaconne in the horror flick?" I said it correctly, *shaw-kon*.

"Not someone. Something. A dismembered hand."

"A left hand? On the piano?"

"Yes, how did you know?"

"The chaconne is the last of five movements Bach originally wrote for solo violin. But Johannes Brahms transcribed it for piano—" I stopped. "Sorry. You don't care about any of that."

"My dear," Zuriel said, and she reached across the arm's length between the rocking chairs, her hand finding my forearm, squeezing it, my waterproof jacket rustling beneath her touch. "I care about anything that makes your voice smile, like it is right now."

I stayed another hour, reading to Zuriel from her Bible. She embraced me before I left, tight enough that I feared her shivery bones might crumble and she'd sink to the floor in a puddle of floppy skin. But she survived the hug.

So did I.

Back at the cabin I picked up the scattered books, shelving them first in alphabetical order, then organizing them by color and size, and then reshelving them in alphabetical order again. I had no desire to lie down yet. It wasn't sleep I wanted to avoid, but those long minutes before it came. The previous nights at the inn had been difficult; Beth told me I'd been washed whiter than snow, but I felt cruddier than before, like smokers' lungs, encrusted in tar and cancerous muck. Shame filled me as I remembered my past, but also loss; would the rest of my life now need to revolve around

Bible studies, church socials, and prayer meetings? God stuff. It all sounded so boring. Mundane. And, while it seemed to satisfy Beth and Maggie, and the rest of churchgoers around Jonah, they knew no other life. I wondered how I could find complete delight in something I was unable to see or hear or touch.

In the kitchen, I opened both cans of Campbell's and, too lazy to heat the saucy Os, dumped them into a Tupperware and ate them cold while I watched television. I finished three-quarters of the pasta and threw the rest in the plastic trash bag by the front door—along with the spoon and bowl. I showered, feasted on my remaining chocolate bars, and fell asleep long after the late-night talk shows turned to infomercials for painless facial hair removers and abdominal exercise machines.

I didn't drag myself from the couch until midafternoon, though I dozed on and off until then, chasing the rabbit trails of discordant dreams and memories. Showering again, I sat on the floor of the stall, forehead against my knees as the water drummed the top of my scalp. I dressed in the same clothes I'd worn yesterday; I'd probably wear them again tomorrow.

Only one more night.

It felt odd, disconcerting, to be eating in silence at the Watsons' table. My impending absence clamping down upon us like a bell jar, sucking away our conversation. At first, Beth tried to fill the void, telling us about her plans for the nursery; she'd already painted the walls a soft blue, and sketched out the beginnings of the mural—a large, twisting oak tree with wise, old branches and a swing hanging from it. But she eventually gave up, the airlessness no match for her forced enthusiasm.

We chewed more politely than usual, without our words to disguise the smacking and chomping. I ate three helpings of mashed potatoes and little else. Maggie had spoiled me with her delicious spuds, to which she added an entire stick of butter, a pint of heavy cream, and a whole bulb of roasted garlic. She also made dessert. Chocolate cake. Memory's cake. Except Maggie's version looked beautiful; she had trimmed the edges and sifted the confectioner's sugar through a paper doily, using it as a stencil, leaving a sweet, lacy design on top. Memory simply spooned on the white powder without waiting for the cake to cool, so it melted in clumpy globs.

Beth set a wedge of cake in front of me, and I scraped my fork over it, shredding it, crumbs falling onto the macramé place mat.

"I'm sorry, Sarah," Maggie said. "I thought—"

"I'm just full," I said.

Maggie took my plate, and she and Beth cleared the table. Dominic kissed his wife on the forehead and excused himself. I sat, staring at the fingerprints on my water glass.

"I should go," I said.

"Do you need help packing?" Beth asked quickly. "Just let me rinse these last few dishes."

"I'm packed."

The finality of my words rattled in my ears, and I watched Beth's narrow shoulders jounce with each stroke of her sponge. She ran the plate under a stream of blistering water— I saw the steam rising from the sink—and stuck it in the rack, wrenching off the faucet and twisting the towel around her dripping hands. Still, she stood with her back toward me, shoulders continuing to tremble. "Stay," she said.

"I don't want to dirty the sheets for one night."

"No," Beth said, turning now, tears on her face. "Stay here. In Jonah."

"Beth—"

"What do you have to go back to?"

Nothing.

Maggie wrapped her arms around her daughter, and I stared out the window. All I'd ever wanted, it was here, in this town. People who loved me, people who wanted to love me.

I had found my family. My home.

But it was too much, too soon. Like a child wishing for sweets—marshmallows and donuts, gumdrops and milk shakes—and having them all piled in front of me, only to find myself with a monstrous stomachache after glutting on my heart's desire. I'd never been good at moderation, and I had no idea how to behave as a daughter, a sister, a friend. I was afraid the longer I was in Jonah, the sooner I'd give everyone enough reasons to stop caring about me.

I needed proof, as well. Beth had called me a new creation, and spent hours explaining what that meant, lobbing around words like *forgiveness, condemnation, salvation,* and I, dizzied with these new concepts, didn't know what I believed. If I stayed, I would never know if this faith truly belonged to me, or if those changes in me—the ones Beth said she saw so clearly, but I didn't see at all—were because of Maggie's prodding or Beth's lily-white influence, or my desire to please Jack.

"I can't," I said. "I have some things I have to do, alone."

They expected my answer, I think. Neither argued, nor pleaded. Maggie hugged me, and then went to her bedroom;

I thought I heard her crying. Beth gave me a bundle of pastel index cards tied with a white grosgrain ribbon. "Verses," she said. "Color coded by topics I thought you might . . . need."

I flipped through them. *Trust. Temptation. Discouragement. Hope.* "Thanks."

"Tell me I'll see you again."

"You will."

"When the baby's born?"

"In the middle of December? I won't be able to get here. You know that."

"Then in the spring."

"If I can. Who knows where I'll be a year from now."

"Sarah, this isn't just about you. It's about me, too." Beth crossed her arms over her stomach, each hand on the opposite hip. "Yes, I'm being selfish, but I don't think you understand how much . . . you've done for me."

It felt bizarre, being needed. But nice, too. Kind of bubbly. I reached up and tugged Beth's ponytail, like I'd seen Jack do many times before. "You'll see me again," I said. "I promise."

She rubbed her fingers beneath her teary eyes and nodded.

"I'm going to go now," I said. "Take care of that baby."

Beth went to her bedroom. I drove back to the cabin and packed the truck. Then, still dressed, I sprawled across my father's bed and went to sleep.

chapter FORTY-EIGHT

I heard scuffling and woofing after I knocked on Doc's door, and several *Shhh, get down*s from within the house. Finally, the latch turned with a *clink* and the door opened. Doc, bent over in his robe and slippers, no glasses, squinted into the white morning air and held Nola's collar so she wouldn't dart away.

"What are you doing here at this ungodly hour?" he asked.

"It's not ungodly if the sun's up," I said. "What's she doing here?"

"The shelter called a couple days ago—said her time was up, and if I didn't want her to be put down, I needed to come get her." He stretched across the dog to the coatrack and grabbed her leash, hooking it onto her collar and standing up. "I figured it was a bit lonely around this place."

"She doesn't like to be alone, either."

Doc lifted his foot toward me. The toe had been chewed out of his suede moccasin. "I know. I have two other pairs of shoes that look the same. And three pillows." He didn't seem annoyed by the damage, but giddy almost, like a proud papa announcing his daughter had made the dean's list. "You're leaving now."

"Soon. Rich Portabella's shop opens at eight."

"You still have my card?"

"Yeah."

"Good. Keep it. And if you ever need anything, you get ahold of me. Anything."

"I will."

"Promise. Even if it means I have to bail you out of jail in the middle of the night."

"Thanks, I guess."

"I'm just saying there's nothing you can do that will surprise me. Remember, I changed your diapers."

Doc and I, our lives were inextricably linked, grafted into each other. In many ways, he'd been my father the first year of my life, holding me over his head and wiggling me until I laughed, feeding me and, yes, changing dirty diapers. Perhaps he sang to me as he rocked me to sleep—hard to imagine now, but not impossible.

We stood there, silent—him just inside the door, me just outside it—wondering in the awkwardness if we should reach across the threshold and hug each other, or maybe shake hands. That was the intimacy we shared, our feet, our lives, so close we felt as if a sinister gaping chasm separated us. We were the same, both north poles of two magnets, drawn together by our pasts, only to be shoved apart by our sameness. One of us would have to flip if we ever would, truly, come to know each other.

That seemed a lot to ask.

In the end, I patted Nola on the head and gave Doc a befuddled half smile, shrugged and said, "Well, see you." He nodded and reminded me once more to call him if I needed something, before shutting the door.

I drove to see Rich the Mushroom. He waited for me, paperwork on the glass counter, little sticky arrows pointing at all the places I needed to sign. I took time to be clear and neat, matching my signature to the one on my driver's license so there would be no question I was me. I made arrangements to transfer the deed to my father's cabin into Jack's name, thinking he may be sick of sleeping on a sofa every night. I know I was.

Rich stuffed all the papers into a manila envelope, handed it to me, his fingers coated with powdered sugar from the donuts on the plate beside the stuffed raccoon.

"You're free to go," he said. "How's it feel?"

"I don't know yet," I said.

"I have to say it—I'm surprised you made it this long."

"Me, too."

"So, what's the first thing you're gonna get with that money of yours?"

"I don't know," I lied. "I haven't thought about it." As soon as I made it back to the city, I planned to head over to the pawnshop on Delancy Street to see if my old violin was still there. I wouldn't mind having two.

"Well, you come back and visit us," Rich said, pumping my hand and then licking his sugary fingers.

I wiped the powder on my jeans, pushed open the door. "We'll see."

I'd considered leaving Jonah without saying good-bye to Jack, but I was never good at ending things quietly. Some part of me enjoyed a messy scene, an insult-hurling argument that made walking away so much easier. Even though I doubted I'd get that closure with Jack, I still found myself in front of the Grange hall, wondering what I would say to him.

He opened the door wearing jeans and a gray T-shirt, no socks. I hadn't seen his bare feet before. They were nice, narrow, without that patch of hair most men have on their bony mid-foot. And his second toe wasn't longer than his first. A pet peeve of mine, long second toes. I dated a guy once whose second toe was the length of his index finger. He'd enjoyed showing people, tugging off his socks at parties when the action lulled, wiggling it and picking up pens and cigarettes and pretzels.

I didn't sit. Neither did Jack. He leaned against the corner of his desk, arms crossed over his chest, shielding himself from me, I thought. So I backed into the wall, head banging into a framed Norman Rockwell calendar cover.

I wanted to apologize for that afternoon after the memorial service, for the kissing and the telling. I wanted to confess my feelings to him, to hear myself say them aloud, and beg him to be the man I'd been waiting for—the one who'd stay no matter how many dishes I hurled at his head, no matter how many stupid mistakes I made while I bumbled and spun like a pebble in the ocean, slowly, painstakingly being smoothed by the mighty waves.

Instead, I told him, "I have your sweatpants in the truck. The ones I borrowed way back in January."

He bit his lip, blew a quick puff of air through his nostrils. "I'd forgotten about those."

"Well, they're in the truck," I said again. "I'll get them, bring them in to you."

"No, I'll walk you out. But first, here," he said, giving me a yellow Post-it Note with the name of a church on it, and a man's name and phone number. "I know him from seminary. He's expecting you."

I folded the paper and crammed it into my back pocket. "And if I don't show up?"

"He'll tell me. And then I'll have to send out the troops to find you."

I turned my head away from him. He didn't say he'd come rescue me himself.

He followed me to the truck, opened the door for me, slammed it after I settled into the driver's seat. I rolled down the window and passed his pants through, then stared ahead to the empty road, pressed down on the brake, and slid the key into the ignition. The big, dramatic, silent good-bye. I'd show him I didn't need anything from him. But he touched my arm.

"Listen," he said. "If you ever want to call me sometime, just to talk, I wouldn't mind. That is, of course, if your new place has a phone."

"If my new place has a phone," I said. "I would like that."

A sober breeze swept over the two of us, wafting my hair across my face. I shook my head, but my hair clung to my skin. Jack reached into the cab and nudged the obstinate strands behind my ear. His hand, warm, gracious, lingered on my cheek. I shut my eyes and pressed into it, my fingers encircling his wrist, squeezing until I felt his pulse against my palm. We listened to the wind wailing through the evergreen needles, a banshee coming to take Jack from me. I shivered; it still felt like winter.

Finally, he turned away, slapped the top of the truck a couple times, and walked back to the Grange hall. I pulled down the visor and watched him, mud sucking at his boots, shoulders rounded and hands jammed into his pockets.

Beth had told me to pray, to pray about anything, everything. So I begged God to make Jack want me, to force him to turn around and run to the truck, rip open the door and kiss me like he did the afternoon of Memory's service. But he went inside without looking back. My throat knotted, and tears dripped warm over my mouth. I swiped them with my tongue. The taste of loss, returning like a stray dog fed too many times.

"Fine, then. Go," I mumbled, changing my prayer, demanding God remove all my feelings for Jack, to toss them into a pit as deep as His love was wide. I'd go into the city, find a nice guy at my new church, some ordinary computer programmer or bank teller maybe, and forget all about Jack Watson.

I buckled my seat belt with a determined snap. Hesitated. Something tugged me from within, and I felt as if a moth were hovering close to my ear, wings tickling my jawbone, my neck. Without thinking, my hands folded into my lap and my eyes closed.

"God," I said, "I guess I should be praying for your will to be done. I don't know if I really mean it. But I want to."

The heaviness in my chest didn't completely disappear, but it was blanketed by another sensation—something warm and shimmering, and whispery, and still. I sat in silence for a moment, and then turned the key. The truck rumbled to life.

I glanced into the mirror once more, but instead of Jack's door, I saw my own damp eyes, my red nose. But I was smiling. I shifted the truck into Drive, pushed up the visor so I wouldn't be staring at myself grinning like a fool for the entire trip, and started back down the mountain.

Acknowledgments

I've found the number of people I need—or want—to thank increasing with each turn in the journey.

To Carol Johnson and David Horton at Bethany House for taking a chance on an unknown. The Lord has used you to bless my life in previously unimaginable ways. And to my editor, Karen Schurrer—thank you for making *Home Another Way* more than it was before.

To my wonderful agent, Bill Jensen—with a "sen" not "son"—who tells me to e-mail him anytime, handles all the phone stuff I hate to do, and plays a mean game of Scrabble. I can't thank you enough for your part on my road to becoming a *really real* novelist.

To my parents, who have supported me, in my best and darkest times.

To Claudia Bell, Melissa Beilstein, Krista Clements, and Sharon Dykshoorn, for your patience with Jacob's extended play dates—you have blessed me more than you can know. To Jo Burl, for your sage advice, and Marilyn Merry, just for being you. To my awesome Web designer, Rebecca Diamond— you rock! To everyone at Redeemer church, I could not have finished this book without your prayers, and I covet them. Keep them coming. To Angela Hunt and Nancy Rue, for your encouragement—you both had the words I needed that weekend in Philly. And to my online writing buds, Melanie Rigney, Michele Huey, and Virelle Kidder (especially Virelle, who loved me and took me beneath her wing the moment she met me)— your words of wisdom and advice have been invaluable.

And finally, to Jacob, my hugga bugga boy. I love you more than mint chocolate chip ice cream in waffle cones, the New York Yankees, books, and football combined. And that, as you know, is a lot.